Praise for The Golden Gate

In writing this novel, Gillian Butler has used her considerable experience and knowledge of adult relationships together with her awareness of the complexities of adolescent development, to provide a rich and totally engaging account spanning a couple of crucial years in the lives of Simon, a highly-driven prize-winning bridge designer, and his wife Ruth, who runs a biodegradable packaging company. The book provides colourful illustrations of how relationships can unwind, especially when subject to intense ambition combined with misunderstandings. But, and most importantly, it demonstrates the healing power that can come with development of self-awareness and of willingness to forgive. The result is a novel that leaves the reader with a warming sense of hope. Gillian deserves our congratulations on how successfully she has achieved this satisfying and indeed much-needed outcome, especially during our current troubling times. We await further works from this clearly talented new novelist with considerable anticipation. - *Keith Hawton, Emeritus Director of the Centre for Suicide Research, Department of Psychiatry, University of Oxford*

How can we design a bridge if we are not able to see the gap the bridge should span? We go on a journey with Simon, a bridge designer who is blind to the deep rifts between him and others. We tumble into the intricacies of life in London with colleagues, friendships, family and the wider world. Through exploring conversations of how daily life is unfolding, Gillian Butler gives us glimpses of people's internal mental imagery which raises startling psychological insights about what is really going on. The book delves into how external interests can reflect the internal mind, the profound para-doxes between success and failure, and the discrepancies between what is said and what is felt. - *Emily A Holmes, Professor Uppsala University, Swedish Royal Academy of Science (KVA. Hon Fellow Royal Academy of Arts UK*

Simon Westover is a normal modern man. And that's the problem for his endlessly competent wife Ruth, for his family, colleagues and friends. Simon designs bridges and is passionate about their capacity to make connections and join people and communities together. The bridge-building serves as a metaphor for what Simon is unable to do in everyday life. For him the main point of life is winning. Simon is mesmerized by success, and therefore by the possibility of failure. Through a series of traumatic events Simon comes to realise that the boundaries of moral responsibility must include the ability to see the world from the vantage point of others. Real success isn't possible without this shift of vision. So Simon changes, albeit slowly, through a series of lightbulb moments that keep the pace of the novel going.

Gillian Butler, a well-known clinical psychologist and an exem-plary understander of people, leaves us with a sense of optimism about human resilience and the capacity to absorb and learn from challenging experiences. This novel is also about the problems of masculinity. Now that women have shown themselves capable of doing everything, what is there left for men, uniquely, to do? On almost every page we are grounded in the details of what families like the Westovers have to do just in order to survive daily life. *The Golden Gate* is truly a novel for our times in more ways than one. *Ann Oakley, Professor of Sociology and Social Policy, UCL, and novelist.*

Early in this debut novel, Simon Westover, an award-winning archi-tect, states, "My dream is to build a bridge that will make a differ-ence. Innovative and beautiful. Crossing a gap that no one thought could be spanned." The Golden Gate Bridge serves as his yardstick. Thus begins the dramatic tension in this adeptly structured narrative. Simon's bridge designing success belies his ability to truly connect with others, especially with his wife Ruth. His self-absorption, in fact, widens the gap between himself and everyone in his emotional world. The closer he gets to his perfect bridge, the farther away he moves from others.

Gillian Butler creates a network of imagery and symbolism that enlivens her narrative. The bridge icon remains central throughout, evoking the desire for change and transition. Musical compositions extend the novel's themes, emphasizing the tension between order and improvisation, abstraction and emotion. Simon's family history emerges to help clarify important, opposing perspectives, delineating his choices. Indeed, there is much to watch and learn from in this story of Simon's literal and figurative bridge building and his important emotional education. - *Lawrence Markert, Professor Emeritus of English, Hollins University, Roanoke, Virginia, and poet.*

The Golden Gate provides readers with close observation of Simon and Ruth's thoughts and emotions during a period of personal upheaval. As the book unfolds, we are witness to how identity is formed and can shift in response to both subtle and earth-shattering events. As Simon and Ruth navigate their yearnings and fears of true intimacy, the complexities of trauma, gender roles, and redefined family dynamics, their journey shows that personal transformation is neither simple nor guaranteed. Written with elegant, spare prose, *The Golden Gate* is a deeply moving and introspective work that lingers long after the final page. A novel to be read, reflected upon, and savoured. - *Christine Padesky, Author of Mind Over Mood*

The Golden Gate

GILLIAN BUTLER

Published by Forward Thinking Publishing

First published 2025

Published by Forward Thinking Publishing

Text © Gillian Butler 2025

A catalogue record for this book is available from the British Library.

ISBN: 978-1-916764-07-1

Typeset using Atomik ePublisher from Easypress Technologies.

For my grandchildren
Alice, Eleanor, Jessica, Alex and Thomas

Contents

Part 1: Ordinary Difficulties

June to December 2008

Chapter 1

Simon

Simon races back to his office. Excellent. He dumps his briefcase on the desk, turns his back on Hammersmith Bridge below and gets out his phone to call his wife.

'Ruth! I've won the Thames Footbridge prize! The judges were unanimous. They said it's completely original.' He shrugs off his jacket, loosens his tie and walks to the window with one hand running through his hair.

'Oh, that's completely wonderful! I'm so pleased for you and not a bit surprised. It's what you deserve.'

'Come and join us and celebrate with the whole team.'

'Have you forgotten where I am?'

'What?' He stares at his screen. 'Oh my god! I wasn't thinking. You had a meeting in Birmingham. When will you be home?'

'I'm on the train. I'll drink to you with Virgin tea.'

'Love you!'

'Me too.'

He stands stock still and frowns at his reflection in the window. Serious stuff this, the biggest win yet. Wish Ruth could be here. Without looking he sidesteps the sharp corner of the glass coffee table.

Brilliant. The international Portuguese competition next. Head-to-head with the great and the grand.

He looks round at all the books and papers in heaps on his desk, on the glass table and on the floor. He sighs with pleasure. It may look like a muddle but it's not. It makes for surprising juxtapositions and that adds inspiration. The chairman of the examiners at his graduation show said it all: 'Simon Westover. He's something special. Keep an eye out for him.' Oh yes!

When he opens the door of the big meeting room there's a hush followed by a double-decker crescendo of welcome. Platters of pastry cases with pink and green fillings cover the long, polished table. He stands at its head and looks at everyone looking at him. Wonderful people. Each one chosen with care; talented, enthusiastic and excited to have the chance to innovate. All held together by Hannah's superb administrative skills and she must have found time to lay this on as well as doing everything else. He nods in her direction and, with one hand held high, he calls for silence. He has a glass of champagne in the other.

'This is a truly wonderful day. I'm so pleased to see you all. Thank you so much.' He sips the champagne. 'Without all of you, without your energy, talent and creativity working with me and behind me, without those of you who stayed late to sort endless paperwork and messaging muddles, and without those who carried away overflowing bins and bags and boxes and tried to keep my room looking respectable despite a never-ending supply of coffee mugs and muffin papers … this would never have happened.' He gasps. They laugh.

'Let's drink to those who succeed in spanning uncrossable gaps. To the difference they make to everyone. To the amazing contribution bridges make to the way we live.' He raises his glass and his voice:

'The sky's the limit. Let's go for it'.

Ruth

The train sways as it speeds round a bend and Ruth struggles to keep her balance without spilling her tea. She takes a sip and grimaces. It's scalding hot and has no discernible taste. So here we go again. She puts the paper cup aside and spreads all ten fingers out on the table in front of her, staring at the backs of her hands. It's great, but already he sounds as high as a kite.

The world outside is a blur and the wheels rattle and hiss. She fidgets, trying to get comfortable while the train jolts her this way and that. Her steadying hand on the temporary workstation in front of her helps a bit, and she holds on until the headlong rush settles into something more like a midstream flow.

She's been steering her team through the difficult decision-making that comes with a global financial crisis and the day was filled with awkward and prolonged discussions. Enough to drain anyone's resources. Her job, she knows, is to soak up surrounding tension, but now her head feels like an over-absorbent sponge. What can you expect if you're in charge of a new business? With her elbows on the table, she puts her head in her hands and closes her eyes.

Another triumph for Simon. Is he keeping count? Or has he delegated that to me? She closes her laptop. It's definitely an accolade to add to his balance sheet, but tunnel-vision will be back in place tomorrow. However well he does it's never enough.

More than a decade together now and we're doing okay, Ruth thinks. Even better given our joint earning power, but still he knows nothing about anything at home. He doesn't notice an overflowing bin or an empty fridge or have to decide what to do about the broken hinge on the shower door. Without thinking her hand reaches for the tea. She takes another gulp, shudders, and shoves it out of reach.

We've been a good team. In lockstep for the kids, and mostly in agreement for the balancing acts like work-and-play stuff. We've pushed on separately in our working lives hard enough to be able to tell a couple of parallel success stories. And we've discovered how to contribute to things we truly care about. Building bridges for him. Protecting the environment for me. Our different worlds could have pulled us apart, but they haven't. Her hand touches her brow. It's all so full on. So much taken for granted.

Stop. Shake the good bits to the top.

Simon's certainty. His surefooted expertise. His hand-picked team of architects and engineers are creative and loyal and interesting.

You can't help noticing how much they enjoy the work they do. But it is odd Ruth thinks that he needs her to rubber-stamp his achievements given he's such a successful leader.

He's good in a crisis. He'll work all weekend to help someone meet a deadline. She can see the papers piled all over his desk and the floor in his tiny first floor study, door shut to exclude family intrusions. Fine to ignore the boring stuff at least some of the time. Keeping things going isn't that difficult, though there certainly are compromises. Like not seeing friends and mental juggling. She picks up her phone. Puts it back down. Ruth can't remember when they last went to a movie.

Compromise for Simon is something quite else. He'll phone out for a sushi. Or ask Susie to put Isabel and James to bed while we go to the local Italian and enjoy another bottle of his favourite Barolo. Much more relaxing without the kids.

True. But he's the one who says it. Ruth opens the front door too late to join Simon's celebration and home smells good. It's a generous space with plenty of room to breathe and tonight it's as quiet as a smoothly flowing river.

The hallway has a high ceiling, sea-green walls and big windows. There's a photograph on the table of a water fight between Simon and the kids. Two children all limbs and laughter and Simon, pretend-serious, with soaking wet hair. Ruth drops her brief case onto the usual chair, hangs her coat on its hook without looking and shuffles through today's mail. Nothing urgent. She looks up. Coats and school bags on child-level pegs with shoes more or less in pairs beneath. The clutter of family life is well organized. Reliable, good-natured Susie has left a note on the kitchen table and gone to bed.

Ruth checks on the sleeping children, looks at her watch, kicks off her shoes and turns on the bath taps.

Immersed in warm water she thinks again about Simon's certainty. It does seem odd now to have been so certain about trusting each other right from the start. No questions asked. As if he knew how to pass that certainty on. It probably helped to be so young and immature too, and relieved not to be dealing any more with the kinds of difficulties that force you to grow up fast. There were more than enough of those. The only uncertainty he ever showed was about becoming a father and that's when he spoke about the horror of school days spent trying to balance the need to win with a fear of disapproval. His nightmare parents occupied centre stage wherever they were. She sighs. They're the only grandparents Isabel and James have and they don't even remember their grandkids' birthdays.

We've been good for each other, Ruth says to herself. Creating a present we believe in has delivered us from untold numbers of fears and worries.

She sinks comfortably into a familiar warm bed and closes her eyes. It's not as if I can't manage it all. Thanks to Susie.

Swish. Ker-clunk. She half wakes at the sound of the front door closing. Then silence.

Simon

Downstairs Simon flings his coat over the banister and stops to look at a picture hanging nearby.

Simon loves that picture. It's both inspiring and comforting. And it belongs exactly where it is, right by the front door.

It was a present from his grandfather just before he died. In it, the Golden Gate Bridge glows dark red in the setting sun. Not gold but a gate into a golden world. Below boats battle with a rough sea in high winds. The hills on the far side look peaceful and accessible. Wind-whipped pedestrians head across the bridge, struggling to keep on their feet. Its spectacular 83,000 tons of steel suspended in the sea-salty air and just as stable as the paving stones outside the front door. Safely anchored at both ends. Impervious to the gales.

'That's it,' he says to it, face to face: 'that's the way to go.' He stumbles up the stairs carrying his shoes to tell Ruth about his evening and to share his excitement about entering the Portuguese competition. An international prize for a huge bridge across the river Douro that for centuries has separated the communities living on both its banks. Important. Transformative.

'That was fantastic,' he says, throwing off clothes that miss the chair. 'I wish you'd been there. I so wanted you to hear what they said.'

He slides into bed beside her, sinks into her warmth and closes his eyes. His imagination, set free as the activity winds down, presents him with a procession of imaginary bridges. They float over chasms. Or rise up in layers to accommodate trains, then lorries, buses, trams and cars, then bikes and pedestrians and children going to school. Bridges seen from above appear to skim the waves. Those seen from below vanish into the blue. In this dream world, he switches perspectives at will. Imagination and talent. Artistry and technical know-how. Ready. Productive. Satisfying.

Ruth merely murmurs and turns over to create their usual limb-nest.

Hannah

Hannah understands the myth: the good and beautiful princess meets the charming handsome prince. They fall in love and beget children who hear the tales about what happens when there's a natural fit between goodness and love. Simon and Ruth had no choice. They were the two most beautiful people on all of the post-graduate courses in their year.

Short, plain, delightful, and acutely observant Hannah had followed Simon to the graduate registration desk the day they all enrolled. Ruth was up ahead, stunning in her skinny jeans and homespun sweatshirt, the light catching her bright brown hair. Hannah witnessed the first glance between them. Mutual recognition she thought. No choice about it.

The apparent rightness of it made her laugh. Nothing is that predictable. But the next morning they were having breakfast together, late, in the common room. Simon, 6 foot 3 with long legs and dark curly hair, peeling back a muffin paper and flapping his elbows to add emphasis to what he was saying while Ruth warmed a pair of surprisingly large hands round her coffee mug. Face to face they looked like a couple of good luck charms, double strength as a twosome.

The inevitability of the match between them brought to life the myths that lurked in the hidden corners of many of their contemporaries' minds.

Of course, they drank too much at times and played when they ought to have been working. They muddled their accounting and struggled through to the end of term. But they were definitely better together than apart. Hannah, to whom friendship came easily despite her well-developed faculty for criticism, was not the only one who relaxed and became livelier and more adventurous in their presence. Years later, with a reputation for being smart, sharp and unselfish, and still with no long-term lover, she met Simon at a conference and he asked her to join his new team. She needed no persuasion. He needed a good administrator and she wanted an exciting new venture.

She's sure she made the right decision. Celebration over, she resettles the chairs round the polished table in the big meeting room, picks up a few stray crumbs and opens a window wide. Simon really is a super-achiever. He was always winning prizes, and now he's discovered he can fly even before he's 40. His tactless way of dealing with other people might hold him back, but he's a good learner. Maybe he'll change. It's certainly time he bought himself a smart suit.

Ruth

Ruth is enjoying a waking dream in which a grey-green dolphin flies through the spray as if hemming the waves. She blinks and it's gone. Definitely not one to be harnessed or trophied.

She stretches and turns over. Running Grainbox is fantastic. She opens her eyes. Starting a new business has been hard, but it's satisfying. Far better than organising a birthday party for young children. Besides, there's a huge demand for biodegradable packaging, and Grainbox is well ahead of the game.

She can hear the usual riot starting down below, policed by Susie.

'I'm not eating those. They're soggy.'

'You're in my place. Get off.'

'James. Will you please sit down and don't kick Isabel. No. Come back. No toys on the table when you eat. Put that down where it belongs. Mind the milk.'

Coats on, bags packed for school, the children race upstairs, give Ruth a hug and shriek all the way down again, a smudge of Simon's shaving soap on each nose.

'Bye you two clowns,' he shouts after them. 'See you tonight.'

The door bangs shut. Susie's in control. Ruth and Simon drink their coffee in the quiet of their kitchen.

'Look. I've found a villa in Umbria.' Ruth shows him her phone.

He glances at it. 'We went to Italy last summer. Why not Portugal?'

A casual suggestion? Perhaps. 'Why Portugal?'

'Why not?'

She remembers.

'This is a holiday. Not a work trip.'

'Yes, but I need to visit the Portuguese bridge site. We could have a holiday there too.'

'No!' Ruth interrupts him sharply. 'You promised we'd have two weeks together without working and we do little enough as a family as it is.'

'They're fine, those two. They'll be OK. Seeing the site wouldn't take more than half a day if we found a place nearby.'

Ruth puts her coffee mug aside. 'There's more to life than work Simon. Why don't you just give the next competition a miss.'

'What? Why would you say that?'

Ruth looks at him, mouth closed.

10

'Entering competitions gets you known and raises your profile. And this one in Portugal's going to attract huge attention. Exactly what I need after the Thames Footbridge.'

'No.' Ruth repeats. 'The holiday's for us. Just the four of us. It's a break from work with screens off for all of us. Not an opportunity to pack in even more.

Chapter 2

Ruth

You never know, this could be OK. The house seems great. Ruth lies back on the orange and purple striped cushions of an almost perfect lounger and closes her eyes. She takes a long slow breath.

What an exhausting journey. The children were freewheeling all over the place as if they thought nothing they did was dangerous. An intrusive image pops up, again, of a total stranger grabbing James off the baggage handler as he rides perilously close to the suitcase chute. Like rescuing a duckling before it's swept over the weir. Extraordinary to be so trusting and so certain others will look out for you. It's time they learned to look out for themselves. Or for each other. Thank God they've crashed.

Ice cubes clink as Simon places a glass in her hand. 'Got here,' he says and collapses into a wicker chair on the terrace.

Not possible to phone up for a delivery in rural Portugal but, as requested by Ruth, the agent has left an arrival pack for them in the fridge. Bread (hard and somewhat grey), two bags of nuts that the children snaffle as soon as they see them, and salad in profusion arranged round a nameless smoked fish. Fresh peaches, grapes, figs and oranges in a glass bowl, and a blue and yellow plate of almond biscuits that turn out to be sticky and soft. A bottle of Portuguese white is cooling in the fridge.

They eat in the dark by the lights round the pool. They reject most of the bread and the bony bits of the oily fish, enjoy the salad and fruit, then discover the bendy biscuits are delicious. Laughing like conspirators, they hide them from the children and collapse into bed. Too tired to make love they relax into a well-worn and easy physical closeness that leaves Simon comatose and Ruth knowing she is loved but not feeling cared for. Accommodating to his wishes would feel better if he'd said thanks for swapping Italy for Portugal.

At 3am Isabel has a nightmare. Simon fails to console her. She ends up with Ruth and he ends up, all 6 foot 3 of him, in a child's bed, feet out in the breeze.

At 4.35 James starts whimpering. He's trying to stir himself. Too late. He pees as he struggles to the bathroom and collapses onto the floor in tears. Simon does his best. Strips off the wet clothes, roughly mops the floor with them and a sheet, dumps everything in the bath and takes James with him into the only dry bed. James goes straight back to sleep, flinging spiky limbs to right and left, and occupying far too much space.

'Well, he didn't do it on purpose.' Ruth is tired and cross and so is everyone else. Simon's attitude of personal injury is absurd. Unnecessary.

The children refuse fruit and bread for breakfast.

'Yuk. It's made of doormat crumbs.'

There's coffee but no milk.

'We'll go shopping.' Ruth makes a snap decision.

The local town has no supermarket. The drive to the big one is long and hot, and on the way home James howls. He's lost his choc-ice. The howls turn into hilarity when Simon releases a fart-squelch getting out of the car, and hops about swearing loudly. Melted chocolate has soaked through both the back rest and his shirt and has congealed in a messy brown stain.

'Bugger,' he says. He glares at James. 'However did you manage that?' He walks off. Ruth fetches kitchen paper and a knife to deal with choc-ice on car seat and goes back for the washing up liquid and a bowl of warm water. She hears Simon humming in the shower. Frowns and goes back for the groceries.

Then she enters negotiations with the Portuguese-speaking agent who prevaricates before agreeing to supply another mattress and threatens to charge full price for it. Clean sheets forgotten. Ruth chases them up. The children refuse to eat anything but cereal for lunch then, revived, they set off to explore their new territory.

It's down-time for adults, Simon indoors and Ruth on the lounger. Quiet until her overworked brain is alerted by the strange sound of silence. The children. Where are they? She sits up fast, destabilizing the almost perfect lounger. They're riding a blow-up whale round the pool and feeding each other bendy almond biscuits from the blue and yellow plate in perfect harmony. They giggle as the plate slips into the water and see-saws to the bottom of the pool. Pity about those biscuits.

Oh!

Don't scare them. Ruth leaps quietly to the rescue and lowers herself into the pool looking like a jellyfish with legs instead of tentacles, yellow sundress floating around her, and joins the party. Isabel is eight and she's passed her 10 metre test. She's tall enough to open the gate to the pool. James is six and he can't swim. She guides the whale to the shallow end, lifts him onto the steps, and together they go in search of armbands. Then she opens a new rulebook.

- Only grown-ups can open the gate to the pool.
- Never swim unless a grown-up is watching.
- Always put armbands on before you go through the gate.
- No food in the pool.

At first all of them are uncertain whether to sleep by day or by night, in a bed or on a lounger, together or apart but by day three the recovery process is up and running. Time to deal with an interfering niggle.

'So,' Ruth says to Simon as they eat dinner outside. 'When's it going to be? When are you going to abandon us?'

'What?' He stares towards her silhouette. 'What do you mean?'

'To visit the bridge site. That's why we're here isn't it?'

'Ruth, you agreed. We both agreed. Don't get annoyed. It won't even take a whole day.'

Did she agree? Or gave in to keep the peace?

'I know. It's good here with just the four of us, and the children love having you around. But it's going to interrupt the feel of it. The being on holiday ...'

'It'll be fine. It won't take long. I bet they'll hardly miss me.' There's a long silence. 'You could come too, you know.'

'For goodness sake. The kids would be bored stiff. We'd be hot and bothered and in the way.' She holds onto the arms of the chair. 'Why don't you get it over and done with?'

He agrees, and Ruth does the planning. Simon will drop them at a park with a pool and pick them up on the way home.

'You drive,' Ruth says. It's Simon's day for being in charge, and once he's left them in the park they all relax.

The pool is a huge success. Isabel and James, play in the water on a hot day, make friends and laugh and invent ways of communicating with anyone, language no barrier. Someone gives the children a drink and Ruth buys two bunches of purple grapes to share. She installs herself on a wooden day bed with thick green cushions and opens her book 'A Thousand Splendid Suns.' Great. The tensions of the life she has helped to create begin to fall away. She loves being able to cover all bases despite the high demand. It feels competent. Now something for me.

Lunch consists of a strange selection of snacks, including more bendy biscuits, in the shade of an oak tree, damp towels spread out to dry. They make a family group of day beds. Ruth distributes plastic bottles of water and they settle down to play, read or doze.

Until Ruth's phone springs into life.

Liz, temporarily in charge of Grainbox, is worrying about the financial crisis. Ruth resists her vision of shock waves threatening to swamp the whole thing and places her feet back on the ground. There's nothing she can do about that from here.

'It will be fine,' she says. She focuses on worry limitation and arranges daily check-ins with regular emails. Hope that's enough.

She picks up her book and frowns. Turns back a couple of pages and the frown vanishes.

'How did it go?' Ruth asks when Simon comes to pick them up. 'Did you get what you needed?'

'Fantastic. Inspiring. Difficult. It makes a huge difference to see it for real, especially in the heat. River banks at different heights. Not unusual of course, but it makes it harder to design something balanced, and stylish and beautiful from every angle. Need for huge amounts of traffic and trains too … Technically it poses difficult problems. Interesting …'

She turns off as he goes on about the technicalities. His mind is utterly engaged, attention directed towards one challenge after another. She offers an occasional ummm, or ohhh and the children sleep.

At home, she unpacks, gives the kids the kind of wash her mother called a lick and a promise, shoves their stuff in the washing machine, microwaves them a meal and resorts to the TV pacifier. She comes to rest outside feeling as if the bunch of rubber bands that has taken up residence round the grey matter inside her skull is tightening up again. It's the divided attention effect that comes from splitting herself between so many bases including a barrage of messages from the marketing team at Grainbox. Result: buzzing in the brain.

'What's to eat?' asks Simon, oblivious, handing her another clinking glass.

'I haven't a clue,' she says, discovering how to open a soul-window. Does he ever tune in to anyone but himself? Does he understand what 'together' means? Is everything he does only about winning the next prize?

'Why don't you see what's there and bring something out here? … and get the children into bed while you're at it?' Not a command, but two or three notches beyond a mere suggestion.

She goes for a swim and hopes it will settle her brain.

Chapter 3

Dani

The afternoon sun highlights the limbs of two children against the red, blue and white tiles of a Victorian hall floor. Maya is pulling on her shoes without undoing the laces. Kiri stands behind, syncopating the tapping of ten fingers and one foot. She's waiting her turn.

'I'm going. Ready?' Dani grabs his shoulder bag and key-checks the pocket of his shapeless jacket.

He puts his head round the kitchen door. 'We won't be late.'

'OK.' Amit looks up from his paper. 'Have a good time.'

'Wouldn't miss it for anything.' Dani says. They grin.

'Why don't you come too?' Maya yells to Amit as she grabs her coat.

'Me? No way.' He laughs. 'Far too terrifying. Besides, I'm cooking. Chili challenge for supper.'

Dani and Maya bounce off down the road. The front door bangs as Kiri runs to catch up, one arm searching for a sleeve.

In Kew Gardens Dani stops. It's a beautiful day and his two girls, with pistons for knees and elbows, add spontaneous action to the stillness of a World Heritage site designed in the eighteenth century. He catches his breath.

Maya and Kiri head to the tree top walkway. They're right, he thinks, it's paradise in the sky. You can stand on tiptoe at the top to see over the rails and look down on the birds and flowers and tree tops. A top-down view instead of the usual bottom-up one. Bright colours added.

They climb up together, and the magic turns out to be reliable. Sun in the trees puts phizz into the imagination and the children invent new worlds for each other.

Kiri imitates bird calls. Maya imagines living in a tree house.

'We'll get Amit to start an open-air café up here.'

'With seats swinging from the branches.'

'And only hard things to eat so there's no spilling …'

Re-rooted back on the ground, the words that Dani couldn't find when he had needed them last night, suddenly come to mind. Amit had bombarded him with questions. Again.

What are you going to do with yourself? Amit had demanded. Why don't you use that big brain of yours and find something serious to do?

Dani had tried to stop the onslaught by telling Amit he was fine, but now he knows what he wants to say: I'm looking after our girls. They need me and I need them. That makes me happy.

Later that evening Dani was surprised to find how easy it was to say this to Amit, and he added a heartfelt explanation.

'It's not that I'm not bothered. It isn't that I haven't thought about what I'm doing. I have. Seriously. And it means I can give Maya and Kiri the time they need. They're already 11 and 8 so it's not for ever.'

Amit put an arm over Dani's thin shoulders as he replied. 'And that way you set me free to go all over the place. But it shouldn't go on too long, all the same.'

Onslaught over.

During his next visit to the running track Dani goes for the feel-good factor rather than a stretcher. He's happy because there's a gang of teenagers in the changing room and he is the one who negotiated special rates for them. That worked.

He looks up as he's overtaken by someone with exceptionally long legs and pushes himself on for a pace or two. There's something familiar about the back in front of him. His head sinks forward again, and his gaze re-roots itself on his running shoes.

A couple of circuits later the man in front slows down. The gap between them closes.

'No,' Dani says to himself, audibly. 'It can't be.' His heart pounds, not only from running. The athletic stranger with dark curly hair walks away.

'Hello. Hang on a minute …' Dani struggles to make himself heard.

The stranger glances round and Dani flings both arms up in the air. He waves. The long-legged runner turns away.

Oh. No. 'Stop! Don't go!' Dani pushes himself on. I can't let him go. 'It's me. Dani,' he gasps.

The stranger stops and takes another look. Slowly he begins to smile. By the time the smile has reached his eyes Dani has crossed the gap between them. No need to hold back. He envelops him in a bear hug.

'Dani!' Simon says and holds him away. He looks closely at his face before returning the hug. 'It can't be you! After all this time. I didn't recognise you without the hair. What are you doing here?'

'Running of course.' Dani laughs.

It's like being caught in a whirlwind as they both talk at once. Where do you live? What do you do? Are you on your own? Got a family? How's it going? What happened after you left school?

Dani moves the moment on. 'Time for a coffee? I so want to know what's happened to you.'

When they reach the café, he leads the way to a table in the window. Simon's thoughts are whirling. When did we last see each other? Wonderful to be together again. Dreadful to have been out of touch so long.

'How long is it?' Simon says. 'Can it be twenty years? Weren't you fifteen when you left school?'

'That makes it twenty-two. Yup. What do you do now?'

'Design bridges. I love it. I won a prize for the last one, a footbridge over the Thames. I went solo a while back, and I've built up my own team. It's exciting.'

19

'What happened to your grandfather? He was such a lovely man.' A stream of memories suddenly opens up.

'Oh! He died. Six years ago. I still miss him. Do you remember his picture of The Golden Gate Bridge? I've got it for good now. It lives by my front door.'

'So that fits together.'

'What?'

'With your liking for bridges.' Dani hesitates, '… and your parents?'

'I never see them. They made some new friends and travel a lot. They're no more interested in our children than they were in me.' Simon shrugs. 'They live in South Africa now.' He provides just the facts. No surprises there.

'What about you?' Simon asks.

Dani clicks open his phone and shows off his girls. 'Maya loves designing houses and Kiri is always singing. She has the best sense of humour.' His eyes linger on their faces. 'I'm with Amit. He's from Malaysia. We've been together fourteen years. And we're pioneers in the world of civil partnerships. And in the world of adoption.'

'That's amazing. What do you do?' Simon asks.

'Amit's a mathematical whizz and management consultant. He's the success story. I manage a local charity shop and organise the volunteers and lead fund-raisers. Mostly I look after the children and the house. Amit's a wonderful cook, but he's away a lot.' He leans back in his chair. Relaxed. 'I'm not a bit surprised you're an architect. Just the right place for someone with so many talents.' He looks straight at Simon. 'What about your family?'

'Ruth started a business that supplies biodegradable packaging. She's called it Grainbox. Isabel is 8 and James is 6.' He finishes his coffee. 'I should be getting back to them. Let's meet again. Soon.'

'So good to see you.'

They fix a date for more running, together, and part with another hug.

Dani walks home almost as fast as he was running. Wonderful, he says to himself. There never was a better friend. Or a more interesting one. Amit will love him. They're similar in a way. Both prolific polymaths.

But some of Dani's memories make him shudder. He's glad to hear Simon's parents are out of the picture. Now he's learned the terms he knows exactly how to describe them: emotionally illiterate and seriously neglectful. Everyone who knew them understood the Westover's only child was a credit to them. They'd heard the boasts. They knew that Simon always came out top whether training for athletics or choosing the exact combination of arts and sciences that the school discouraged. Prize-giving days were embarrassing. Westover this. Westover that. Maths and German. Art history and physics. No one else got a look in. He went on accumulating ever grander trophies.

'He's no bother,' Simon's father said.

'No trouble at all,' added his mother.

But that wasn't the way Dani saw it. Either Simon brought home another prize or he wasn't worth bothering with. Their attitude was chilling.

Dani remembers the endless after-school hours he spent at Simon's home without ever feeling a sense of real connection. There was no hint of friction but the only thoughts those parents had were about themselves. They had no idea what mattered to Simon, what he wanted, needed, or worried about. Dani was shocked by a sudden flashback memory of him sitting at their kitchen table in front of a sticky plate of pasta that he couldn't swallow. Right back there in an instant. Unable to open his mouth or breathe freely. Witness to an unsmiling inquisition. He heard Simon's parents say:

'Maths OK?'

'Ready for chemistry tomorrow?'

'Did you rewrite the essay you showed me? When's it due?'

'Dani you'd better be off now. Simon has work to do.'

It seemed endless. They kept the tally of Simon's achievements as if they were counting a pile of treasure. Now he has his own children Dani wonders how Simon survived.

Probably because of Simon's grandfather. He was a turmoil of a man with an untidy house full of books, music, carpentry tools and muddy boots. He had an unstoppable grin and he knew how to make schoolboys laugh. He taught them to toss pancakes, to understand trigonometry, and to enjoy wholly demonstrative male hugs. His house was a place of warmth and freedom, and Dani knew that Simon had his grandfather to turn to when he was suddenly moved to a different school.

Parents of a younger child complained to the headmaster that Dani was leading their son astray and that he had a careless attitude towards achievements. They had spotted Dani with an arm over their son's shoulders and said their son had developed an unhealthy degree of attachment to him.

The matter was dealt with quietly and quickly. Dani's parents were persuaded that a more creative school would suit him better and he was moved. The friendship with Simon ended there and then.

Dani suspected that Simon was bereft. His parents wouldn't have noticed.

Simon

Simon is cushioned in his favourite corner of the sitting room sofa. Not reading. No music playing. He can't keep still. Thoughts of Dani and of Ruth pull him this way and that as if they were connected even though they've never met. Ruth watches him from her armchair in the window.

'Tell me more about Dani. Your grandfather told me how fond he was of him, but not a lot else. What makes him so important?'

Simon hesitates. 'He was the best friend I ever had. We met in the first year of secondary school.'

'So, what's he like?'

'When Dani was at school it was common knowledge that he didn't care.'

'What? How does that make sense?'

22

'There wasn't anything you could do to upset him. You could tease him, taunt him, up-end him, laugh at him and he would always remain your friend.'

'Sounds too good to be true.'

'Maybe. But it wasn't. Lots of people found it impossible to believe. And they teased him mercilessly and took advantage.'

'Dani's real name is Daanish. His grandparents arrived from Kolkata immediately after the war with large numbers of his family following soon after. His sister Sita got leukaemia when they were in primary school. He helped look after her until she died, shortly before we met.' Simon leant his elbows on his bony knees. 'We listened to music together. We made each other laugh.'

'Is that what made you friends?'

'Partly. We were good for each other. Almost instinctively. He was like my other half. He seemed to understand what I meant even when I couldn't put it into words. And the way he was singled out and picked on at school was horrible. I stood up for him.'

'Uh uh …'

'Fighting battles. Not just verbally. Dani was never going to fight for himself.'

'Did it get you into trouble?'

'Yes. My grandfather patched us up if we needed it. He treated Dani like another grandson.'

'I wish I'd known your grandfather better.'

'Without him I'd have been totally lost. He protected me. And rescued me. I cut myself off when Dani left school. I couldn't talk about it. My parents were useless. They didn't even notice how upset I was.' Simon's route through the past sounds less smooth than it used to.

'Your grandfather told me something else…'

'Oh?'

'He said that Dani had an instinctive way of tuning in to people. He hit all the right notes without even trying. He was happy to show his feelings and good at talking about them. He said it was as if he gave you a new vocabulary.'

23

'He didn't say that did he? That's amazing. I never realized …'
Simon rubbed a hand across both eyes. 'I was probably too young
to understand but I could be myself with Dani. I never could be
like that at home.' He stops. 'Let me think…'

All that emphasis on achievements … even the smallest hint of
failure could dump you in the ditch. It was threatening. Terrifying
at times. And the feeling that might happen again still comes back.
Not often, but it's always there in the background.

'It's complicated,' he says and shakes his head. 'I'm so happy to
see him again.'

'Why haven't you told me about him before.'

'I don't know. I think I didn't realise what I was missing. And it
seemed best to leave the past behind.'

Ruth

As the autumn winds gather strength the cogs and wheels of the
Westover family life move on. The children are in bed, Susie is out
and Simon and Ruth sit at the kitchen table, plates pushed aside,
wine glasses within reach.

Ruth takes a deep breath. Simon notices that something's not
right and squares up a fraction. Ruth wills her big hands to keep
still but they seem to have a mind of their own. Simon watches
them and blinks. Purses his mouth but says nothing.

Ruth looks up and then away. 'I feel as if we're barrelling along
the same road in separate cars,' she says.

Simon reaches for the bottle and tops up his glass. 'Hardly
surprising,' he says. 'Two working lives in perpetual motion and
both of us doing our own thing. At least we're independent and
not living in each other's pockets. Both of us are on the up, even
if we're going at different speeds.' He turns his glass round by
the stem.

He's not hearing me, Ruth thinks. She tries again. 'It's all work
and no play now, for both of us. As if we're on totally different paths.'

'Yup,' he says. 'Work's gone well. And fast. I don't get time for much of a breather. Nor do you though.'

'Well … I've had lots of worries to sort and problems to solve since the financial crash. It's not all plain sailing you know, and you're not exactly in the business of sharing the load here.'

'I put the children to bed tonight!' His response is as automatic and as fast as a knee-jerk. He frowns. What's she on about?

'It sounded like a riot from down here. Shrieks and yells and laughing and splashing. Bouncing and ragging about from all three of you. Then tears when you ordered them to bed. How could they possibly settle down? Why is everything you do so high octane?'

'They like having fun, don't they?'

'But what happened in the end? The bathroom full of wet clothes and towels, and I'm left mopping up faces and floors as well as settling them down. Why don't you notice your effect on people?'

'What?' He snaps to attention. Volume not in control. 'I do. Look at my work team. Ask them.' That's not fair, he thinks.

He hears her take a deep breath. 'OK. I do know,' she says more slowly. 'That's a big success story. Largely due to you. But I'm talking about us not them.'

'What do you mean?' Simon puts the wine glass down and looks at her. 'About us? In what way? Have I done something wrong?'

She looks at the table.

'It's as if you and I are standing back-to-back, facing the wind and the rain and the patches of sunlight, but never look at each other directly.'

'That's nonsense. You're talking in clichés … Get real …'

'As if going out there to keep on winning is all you're on about and nothing else matters. As if your relationship with me and the kids is take-it-or-leave-it … one-dimensional.' She is flushed now. One hand moves to her throat. 'What's happening?'

'Nothing. What's the matter?' Simon's fingers run through his hair. First one hand then the other flattens down the waves. He pulls his legs in under the chair. 'Nothing's happening. I don't know what you mean ...'

He puts a hesitant hand out towards hers, now lying flat on the table between them. Not far enough. She moves hers back.

'Then think about it.'

'Wow. That was sudden.'

Silence. He gets up. Picks up the empty bottle and chucks it into the recycling with a clatter.

'I don't think you have the slightest clue what I'm talking about.' She looks at him straight.

'Don't I?' Words fail him. He walks away and leaves her at the kitchen table.

'I don't know how long I can go on like this.' Ruth whispers.

He turns back, hand on the door frame. 'What?'

'You heard.'

'Is that really what you mean?'

'Uh-uh,' she says quietly, without looking up.'

He goes on into the sitting room.

When Ruth eventually decides to go to bed she sees him from the hallway, slumped into a corner of the big cream sofa. As she walks by, he uncrosses his legs then recrosses them and she hears a mutter. 'But everything's on course. There's no need to worry.'

From the hallway she watches him lean forwards and put both hands to his head. She's two or three steps up the stairs before he speaks again and she pauses to listen.

'I can't bear it when you're angry with me.'

Did I hear that right? She asks herself.

Chapter 4

Ruth

The light has only just dimmed on a September evening that still feels like summer. Ruth walks across the park just ahead of Simon on their way to have Friday night supper with Dani and Amit. Maya and Kiri are staying with friends and Susie is with Isabel and James.

Ruth had arrived home from work late and the moment she opened the door Isabel rushed at her holding out a crumpled drawing with both hands.

'James scribbled all over it,' she yelled, tears dampening her cheeks.

Simon was slouched on his usual sofa corner listening to Stan Getz, either oblivious to, or ignoring, the tumult coming from the kitchen.

Susie had just managed to de-escalate the crisis so Ruth took James upstairs and let him play with the bath taps while she changed into her favourite blue sweater. Isabel, with a clean sheet of paper in front of her, got straight back to work as if nothing unusual had happened.

'Bath ready,' Ruth shouted down the stairs, and they left Susie to take over.

Now it's hard not to stride out at full speed. Ruth pulls out the scrunchie she had forgotten to take out of her hair and shakes her head. Getting to know Dani and his family has been great. At last there seem to be some people Simon can relax with.

'Good to be going out, just us,' she says. 'The more I see of them the better I understand why you and Dani were such good friends.'

27

'Are.' Simon corrected.

She gave him a sideways look. Bit her lip. 'He isn't a bit how I expected.'

Simon shrugs. 'Oh?' Silence. 'Odd how meeting the partner of someone you know well can tell you more about them,' he adds.

'Oh?' She knows it's not helpful to match the terseness but she does it all the same.

'Well Amit isn't in the least musical, and music was always important to Dani.' Simon puts a hand to his temple.

'You sound puzzled.'

'Dani's so curious. Always interested in new stuff. He's creative and adventurous. It's not right for him to be a stay-at-home person.'

'Oh?' She searches behind the honeysuckle for the doorbell.

They're greeted with warm smiles and delicious smells.

Amit is wearing a navy apron with thin blue stripes. He loves to make a meal for friends and nothing will stop him talking as he cooks. Simon and Ruth already know what good company he can be, and his roundness is definitely part of his charm.

Ruth catches sight of Amit's feet. Amit's shoes have red toes, blue heels, and yellow sides stitched onto standard brown soles. 'Amazing shoes.'

Amit grins. 'Glad you like them.'

They talk as they watch him cook. He crushes the garlic, reaches for the spoon, picks up the chopping board, slices a cucumber without looking and keeps on talking, listening and cooking with an astonishing capacity to multi-task. He's totally focused and infinitely distractable both at once. He never stops moving but none of that interferes with the stream of conversation.

Simon

Simon's attitude to the financial crisis is simple: the Westover group will survive. He doesn't want to talk about it, especially to Ruth. Listening to pessimism is useless. Boring. But the summer has given

28

everyone a shock, so no one can leave the topic alone and that goes for Ruth and Amit as well.

Amit is the optimistic one.

'I reckon there'll always be other possibilities. Other markets. Just have to keep an eye out for opportunities and move fast when you spot one.' He dips a spoon into the pot, blows on it and tastes. He thinks about it whilst he opens a cupboard full of spices and searches through the jars.

'Here. Let me fill your glass.' He looks from Ruth to Simon. 'And yours.'

Simon moves his glass within reach. Amit's an attentive host as well as a good cook. He pops the lid back on a spice jar.

'Didn't your family come from Birmingham?'

'What? Me?' Simon looks from one to the other.

'Simon did. Not me.' Ruth says and turns back to Amit. 'Not so easy for my business to adapt when everything keeps changing. I used to be ahead of the competition. But as soon as I've got something up and running others jump on the bandwagon. There are so many new ideas all the time it's impossible to keep track.' She laughs. 'Like watching you cook!' She rests her elbows on the counter and balances her chin on interlaced fingers. 'But seriously, it's worrying.'

Simon's eyebrows rise. She can't really be worried about her business can she? Is that what makes her so on edge?

His mind wanders off and he resurfaces to find that now they're talking about doing something together with the children.

'We could go skating,' Ruth suggests.

'Not me.' Amit laughs. 'The pantomime?'

'The Richmond one is meant to be brilliant,' Simon says. 'But we've never been quick enough to get tickets.'

'I'll do it,' Dani offers.

Amit is not one for exercise. 'I don't want to put the kids off. Better for them to feel free to do anything at all.' He's stacking up plates. 'Whatever turns out to suit them.'

'Yup,' Dani says. 'I don't mind what they do.'

But, Simon remembers, the first thing Dani told me about Maya was that she loves making houses.

'How d'you get to make homes?' Maya had asked. 'What d'you have to do? Do you have to be good at maths?'

'Well, yes. Are you?'

'OK I reckon. But I'm useless at making models. Were you good at it?'

'I totally destroyed the first one I was really pleased with,' Simon had told her. 'I left it on the bedroom floor and trod on it in the dark.' They had both laughed.

Simon turns back to the present. There's nothing that grabs Isabel or James in that way, he thinks. Kiri's always listening to something, or humming, or making music. Like Dani. Strange, given they don't share any genes at all.

Surely children need a bit more guidance than that? So they can make the best of themselves. Parental pressure is definitely to be avoided, but still. You shouldn't go too far in the other direction.

Being around people who think together out loud in such personal ways is disturbing. They seem to let go of habitual layers of protection without any fear of being cast into outer darkness.

Ruth

Ruth needs regular contact with the outside world, however watery it might be. Without it she feels stifled and scratchy. So she plans expeditions for everyone and that helps all of them develop new lines of friendship. Strands that reach within and between the generations.

A new greenfield site has been developed along the local canal and it provides a slice of natural countryside in mid-city that makes the air smell different. The story of reclamation has been depicted on a laminated board placed against a backdrop of shining holly near the entrance. It shows groups of volunteers with the discarded bikes and shopping trolleys they've dragged out of the mud, and people in shirt sleeves using unfamiliar tools to cut branches back from the water.

Ruth wants everyone to know how quickly the natural world recovers when it's been saved from being a rubbish dump and released to do more of its own thing and she takes them there for a walk one Sunday. Four children with billowing anoraks race on ahead and Amit goes with them, his black and silver wellies catching the light. Ruth and Dani walk together and Simon follows behind listening to them talking about their past, and thinking about how much Ruth loves wetlands. He hears Dani say it.

'Underlying water systems. You're passionate about them aren't you.'

'Yes,' she says. 'They're crucial. Everything depends on them. Including us.'

She tells Dani the same story she told him when they first met, in almost the same words.

'We lived in Shropshire, by a river. There were reed beds in the water meadows at the back of the house that had spread through our garden fence, rotting the posts that held it up.' Ruth describes the landscape of her childhood as if she could see it.

'There were wagtails that pivoted themselves up and over the rotting slats of the fence and walking along the river under the willows there were patches of water weed where water voles sat using both hands to feed themselves. You had to tread carefully or they plopped into the water and made for holes in the riverbank, creating a V-shaped bow-wave with their noses.'

'If you crept along quietly you could get close enough to watch.'

Ruth was wearing a myriad shades of blue when he heard this story.

'I loved that place,' she goes on. 'That watery world was full of light. A light that spread out and up from the ground. When you came indoors late on a summer evening it was a shock to discover that inside it was dark.'

The path is narrow. Two in front. One behind.

31

'Just you?' Dani asks.

'Just me. My parents were quite old when I turned up, and all three of us loved the outside world. We spent hours together out there. Indoors was the service station, especially in summer. Just for washing, cooking, sleeping ...'

She explains how all their sensitivities drew attention to the outside world at the expense of the indoor one and about discovering why the activities of living things look so purposeful.

She picks a stem of dried grass still hanging on to its seedcases and spins it round between finger and thumb. 'We all loved that place. Not just me.'

'I had no idea,' Dani says. 'I thought you came from suburbia, like the rest of us. I'd never have imagined you that way. So immersed in the elements.'

She knows where she belongs in this world, Simon thinks. I never had a clue.

'We never thought of the water as dangerous. But the damp was a killer. It's difficult to heat an ancient cottage built alongside water meadows. Mist seemed to live inside as well as out, especially in the kitchen. Going to bed, except on the warmest summer days, meant wearing socks and curling up tight to create a small warm patch. Stretching out or turning over made you shiver. When Dad was in work, we kept warm. It was much harder after the railways laid people off.' Ruth pushes a strand of hair behind an ear.

A moorhen skitters across the canal water ahead.

'Mum's chest infections gave her a permanent cough. That winter she was caught in the floods and spent the night in the car. When she got home she couldn't get warm. By the time Dad realised she was ill she had severe pneumonia.'

Simon clenches his fist in his pocket.

'They were slow to get help,' she explains. 'Though I don't think Dad ever told me the whole story. She started to struggle to breathe so he called the doctor. By the time an ambulance arrived she was in a coma. She died the next day. Before I could get there.'

Simon's hand reaches out towards Ruth but not far enough to interrupt.

They walk on.

Ruth goes on. 'Dad was nearly 20 years older than Mum, and he didn't manage well on his own. He had a fall, and that was it. We got him into a home, but he only lasted a few months longer.'

Dani lays a hand gently on Ruth's arm.

'I spent my first summer vacation there. Alone. Sorting things out to sell the cottage. Mum, Dad, our home. So many losses all at once. It was overwhelming.'

She stops and looks down into the water.

'The cottage has had a new lease of life though. And the money helped me out at uni. It paid for my master's and got my business started.'

They come to a bench and Ruth and Dani sit down. Simon joins them.

'Simon knows all about it,' Ruth says, turning towards him, 'though we didn't get together until after that.' He nods.

'Those wet worlds are worth preserving, even if they can be killers. I know that goes for the dry places too, but they'll never mean as much to me as the soggy ones. Full of cold wet life of all sorts once you know where to look.'

She laughs. 'It's embarrassing I suppose to end up trying to transform the wasteful world of packaging for fear of losing the wetlands.'

Dani looks from Ruth to Simon and back. 'Both of you have this amazing sense of direction,' he says. 'No wonder you're together.'

'What?' Simon asks. How come we end up at cross purposes so often then, he thinks but does not say.

'You both have an energy that drives you on. You to change the world.' Dani looks at Simon. 'To make something stupendous. Ruth to preserve it.'

'Oh!' Simon's eyebrows rise. 'Yes. Maybe you're right.' He laughs. 'Internal motors keep us going. Hers comes from her convictions, but mine's more like pressure from behind. Do it, or else … . .'

'Or else what?' Ruth asks.

Simon has no answer to this.

Ruth is thoughtful. 'For me it's completely independent of what anyone else thinks. No need for prizes along the way.'

Simon rubs the corner of an eye with a knuckle, as if surprised by Ruth's answer.

'I'm the odd one out then,' Dani says, and hesitates while he looks back along the canal path.

'And? …' Ruth asks.

'I have no idea what it's like to feel that kind of drive. Or why some people have it and others are perfectly happy without. Like me.'

'But isn't there something missing?' Simon asks Dani.

Simon

Halloween gives everyone another excuse for getting together, once more in Dani and Amit's house.

With the lunch over, Maya takes charge. 'We're going to make a haunted house on the landing. OK?'

Dani passes close to Amit as he carries a load of plates from the table to the sink, a tea towel draped over one shoulder. They lean shoulder to shoulder. Shrug then smile.

'OK,' Amit fills the kettle. 'Move everything back afterwards. Everything. Back to where it came from.' He turns, switches on the kettle and reaches for the coffee.

With children out of the way it's easier to hear yourself speak.

'How's work? What are you going for next?' Simon asks Dani.

'What? Not sure!' He chooses a CD, presses play and turns the volume down.

'You?' He asks, slumping onto the mismatching sofa cushions.

Simon's fingers are moving with the music. 'Miles Davis. Kind of Blue. Remember how often we used to play it?'

Dani nods.

Simon crosses his legs. The music travels from head to toe. His foot disperses surplus energy.

'My dream,' Simon says, 'is to build a bridge that will make a difference. Innovative and beautiful. Crossing a gap that no one thought could be spanned. I need a perfect engineer to work with.'

The music plays on.

'But you didn't say. What would you go for?'

Dani shrugs. 'I'm not bothered.' He drinks his coffee. 'Got everything I want right here.'

Simon looks around. It's comfortable. Books crammed on the shelf, music, papers and games too. A jam jar stuffed with pens and pencils. The edge of a carrier bag poking out from behind a chair. A keyboard, uncovered with heaps of sheet music on the floor beneath.

'I've been lucky. This is what I've always wanted.'

Simon raises his eyebrows.

'There's nothing else I want.'

'I meant something you want to do. Not have.'

'Never crosses my mind.' Dani laughs. 'I like managing the charity shop. It's easy work. Nice things there and nice people. Running the home takes all my energy.' He's totally relaxed. 'The shop has nice cushions too.' He pats the one that has fallen between them. It has sequins sewn into pockets along the edges.

Simon lets it go.

A burst of laughter comes from Amit. 'Yes, you're right,' he says to Ruth. He leans forward in his chair. 'There's always a risk that I'll get sidetracked somehow or other, but I suppose that makes it easier to change direction.'

'Much harder for you. I think you need a whole new marketing team. Or a visit to Brazil. Or perhaps you should go back to uni to catch up on all the new stuff.' He stops, fingers still on the arms of his chair. 'No. Better still. Employ a new graduate off one of those environmentally sensitive courses, whatever they're called.'

Ruth laughs. 'You're certainly full of ideas. But I was leading the field only a few months ago. Now I'm in danger of being overtaken. It's worrying.' Ruth pushes her hair back. 'But I do think about the kids. I don't want to miss out.'

'It takes two to keep everything spinning. Perhaps I'm a natural juggler. I love the feeling of all those balls in the air at once. Constantly testing your dexterity. Pushing the limits.' Amit looks up.

'Lucky I'm a good catch!' Dani says.

'I can't get the balance right. I love to work,' Ruth says, ignoring the others. 'It's important to me and I'm useless if stuck at home too long. I get bored and irritable. Then I miss everyone when work takes me travelling and I end up feeling guilty.'

Oh? Simon looks up at her and frowns.

'You need a house-husband like Dani!' Amit says. 'He keeps everything going when I'm away. I do wonder though if he won't one day decide he was only half right.'

'Lost you. How d'you mean?' Ruth is frowning.

'Well, he's so talented. What'll happen to the creative side of him if he stays home all the time? When the kids fly off, we'll bore each other silly.'

'I doubt it.'

Suddenly there are shrieks from upstairs. It sounds as if a fiend is stomping about on the landing.

'Oh dear. James has lost it again.'

Simon's glad it's Ruth who will go to the rescue.

Ruth

At the top of the stairs she takes it all in at a glance. James sees her coming and knocks over a chair with a crash as he tries to grab the sheet that covers the girls' version of a spooky attic.

'James, stop it.'

'Leave us alone.'

'Go away we don't want you.'

James turns to Ruth and yells: 'They won't let me play ...'

36

She tries to hold onto him and gets thumped with two fists. She hangs on.

Dani comes to the rescue. Ignoring the fiend and his mother, he turns to the three girls. 'He keeps pulling things down…' 'He won't listen…' 'We want to make it dark inside and he keeps opening it up …'

'OK. Could you wait? Do another one on bonfire night?'

They negotiate. The impetus goes out of them.

'Right James. Now you can take it apart.' Ruth lets him go. He pulls the sheet that was functioning as a roof off the banisters and puts it over his head.

'Whooo hooo.' He waves his arms. Trips. A fallen ghost, but no longer snivelling. He tramples through the girls' domestic arrangements.

'Stupid.' A passing shot from Isabel.

Having let go of the current plan the girls are no longer bothered. They right the chairs and replace the bedding, the bathmat, and numerous squidgy animals.

'Get your coats on. we're going out,' Dani says, and leads the way downstairs followed by a flurry of legs, arms and hair. Ruth gathers up a scattering of paper, felt tips and used Sellotape. She grabs her coat and James's and follows Dani outside.

They come back as the light fades to find the house smelling of chocolate and peppermint and Simon dozing on the sofa.

'Wake up, Dad.' James thumps his knee. He stirs and stretches. James pulls him along to join the party in the kitchen.

'Here's a fishing rod each,' Amit gives everyone a wooden rod with a hook on the end dangling from bright red string.

'Bugs and spiders to deal with.'

A huge bowl covered with a cloth is in the middle of the kitchen table.

When everyone's ready, kneeling on chairs or stools, Amit whips the cloth off the bowl and they go fishing for peppermint-chocolate creepy crawlies.

'Whatever you catch you have to eat.'

Amit switches off the kitchen lights. A pumpkin with a toothy grin is lit from inside by a candle.

'Here Ruth.' Amit hands her the matches.

Ruth lights all the candles she can find and the four adults watch the fun.

Afterwards Ruth and Simon walk home. Isabel and James run on ahead.

'That was great,' Simon says.

'It was,' she says, and leaves it there. It was good to feel the warmth between Amit and Dani. But saddening.

Something has changed in Simon, Ruth thinks. It's impossible to talk to him properly anymore. His self-absorption is outrageous. Now that he's ticked the family box, it's as if he can concentrate on getting where he wants to be, regardless. But I'm not going to let myself get stuck in a box of his making.

Chapter 5

Ruth

Ruth is packing. It's an emergency. Her Spanish source of biodegradable packaging material has been invaded by competitors willing to pay over the odds for plant-based wrapping. She has difficult decisions to make and her mind is at full throttle, at this point in organizing mode.

She scans down her internal list. Flight booked, text sent to Simon (not answering his phone), talked Susie through Isabel and James's after-school clubs music lessons and play-dates, office responsibilities delegated to Liz, online shop arranged to be delivered when Susie will be in. Travel arrangements and contact details have been emailed to everyone, one copy printed out and pinned to the kitchen noticeboard. Done.

No. Not quite.

She sends a copy to Hannah in the office. Can't rely on Simon. Ready.

She sits with the children and they munch after-school fruit sticks that Susie supplies as if she's feeding a conveyor belt.

Isabel taps Ruth on the arm. 'Can I go to Meena's party on Friday?'

'Yes. Susie will collect you.'

'Uh-uh,' Susie says, and peels another pear.

'Are you going in an airbus?'

'No James. It's only a short flight. Do you want to see where I'll be?' She helps him find Madrid on her phone and shows him a picture of her hotel.

Her taxi arrives and she gives everyone a hug, Susie too, and collapses onto the back seat, bags at her feet. Phew! Free. Susie will cope fine. Where's Simon? Why doesn't he answer? Hope he doesn't create havoc in the evenings, Ruth's mind is full of uncertainties.

What next? She fires up her laptop to search for untapped sources of plant-based packaging materials but gives up. Right now, she thinks, a moving taxi is about as unstable as the global economy. Grim.

Simon

Simon comes home to find the children asleep. No clamour. He puts a box of lasagne into the microwave and takes the stopper out of the bottle of red they didn't finish last night. Glass in hand, he goes into the sitting room and puts it on the table by the sofa. He searches for a CD, hears the microwave beeping and goes to collect his food and a fork. Then he collapses onto the sofa.

Done. Ticked all the boxes. Designing the Portuguese bridge has been a huge amount of work and it's finished. The competition will be tough, but his design is exceptional, and it makes use of an unusual range of sustainably resourced materials. Unbeatable. He runs an imaginary eye slowly over his bridge as if it were already complete. A beautifully slender and stunning addition to a dramatic landscape. His whole body holds still for a second. A dream is about to be realized.

He finishes his lasagne and sends a text to Ruth, now high above the Pyrenees:

Application ready. All well here.

Don't let those Spaniards steal your thunder. S xxx.

He's searching for the right music to listen to when the phone rings. Dani. He smiles and stretches out his legs.

'Hi Dani. I'm collapsing. Just finished our entry for the Portuguese competition.'

'How did it go?'

'The engineers were worried that the new materials might not retain sufficient stiffness. They're going to have to carry huge loads.'

'And what's the verdict?'

'I wasn't convinced by the figures at first, but everyone was satisfied in the end. Huge relief to get it done.'

'So, can you come running tomorrow? I missed you this week.'

'Yeah. Sure. 6 OK?'

He chooses Beethoven's Archduke trio. It's like a conversation between friends. Or like different parts of yourself working things all the way through before reaching a conclusion. Always satisfying to listen to. Simon goes to bed early and falls asleep without another thought.

Isabel is crying. Simon looks at the clock, 3am. He hopes she will soon stop, but the crying turns into a wail: 'I want Mummy.'

'She's in Spain.' … Simon is shivering. Irritable. He rubs his eyes and it makes them smart.

'Try to go back to sleep.'

The wailing wakes James. A search for his lost killer whale only succeeds after all the other soft toys on the bed and the floor have been tossed into a corner. Very slowly Isabel types Ruth a message on Simon's phone:

Can't find my gim bag. Miss you. Come home soon. Is xxx.

No one gets back to sleep quickly and by the time it's light, and a normal time to get up, Simon is ragged. Fit for nothing. Susie deals with breakfast, loads the washing machine, finds the gym bag, treks a second time to school to deliver it. When she's back, she tidies up the mess spread by two small but busy lives into every room in the house, and eventually gets herself something to eat.

When Simon rushes back after work to grab his running gear he finds Susie struggling to keep the peace between two tired children while she makes them a meal. She stuffs a wodge of paper hankies into her jeans pocket and dumps two plates of pale green pasta onto the table with an uncharacteristic degree of clatter and inattention. Something is wrong.

'What's up Susie? You OK?'

'Dad's ill,' she says. 'Mum rang. He's in Lancaster hospital. It's serious. I need to get there.'

She has to leave as soon as possible. She has no choice.

His heart sinks. Of course she has to go. But can she finish getting tea and get the kids ready for bed before she goes?

'I'll have to leave soon or I'll miss the next train.'

'I'm so sorry.' Simon says it slowly. 'You get your stuff. I'll order you a taxi.'

He looks at the children. They're watching the adults in silence. Susie goes to pack and his heart sinks. But there really are no choices here. He orders Susie's taxi and pays for it in advance. When the taxi arrives she gets a hug from each of them and leaves without looking back. Simon sends a text to Dani.

Domestic crisis. Can't make it.

'What now?' he says aloud, to the children as well as himself.

'We usually have a pudding,' says Isabel as James shoves his uneaten pesto-pasta across the table. Isabel knows where the chocolate yoghurts are hidden and reaches into the back of the fridge.

A bath gives the children a second wind. They burst into the kitchen in their night-gear.

James runs to Simon and thumps him on the thigh. 'I'm hungry Dad.'

'Can we have supper with you?' Isabel asks.

'No to that one,' Simon says to Isabel. 'It's already well past your bedtime. You can have cereal. Go and find some bowls.'

42

'No.' Isabel is totally definite. She shakes her damp hair out of her eyes but refuses to look at him.

'Not cereal. That's for breakfast.' James is equally definite.

Simon opens a tin of beans and puts bread slices in the toaster. He turns to search for two plates when the doorbell rings. It's Dani.

'Are you OK? What's up? I was worried.' Dani makes himself heard above the shouting but gets no share of anyone's attention and sits down at the kitchen table.

Simon tips the beans into two bowls. 'Nothing is going according to plan here,' he says. 'Ruth's in Spain and Susie's Dad is ill. She's gone to Lancaster. Don't know when she'll be back.' He bites his lip.

'We're just about managing.' He pushes up his sleeves.

'Let me help.' Dani doesn't wait for a reply. He enlists Isabel as a kitchen guide and finds spoons and forks. He redirects James's fire-engine out from under Simon's feet and gets him to the table where the children eat in total silence.

James yawns and Simon takes his hand. They wave goodnight to Dani and Simon leads the way upstairs where he tucks the children into bed, teeth uncleaned and ready to crash.

Downstairs again, the men take mugs of tea into the sitting room. 'Anything else I can do?' Dani asks.

Simon's cheek twitches. His jaw aches from gritting his teeth. 'No thanks. I'll work short days this week and bring stuff home too.'

Just what I need right now, Simon thinks. How can I do anything serious if I've got to manage things here as well?

Chapter 6

Simon

Simon congratulates himself. Children fed and ready for school on time. He shuts the front door and watches them speed off down the hill. His phone rings. He's carrying two green school bags, handles too short to shoulder and keys in the other hand. Can't even answer the effing phone ...

'Ruth! Hi ... How's it going?'

'Still working out the size of the problem. All well?'

'Uh-uh.' Simon looks up. He'll have to hurry to keep up. 'I'm on the school run. Susie's Dad is ill. She's gone.'

'Oh! What's happened? Is he OK? How's Susie?'

'When will you be back?' Simon frowns as he speaks.

'By the end of the week at the latest. I may have to set things up somewhere else. Romania? Brazil? Don't know yet. Are the kids OK? Can you manage?'

'Have to. No choice. I'll work when they're at school. I'll start training for the first multi-tasking prize for men.' No response. Signal lost.

Simon grimaces. Nothing too hard to handle here, but having no Susie is dreadful. It totally interferes with everything. Bother her. In fact, bother both of them. Shit! He thinks. Between them, Susie and Ruth are creating chaos. He shakes his head. Don't be ridiculous. Her Dad didn't choose to get ill when Ruth's away. Ruth didn't choose for her business to be threatened by a financial crash.

He looks up. Isabel and James have disappeared into a mass of children, pushchairs, parents and helpers on the way to school. The kaleidoscope keeps shifting. So many people in the way. He stands still and concentrates. Still can't see them. What the hell? He starts to run and just misses stepping on a wayward pink scooter, green bags flapping as he runs. He reaches the corner. They're nowhere to be seen.

Heart thumping, he looks again. Both ways. There they are, skipping along with some friends, about to cross the road to the school gate. The panic subsides. He gasps.

'Wait!' he shouts, running to catch up while reaching for, and then ignoring, another buzz from his phone. 'Wait right there.' Oh dear. Too many people in the way. Watching. Amused no doubt by the sight of another incompetent Dad. Those kids really scared me. Simon makes the effort not to yell at them.

'But Dad you're so slow,' says James. 'Anyway, you're always on the phone. Why don't you keep up like Susie?'

Isabel, eyes down, shrugs and scrapes a pattern on the pavement with the sole of her shoe. 'We ALWAYS wait for Susie before we cross over. We're not stupid.'

Simon gathers himself together. It's just what they do. Child management can't be that difficult. After all they're not very big.

'OK. Now I know. Run on ahead if you like but keep in sight. Check that I've seen you before you disappear round a corner.' James reaches for his hand. Isabel keeps her distance. But they cross the road together.

Simon hands over the school bags and watches them dissolve into the playground free-flow. It's a relief. He's proud of their independence. Happy to see the friendliness with which they're greeted. He watches their confident entry into the noisy and busy world of school that he had found so alarming at their age and a lump comes to his throat. Lucky them. No need to win prizes just to earn your place at the table. No need to feel vulnerable around your contemporaries.

Time to sort out other stuff. He walks back up the hill. How will it be possible to fit everything in. Why not work at home? Why go to work and risk getting bombarded by others? There's no need to go into the office now the competition entry has been done. Working at home will be much better. More efficient. Might be able to go to the gym at lunch time too. Ha!

As he turns away from the school Simon takes out his phone. 'Hannah, I'm stuck at home. Can you help?' He knows he can usually catch her early so he wades straight in, unapologetically direct and demanding.

'What's up?'

He starts to explain his predicament, then stops short. It's hard to find the right words, and he doesn't need her to doubt his competence.

'Can you bring me the pile of blue folders on my desk? The New Project Group ones. I can work on those here. And if you chair the department meeting tomorrow then I could get them sorted. I'll email you an agenda later today.' He clenches a fist to emphasise the point as he walks fast uphill, pleased that he can find the breath for the stretch. He tells himself her workload is far less demanding than his.

'Simon, I'm completely full up all morning. Come in and get whatever you need. Then you can find someone else to lead the meeting too.'

Silence from Simon as it sinks in that his plan of enjoying a morning of uninterrupted work and some exercise before lunch has become as unrealistic as any other fantasy.

'OK. See you later perhaps.' He stops to think. 'If you're not too busy that is.'

This is not going to be straightforward.

Back home he flings his coat onto the banisters without a glance at the Golden Gate and goes straight to the kitchen.

He makes the coffee that he missed earlier. Sweeps the breakfast debris aside with one hand and opens the paper. The phone rings. Susie this time.

Simon's hopes rise. But then she tells him that her dad died during the night and her voice breaks.

'Oh no. That's awful. I'm so sorry.' Simon is indeed sorry. His concern lasts nearly 20 seconds before the top slot is swamped with worries about how long they will have to manage without her. 'How long do you need to be there?'

'Don't know right now. I need to be with Mum.' She blows her nose. 'There's a million things to do. She needs help.' He listens through a pause. 'I'll let you know as soon as I can, but it'll be a while. I'll email Ruth. And you.' She's uncharacteristically hesitant.

'Thanks for ringing Susie. I'm so sorry about your dad. Keep in touch.'

Simon stares at the milk blots drying on the kitchen table with the feeling that he's been roller-coasted into a kind of reality that he never signed up for. Forced into an attention-demanding world with no advance notice and no brain space. What about work? What about supervising the new projects? And catching up with the backlog left by all that work on the Portuguese bridge? There's no time to adapt to the complications of a woman's world. He sweeps a hand across the table, shuffles his feet about, then pushes his mug away, grabs his coat and rushes out.

The visit to the office takes longer than he hoped it would. When he reaches the school, rushed and hassled, he's carrying a loaded bag of folders as well as his briefcase. From the classroom door he can see James sitting sideways on his chair, arm-wrestling his neighbour as they wait to be set free.

'Hello. I'm collecting James Westover. I'm his dad.' Simon introduces himself to James's new teacher, the fierce Miss Bruno with the winning smile.

'James and Max! No more of that. I asked you to sit quietly.' She glances round the classroom. 'You can go James. Don't forget your coat.'

James explodes into the fresh air and races to the climbing frame. He chucks his school bag away and it skitters across the rubberised tarmac to land against the fence. Miss Bruno turns towards Simon again.

'Will you be at the parents' evening next week? I think it could be useful to think about James together.'

'Is there a problem?' Simon's quick-fire response is met with an eyebrow raise.

'He seems to find it hard to concentrate. Is that something you've noticed at home?'

'No. Not at all. He's always busy.' Never sticks long at anything would be Susie's way of putting it. But he's a bright kid too. That should be obvious.

'I'll tell Ruth. She should be back in time for that.'

'Either or both of you. That would be fine.'

Fine for some, Simon thinks, standing tall and looking down. He wonders what else Miss Bruno might have to say about his son. He may well be as much of a handful at school as he is at home, but isn't that normal for boys? She should know. He can see James hanging upside down from the monkey bars, coat totally obscuring his vision.

When everyone is fed, and the children are washed and storied Ruth rings for a goodnight chat. Isabel grabs the phone.

'Mum ... netball practice's been cancelled tomorrow. Can Meena come to my house instead?'

'Yeah, sure. As long as her mother knows about it and it's OK with Dad. Talk to him about it while Susie's away.'

With her current worry sorted, Isabel disappears on a task of her own. 'James! Come and get the phone. It's Mum,' she yells and lets it slide to the floor. She rearranges her menagerie of night-time companions and settles down just as she usually would.

James steps on the phone. 'Ow.' He can't make it work. 'Dad ... is it broke?' Simon sorts it.

Ruth's voice comes over clear. 'I heard that! What happened?'

'Isabel left the phone on the floor.'

48

'And you stepped on it, right?' Ruth is laughing now. 'Not again,' she says! 'I'm surprised that phone still works at all. How are you then J?'

'Dad let us have fish and chips for tea – and he put Nutella on bits of apple.'

'Sounds good. Did you like it?'

'Yeah. And he found my killer whale.'

'So, you're OK, then. Tuck in and tell me when you're really comfy.'

James wanders to his bed, followed by Simon, who draws the curtain and pulls up the duvet once James is installed beside the fearsome whale.

'In now,' James says. 'Night Mum.'

Simon gives him a kiss, retrieves the phone, turns off the light, and fixes the door the usual quarter inch ajar. Done.

It was talking to Ruth that settled the children down, Simon realises with admiration, relief, and a flicker of envy, and he talks to Ruth as he goes downstairs leaving the bath full of scummy water. He shuts the door on the remains of breakfast, supper and the unread newspaper in the kitchen.

'This is full-on amazing. There's hardly time to breathe. Can't imagine doing it five days in a row. When can you get home? Has Susie emailed you? I've not had a chance even to open the work I collected earlier and James's teacher wants to talk to us.'

'So hard for Susie. I've said just to keep us posted and to let us know when she's ready to think about coming back. I've had such a busy ...'

'I don't see how we can manage without her ... or rather how I can manage without either of you. What can I do?'

'I'll be back in a couple of days. I'll see what I can sort out. It's been a real shambles here. I've been talking to everyone, and hardly had time to breathe. Can't find a solution yet ...'

'That sounds good.'

'My shambles? Or my homecoming?'

Chapter 7

Ruth

Ruth and Simon sit in the kitchen, the wine bottle empty, dish-washer chugging, plans for next week pinned on the board. Ruth moves her empty glass back and forth through a wine-spill, making a purple Rorschach blot on the wipeable surface. She mops it up with a tissue. Her hand rises to her neck.

'Simon, have you thought about what I said before I went away? About us?'

Simon pockets his phone. He sits still, mouth firmly shut, neither looking nor answering. But no longer in electronic neutral.

No surprise there. A muscle in his cheek twitches. It's hard to go on. No time is ever the right time for this. Right.

'I meant what I said, about not being able to go on like this. It's too much. I'm doing more than I can manage.'

'Not now. I'm tired.' He yawns. Stretches his legs. 'Wasn't that great, meeting Dani and Amit in the park? All the kids running about together? It's bedtime.'

'No. We need to talk.'

'We need to sleep.'

'Yes. Soon.'

'Later. Another time.'

She thought he was avoiding facing any part of this. Now it occurs to her that he has no idea how serious she is. It's going to be difficult not to get into a fight. She imagines herself stepping carefully round the fire-pit of an all-out row.

'Simon, this can't wait.'

No response.

Then words spill over. 'I can't go on like this. It's too much. Children, the house, work, you. An endless stream of demands. I'm left listening to nothing but the noise of other people's worries. My head's too full. And it's getting worse. Something's got to change.'

Her lips make a hard line. She's determined not to cry.

Simon shows her an upright palm.

What? How dare he. This isn't traffic noise. Besides he has zero right of control here. Why does he assume he's in charge?

'You're doing too much. You'll be fine when Susie's back.'

'No, I won't. That won't change anything,' she responds with the immediacy of a ricochet. 'The problem is you're not interested in doing stuff here, at home. It's impossible to get your attention and you're behaving as if winning prizes is the only thing you care about. As if nothing else matters.'

'Whatever do you mean?' He glares directly at her. 'What are you suggesting?'

'I said it before. The sharing's gone. The sounds in our heads are miles apart. Being together isn't working.'

'So how do we keep the show on the road?'

Which part of this does he think is a show? The children? And his endless joking and teasing and ragging around with them? Isabel shutting herself off in her own world. James's shrieks getting more and more frantic.

'We don't.'

He looks stunned. 'What? Think of the wreckage.'

Whose fault would that be? Careful, she says to herself. Think before you speak. 'I've been thinking. I'm not just blowing off steam.' She looks at the floor. Simon stares at her.

'Could you manage the children if I moved out?'

Simon places his hands face up on the table, fingers spread wide. It's almost a shrug. 'You know perfectly well I can't. I have to work. I'm in charge of all the new projects.'

Ruth fumed inside. What makes his projects more important than mine? And are there no projects we share? 'Then I'll stay and you go.'

'Ruth! No. Surely you don't mean that.' His eyes meet hers. 'Do you?'

'I do.'

Simon opens and shuts his mouth. He puts one hand to his cheek. Horrified.

Ruth has been heard. At last. But what next?

Ruth has a brief glimpse of relief then she sags in her seat, head in hands, elbows on the table. She's worn out, but the pressure has gone and she managed not to light the touch paper that could well have been explosive. The underlying rumble in her head has stopped.

She gets up slowly. Picks up a basket of clean clothes and moves towards the stairs. Simon sits at the table, quite still with his eyes shut and his arms wrapped right round himself, fingers whitening as they clasp his back. She resists the instinct to give him a hug from behind and heads upstairs to bed. Alone.

It's autumn but the sheets feel hot. Ruth gets up and opens the window. Neither her mind nor her body will rest. She's pulled from the sense of swimming across deep water by footsteps on the stairs. She supposes she must have slept. A grey dawn is on its way.

The steps pause, and then she hears them turn towards the spare room, and sadness seeps out of her body right into her soul. Another busy day to get through. No real time for consideration.

She's right. When she comes home to make a meal for the children and see them through the atrociously unrelaxing end of another school day, she finds a note from Simon:

Flat hunting. Will be in touch.

Chapter 8

Dani

It's alternately raining and shining as Dani walks along the river carrying a load of shopping, and the sun, when it takes its turn, glances off the steel and glass construction beside the Thames. He blinks. It's impressive. But what an unnatural way to make new homes for people.

The huge glass wall in front of him reflects the river water and a flight of grey slate steps that shimmer in today's rain. The river seems to be both behind and in front, ebbing and flowing with the weather as well as the tide, making vertical reflections of raindrops intersect with the horizontal ones of the river and the steps. It's beautiful. Or will be when finished. Rain or shine.

Dani escapes from being wind-blasted into the shelter of the lobby. Elegance is definitely the main intention here. True elegance he wonders, or just skin deep?

Simon has told him he's product-testing a penthouse suite while it's tweaked into shape. He also says he's pleased to have made a good deal, and willing to suffer the noise and mess of continuing work on parking facilities, roof terraces, gym and swimming pool. Dani's not at all sure Simon has got that right. Silent stoicism? his old habit of avoiding emotional realities? It was hard to tell.

Dani's amazed at what is available to people like Simon. How long will it be before the whole complex is finished and market forces push him out? Is this a wise move? Steel and glass feel less permanent than brick and plaster to Dani, where families are concerned. Is he hoping separation from Ruth will be temporary? Simon probably can't afford the kind of home that smart architects love to design. Is that why he chose this place? Is he chancing it? Keeping up appearances? Adopting a veneer of confidence? Whatever. He's not saying what he feels and most of the time he's oblivious to his effect on others. But he's still a friend in need of emotional rescue.

Dani did not expect to feel so completely out of his element. Will this place help Simon adjust to the shock of Ruth's ultimatum? Will the children feel at home here? They'd probably enjoy threading their way round the heaps of sealed packages, discarded cardboard and squashed snail-shells of sticky-tape to get to the lift.

Dani steps into the satin-finished stainless-steel box with rosy pink lighting. Safety-check completed. He presses the button for the top floor. It stays put, exactly where it started. He's blind-scanning for an emergency button when the door behind him slides silently away to reveal another lobby, high in the sky. He reads a sign. You need a special code for the penthouse level. Typical of Simon not to mention that. His inability to show consideration is pitiful and irritating. Dani's heart is thumping but he's distracted by the view that seems to begin far too close to his toes. With his fingers fumbling Dani taps Simon a message. Looking down from this air-conditioned glass tower made his knees shake but looking out from the tree-top walkway in Kew is a total pleasure. Why is that?

No idea.

'Shit. Fuck it.'

There's a thump on the wall somewhere above and a roar of exasperation in a familiar voice followed by a clatter of footsteps on the stairs. A blast of cold air rushes in from a door behind him.

'Sorry! Couldn't find the code.' Simon emerges from the fire escape wearing a chunky dark red sweater with a hole in the sleeve. 'We'll have to go this way instead.' He turns on his heel.

'This is amazing.' The lift-panic has disappeared into thin air but Dani's arms are too full to offer the usual hug.

'Will be, one day. Bit brutal right now.' Simon isn't smiling, or anywhere near huggable. He looks unshaven, dusty and tired.

Dani struggles to keep him in sight as he crashes back through the escape door, up the stairs, through the top lobby, past the unused lift, and straight through the door of number 1201. Simon kicks away his wine-box door-prop and strides through a wide hallway into the main room.

'Here we are. This is it. I was about to start sorting. You've arrived at exactly the right moment.' He looks down, breathes slowly out, then looks up again. 'It's good to see you, Dani.'

They are surrounded with stuff: boxed, cased, bagged and dumped. On a small table in front of an immense wall of western facing glass, the river curving far below, a screen-saver is gently waving. They are in an enormous room that progresses from kitchen, to dining, to sitting to working areas, floor space already cluttered, but otherwise bare, angular and colourless. Dani looks around. He would hate to live up here. He's lost for words.

'Put your bags over there.' Simon points to the granite work surface already covered with used mugs and sugar-grit.

'Coffee?'

'Yes please. Can I see round first? Get my bearings?'

The master bedroom is huge, bare and dominated by the river view. There's a tiny twin room with its own shower, and hidden cupboards in the hallway for storage, washing machine and drier with minimal furniture in place.

'How's it going?'

Simon grimaces. 'Be better when this is sorted.'

So together they sort it. Bedding onto beds. Bags of clothes into the walk-in closet. Books shelved (more needed), and while Simon flatpacks empty boxes, clears the living room floor, and scrabbles through his toolbox Dani takes control of the kitchen. Simon unwraps a small picture and takes it into the hall. Dani stirs the pot. Simon bangs a nail into the wall by the door then sets about disentangling the cables for his music system.

'You've hung up the Golden Gate Bridge again, right by the door.'

'My anchor. Can't go anywhere without it.'

Dani looks up and then looks down. It's an anchor that can't reach the seabed from here but, he thinks but doesn't say.

They sit at the round glass table under a low shaded lamp, wine bottle open, a steaming tagine scenting the room, couscous now ready. Dani opens the last of the bags that he brought with him and pulls out a parcel.

'This is for you Simon, from all of us, to bring you good luck. I hope things go well for you here.'

Simon looks down. Pauses, with a hand to his temple.

'Don't worry! It's nothing grand. Just the basics for a new home.'

Maya and Kiri have made him a wonky but squashy loaf of bread. It's sitting on an olive-wood board, under which he finds a knife, and a small jar of pink Himalayan salt. The children's card explains it all in pictures: Amit holding the knife, the salt from on high for those who live on the top floor, the rising bread overflowing its bowl, and Dani rubbing oil into the board. Inside it says 'Bread so you will never be hungry. Salt to give your life flavour.'

Simon can't speak.

Dani goes gently. He pours Simon a glass of wine and asks him to cut the bread. He hands him the salt with his plate. Simon raises his glass.

'You're a wonderful friend, Dani. Thank you. I didn't expect … I don't know what to say … ' He looks shaken. 'My lot are coming over tomorrow. I refuse to let them cut me adrift.'

'How are they?'

'I really don't know.'

Chapter 9

Simon

December has arrived as if without permission and waking early in his new home Simon feels the weight of it. He heaves himself over and tries stretching. He groans. Nothing seems right. The light's coming from the wrong side. The sheets are tangled. He feels as though he's in a dream that's muddled with reality. His brain cells are fully occupied with images of complex cross sections, 3D projections and discarded hi-viz vests whirling away out of reach at the mercy of a strong current. He can't find a light. Can't tell the time. He searches for his specs but there's no table. He feels around under the bed then stares at the dumping ground of floor space in which his bed is marooned. What next? His phone pings.

His hand scrabbles for it in slow motion. It feels as if it's a whole two minutes before he locates it, prevents it slipping out of reach and taps it awake. It's a message from Ruth. He sees her screen-face and a sharp mix of familiarity, hope and sadness floods right through him from head to toe. Maybe she needs something.

Chair of prize committee rang on landline. Marion? Ring back asap.

Oh my God. Heart thumping, he stumbles into the bathroom, leans both hands on the basin and stares at himself in the mirror. No need to worry … it's a brilliant design, he tells himself. My best yet. He looks down to see a pair of knuckles gripping the smooth white porcelain. Must be my hands, he thinks, trying to get a grip.

Perhaps water will help. They don't need to see me like this. He splashes his face and cleans his teeth and then wakes up to the fact that they want to talk to him. They won't be looking. No scrutiny.

Where? Simon needs to get into work mode and find a perspective. A long view. He goes to the desk in front of the glass wall high above the bend in the river Thames. It's all about crossing over gaps. Always has been. It's what I'm good at. That's what I do. Shoulders back, standing up straight, he dials the number.

No reply.

Double check. They must be there. They've been trying to reach me. It may have been a misdial. He tries again and this time there's pick-up.

'Simon Westover. You rang?'

'Just a minute. Marion wants to speak to you. I'll put you through.'

Standing by the window Simon shifts his weight from one bare foot to the other. The horizon tilts. He slow-blinks twice and takes a deep breath. He reaches for a coffee mug. There isn't one. Merciless dream-current after-shocks refuse to let him go.

'Is that you Simon?'

The familiar voice sounds as straightforward and efficient as ever.

'Not you this time I'm afraid. I thought you'd like to know before it goes public.'

His mind goes blank. There's a long silence. The line crackles and Simon tries to stabilise the horizon.

'Are you still there?'

'Uh-uh.'

'We went for a new star in the field. The only woman. She hasn't done nearly as much as you - yet, but her ideas are really exciting. I think you'll like them. And she's half Portuguese too....'. Marion's voice goes on, and words pass him by until the sound of a cadence tunes him back in: 'I'm sure your work will continue to break new ground. Keep in touch.'

'I'm not about to retire.'

'Oh!' A moment passes before he hears a brief laugh. 'We love your work Simon, and the decision was not an easy one. It was a good competition and you're not easily beaten.'

'Except when it's an inside job.'

'What? Did I hear you right?'

'An international competition with a local winner? What's that about?'

'Simon. That's outrageous. Is that an accusation?'

'Well! What will people say? Local women come out top when political correctness leads the way? Congratulations.' He presses the red circle to cut the call, drops the phone and paces the room without seeing anything. He stands stock still and stares down at the river. At a city that would be brought to a halt without its bridges. His fists are clenched. Jaw aching.

He sits at the table then wonders how he got there. His hands sweep over the cool surface while his feet jitter about on the floor. What time is it?

He looks at his new home. Home? How can this be home? It's a void. Nothing but air in every direction. Devoid of terra firma. Oh my. What can I say to the team? What will Ruth think? Simon is jolted back with a sudden bang. Has a door blown shut? Nothing has changed. Maybe it was the lift. Or the workmen. Talk about new territory. From all directions at once.

He stares blankly at a phone reminder: *11.30 Team meeting.*

How did this happen? What did I miss? Something I didn't check? More questions join the queue. Answering systems all closed.

He hides his face in his hands. Twitches in uncoordinated fingertips mirror the tension that has invaded his feet. How to face them … His imagination delivers a room full of expectant eyes with Hannah's being the most prominent. They swivel towards him as he approaches, searching for a cue on which to hang their reactions.

Maybe they know already. Or will I have to tell them? He opens his eyes but sees nothing recognisable. How could they do this to me? What now? Who will lead the team? What will they think of me?

I'll have to manage …

What a fucking waste of time.

A huge amount of work all for nothing. Drawings, calculations, research, discussions, late-night revisions. The headache of turning technicalities into elegance. Binned. That's the last time I do that. Never again. Ever. Why should I put myself on the line only to be shot at by presumptuous judges who couldn't build a sandcastle better than a three-year-old? Why have an international competition only to pick the local as the winner? What a corrupt bunch of so-called experts they must be.

He thumps the table. Don't be a fool. Get out and do something. Indignation gets him into the shower, into clean clothes and into the lift. The need for coffee forgotten.

Simon nudges his office door open carefully using his foot. He puts his briefcase on the floor and looks up straight into the photograph of Ruth and the kids on top of his bookshelf. He can't think about them now. They're smiling as they watch Ruth pour out drinks on a hot summer day. Auburn tints are glinting in her hair, the most beautiful woman ever. Never even thought of getting close to anyone else.

Stop it. Focus yourself.

Internal software loads in unpredictable chunks. The team meeting. He glances at his watch. Already started. Get it over in one go. He strides straight off.

He hears them as he approaches, mid wrangle. Two bits don't fit well … too many new projects … might not come off … A jumble of overlapping phrases.

Yet again. Hammering away at the problem of balancing new stuff with routine work, expenditure with income. Afraid that new projects will vanish if they take a few risks. Someone needs to remind them how the Westover reputation took off. Where would they be without a series of prize-winning designs? … He wades straight in.

'Hi everyone. Come to tell you they turned me down. Turned us down. Given the prize to an unknown newbie. Half Portuguese too. It'll be public by lunch time. Sounds as if we'll be flung back into the melting pot. Creativity stifled at birth.' He wonders if he's making sense ...

A brief silence is followed by kind words. Sounds of sympathetic understanding. He hasn't sat down yet, and he finds himself feeling for the steadiness of a chair back. His team's loyalty and concern visibly turned towards him. The sounds of shared disappointment come as a surprise. He turns away and busies himself with unsticking the top of a coffee jug and choosing a mug. His favourites all in use, so he's left facing images of world-famous bridges that look more fragile in profile than the thick white china onto which their silhouettes have been transferred.

Simon sits down and tries to listen. For the first time he can remember he wonders how to play it. As team-leader? Team-creator? Ideas-generator? Source of inspiration and motivation? Project controller? Rescuer? No longer as serial prize-winner.

'Who is he?'

'Who? Oh! Not 'he.' It's a 'she'.

'That must be Arantxa Villela. Her work's really interesting.'

'So sorry Simon. I thought that design was your best yet ... original ... breaking new ground ... would have done wonders for our reputation ... there'll be more ... other competitions ... so much work in the pipeline ... ideas useful for other projects ... an inspiring degree of energy ...'

Ideas-person? Creative? Able to join technicalities up with environmental concerns? Team leader? Winner? Simon's internal processes are caught in a loop. The phrases they use to describe him dissolve into cacophony. That's not me. Not now. Not any more.

'Thank you. Thank you. For being here. For helping to put that together so fast. Maybe it was too fast. Now I need to think. I need a break.' He waves both arms in the air. Closes the meeting down.

'Hannah, could you spare me a minute?'

This could be awkward. He seems really rattled, maybe for the very first time.

'You OK?' She closes Simon's office door.

He's on the move and picks something up and stares at it. He puts it down and moves on.

'Could you stand in for me? Run the team meetings? Answer questions about new projects and so on? Lead the team?'

'Ye-es.' He's in shock. Not thinking clearly. She looks at the heap of files on the desk, on the floor and on the glass table. She stands still while she thinks.

'I could find a way of sharing jobs through the team. I couldn't manage it all and keep things running as well. That should work. And it might help some people appreciate what goes on behind the scenes. We'd need a regular check-in time.' She looks up at him. 'There's bound to be stuff I don't know much about.'

'More than you might think Hannah. I've had to move out. Of home. Leave Ruth and the kids. And now this.'

'I'm so sorry Simon … that's a lot to deal with all at once. How are you?'

He stares at her. 'How do I look?'

'Losing this one isn't such a big deal Simon. We need you here. I'll do what I can, but don't jump ship. If you pull up anchor it could destabilise all of us and leave us at the mercy of the worst financial crisis in years.'

'It was all about trying to be constructive,' he says. He reaches out and lies the family photograph face down, flat on top of the bookcase. 'I'm sorry Hannah. I have to go. Now.'

Simon walks straight out of the door without making eye contact. He leaves everything but his briefcase behind.

Chapter 10

Simon

Simon's feet scuff the gravel as he swerves to avoid a scruffy terrier galloping along the river path. It is almost visibly joyful, racing along under the willows that rustle and sigh in the wind. He scowls at it and elicits a piercing glance from its owner as she strides out for the woman and the beast's daily exercise, her turquoise anorak tied round her waist. It's not, he notices, a good match for her trainers.

Another person who can't get things right.

Simon's mental chatter goes into overdrive. Eff them! Blind judges with no imagination. Utterly out of touch. Grinding their own axes or trying to promote women ... Can't recognise skill, ingenuity and elegance when it stares them in the face. Completely insulting.

He stares at the glassy, reflective river. Full tide makes it sluggish. A distant memory of the sudden chill of cold water makes him shiver. He fell in the lake when he was 12 and lost his specs. Supposed to be out of the way, having fun at holiday camp. Half-blinded and grounded instead. Forbidden to go rock climbing or canoeing and shamed into tears. Taunted. Told not to make a spectacle of himself.

He shudders. Bats the side of his head with one hand. Groans. Turns round and retraces a few steps. Ruth lost ...

He's not looking where he's going. The path doesn't seem straight. A man in running gear stops.

'You OK? Anything I can do?'

'Me?'

The runner is young. Unaccountably friendly.

'Oh. I'm fine.' Frowning, Simon pats himself down. 'Looking for my phone.'

It's vibrating. How long has it been on silent? Ruth's familiar face on the screen, as if from a previous era. He scowls. The runner steps back.

Where is she? What will she think? What shall I say? Simon scowls. Nothing. She already knows.

'Simon I'm so sorry. Are you OK? Hannah rang me. She was worried.'

'It's alright. It doesn't matter. It's not important.' Tight lips clip the words short. He slumps onto a bench, elbows on knees.

The runner walks slowly onto the path, gathers pace and moves off downstream.

'What did they say?'

'Not a lot. A Portuguese woman won. Inside job I guess.'

'What?'

'Useless judges. Completely biased.'

'Simon. I know this is difficult …'

'Thought that's what you'd say. I don't want to talk about it.'

'OK. Fine. But don't let prizes define you. You're so much more than that. It's a shock, but it'll wear off. The first time I've known you fail at anything.'

'Uh-uh. So what?'

'Well, winning doesn't give you roots, or anchors, or tie you safely into your life. It isn't why people like you.'

'What are you talking about?'

Simon hears a bird land on the river. Sees the shifting shades of sunlight on moving water and feels a breeze. Have I been stopped while the world goes on? He hears a question. Ruth's. Something about the children and their collection times.

'I can't do it Ruth. I can't be with them. Please.'

'They love being with you Simon. They like messing about in your home … James has made you some pictures. Don't turn them away.'

They'd be perfectly happy with Ruth in charge for an extra afternoon. She's the one they rely on. He can't risk losing brownie

64

points by being distracted and feeding them nothing but crisps and ketchup for tea. Or face their relief when she comes to collect them. Rescues them.

'They're part of your life, Simon. I'll have to sort a huge amount out here to get to school in time. This isn't the end of the world you know. And we're going to have to make a schedule we can both stick to.'

He looks blank.

'I'll swap you today for tomorrow, but last-minute changes are not on. Sorry.'

Children in after-school mood? Noisy. Quarrelsome. Demanding. He can't take it. He won't budge.

Ruth rings off. Nothing properly settled.

She's angry. But Simon tells himself that moving out was her idea, not his, so it's up to her to deal with the consequences.

His stomach churns. Is the gap between us widening?

He's still sitting on the bench when he gets a message from Marion to say she's waiting for an apology.

He jabs the phone right off. Pockets it.

A lump in his throat makes it hard to take a breath. His chest is tight. There's reacting to the present and there's understanding what's happened he tells himself, and that means my bridge will never be built. No one will see its slender lines combine with those of the surrounding horizons. Or discover what it could provide for people who, for centuries, have lived close to each other without being close. Separated by a powerful river. A door has closed. The platform I was standing on has tilted. No handholds. Did I forget to add them? He's shaking. Inside and out.

Back to base. He heads for the new glass and steel building by the river with its big slate steps. Water mirages from the sun and the tide etched on the glass. It's not far. Simon skirts round the office and keeps going.

His body feels as if it's sinking. He shudders at the thought of slithering along looking vulnerable; like a snake with a layer of fragmenting skin. He steps out faster and takes in a long deep breath when he reaches the slate-grey steps.

It's a relief to see his reflection in the shiny stainless-steel wall of the lift. He presses a button in a box and waits to be delivered to a home in the sky. He looks at his feet. When he arrives he fumbles the lock. Staggers through the door and kicks it shut then throws himself face down on the bed and gives up.

With a furious yell he thumps the pillow and finds himself crying like a child. His whole body is shaken by sobs. When the storm passes, he's exhausted. But the onslaught hasn't finished. He turns over and an internal video presents him with a crowd. Family. Friends. Strangers. Ruth last. They turn their heads away as he approaches. You lose them when you fail.

Simon feels a sensation on his back, like his grandfather's hand. The one and only person with the intuition to understand tough times, and the ability to respond with comforting gestures. The kind that stopped you howling and helped you sit up and take stock.

'OK. I will then.' Simon says out loud.

He wipes his face with a fistful of sheet and gulps.

You're not a child. You can't go on winning forever.

It wasn't the achievements that mattered for him. They were just a ticket of entry into the world, like a virtual currency that was activated by being passed on. His mother and father grabbed hold of the congratulations for every one of his successes. What he got was a few, temporary, smiles and acknowledgments. No prizes meant no approval. That was the fuel that kept his engine in perpetual motion. The slightest sign of failure was met with instant rigidity. Mechanical jerkiness with knife and fork. Eyes filled with cold horror. But there weren't any failures. Or even disappointments. Until now. Simons shudders as the elements fall into place.

What did they want? Gratitude? To be thanked for passing on the right genes?

Ruth's my only hope he thinks. I can't let her go.

66

He gets up. Finds the front door open. Closes it and sees the Golden Gate Bridge. He puts out a hand towards the far shore. Such a huge gap.

Simon knows you shouldn't feel sorry for yourself. It's the kind of self-indulgence his parents abhorred. But there's a lot to take in: chucked out by Ruth, hopeless at looking after kids, Isabel keeping her distance, James not concentrating and more than half out of control. Dreadful to have to tolerate the unveiled scorn of small children. Then the competition. Won by unknown Arantxa …

Lucky I'm not the whimpering sort, he says to himself. I'll just have to work harder. Show them what I can do.

He searches for a fleece and finds a scarf. Navy and black hexagons. It's soft and he wraps it round his neck.

Part 2: Considering the challenges

January 2009 to February 2012

Chapter 11

Simon

Shortly after the sharp corner of the new year has passed Simon slips back into the office late enough in the morning for everyone to have settled down. Best to get the re-entry over quietly.

'Happy New Year, Simon. Glad you're back.'

It's impossible to bypass Hannah. 'All well?'

'No problems.' She barely looks up. 'Rumbles from the New Project Group, but they can wait till you're ready.'

Simon goes on to his office.

Let them wait, he thinks. First priority: avoid a postmortem on losing the Portuguese competition. Second: keep track of the flow of profitable contracts. Austerity's beginning to bite. It could be serious. It'll take visible achievements to do the job of earning back credibility. No time for anything else and he starts at once by initiating a close scrutiny of current projects and those in the offing. It's hard work, which makes it easy to ignore irrelevancies such as a growing backlog of emails. Until a message from Marion flashes by.

> *You've been ignoring my emails. I find that astonishing and rude. Your accusation was outrageous, and arrogant. You owe me an apology.*

He slams both hands flat on his desk. Eff you! I will not apologise, he says to himself. Too bad. You're not the only judges in the world. He swipes the message away and pushes back his chair. A gust of wintery wind rattles the window. He stares at the outside world, fingers twitching, then picks up a note left for him by Hannah. It makes no sense at all to him so he puts it back down.

Losing a competition isn't the end of the world. After all it wouldn't be a competition if it didn't have more entrants than winners. He forces himself to read through Marion's earlier messages and their tone works its way under his skin. Details may slip round the corner, but her disapproval is obvious. Don't even go there, he tells himself, avoidance as automatic as a reflex.

OK. She's waiting for an apology. Simon decides to let her wait. After all, he only said what others would be thinking.

He turns to more important matters but can't find a focus. No one is doubting him or complaining. No one is disappointed in the outcomes he reports. But you never know for sure. You have to be super-alert not to miss the scepticism lurking behind an innocent question or suss out whether scepticism has developed over time into criticism. You're never safe.

Simon still dreams of building an international reputation on his love of bridges: on what others recognise as his special skill in designing them. He decides that now's the time to narrow down the focus of the Westover Group. His dreams include a share of the limelight for himself of course, and he can't resist telling Hannah something about them.

Long ago she asked: 'What do you find so fascinating about bridges?'

The answer was ready and waiting.

'It's all about crossing gaps and joining things up. Elegantly. Creating the missing links so nothing interferes with the free-flow everyone loves. People, objects, traffic, ideas. All of them. It's a story of connectivity made physical. Made with bridges. Beautiful bridges.'

He thinks still about ways of combining strength, safety and elegance into a work of art that is of daily practical use to thousands of people. It doesn't matter if the bridge is for commuters, or container lorries, or high-speed trains, or for many kinds of transport all at once. Or whether it crosses valleys, or train tracks or more or less turbulent waters. The same principles apply and using them brings the same level of excitement and enthusiasm. This should be the Westover Group's signature product, he tells Hannah. If everyone agrees.

'I've mapped out a draft plan,' he tells her, 'Though I know there'll be objections. About the risks of specialisation and dangers of over-stretching budgets just to start with. They'll say you can't do something ambitious when shortcuts are at a premium.'

'You're right,' Hannah replies with a sharp look. 'Reining yourself in sounds like an excellent plan to me!' Then she smiles. 'What about connecting with people as well as plans? Taking them along with you instead of going it alone?'

'What?' He laughs. Briefly. What's that about? She knows how important this could be.

It was so good that she agreed to join the group. Someone with sound judgement and a sense of humour. Hannah has been a friend since graduate days who's not afraid of plain-speaking. Not only that, she's always been competent and recently she's acquired an exceptional ability to keep working relationships in good order. It's amazing to see how she arrives at work ready to enjoy herself. Never searching for the next opportunity to shine or looking over her shoulder for fear of being overtaken, but working here because she likes what she does, and she likes the people she works with.

She's totally trustworthy. It's not only the long friendship that allows us to talk straight. It's the way she is.

In the first week of February Londoners have something other than the economy to complain about: the biggest snowfall for 18 years. No one wants to lower the temperature inside today. Simon sees Hannah bouncing across the icy tarmac of the car park wearing her soft beige and brown work clothes and a rather hairy coat with no buttons. Her enormously long light brown scarf is almost the same colour as her hair. No sharp edges at all. He hugs his coat closed and waits for her to catch up before opening the door to the office.

'Thanks for waiting. I was hoping to talk to you today.' She lets the scarf hang loose as she steps indoors, cheeks glowing from the frost.

Simon smiles down at her. 'Oh? … about the New Project Group? … I hear you've been reorganising them.'

'Um …'

By the time they reach the lift the smile's gone.

'Uh uh,' she says. 'Yes. I've really enjoyed working with them.'

Simon has heard rumours, recounted with an unsettling degree of amusement. What's going on? Apparently, they've been having fun. Enjoying themselves exploring the new equipment kept in the conference room. Kept there precisely to keep it safe from careless or ill-prepared users.

Hannah's reliable. That's why she's the right person to be left in charge. That and her capacity to keep calm in the face of volatility. But those new guys are meant to be doing serious work, not playing around. They've got specific projects to work on. Deadlines to meet.

'When's good for you?' Hannah asks as they reach the top floor. Midday? How long do we need?'

'Not long. See you then.' She sounds almost amused.

Simon looks at her closely. Did I miss something?

Reaching his office he ignores the hook on the back of the door and drops his coat onto the nearest chair, burying a heap of papers in the process. Their rustling sound makes him look round at the familiar clutter.

His computer is marooned in a sea of paper. Every inch of wall space is covered with prints and photographs of bridges under construction, including some of the Golden Gate with rows of steel beams yet to be assembled arranged on acres of the surrounding land. Not all of the pictures hang straight. Books and journals, mostly open, scatter his enormous desk, and the gaps they left when removed from his bookshelves look to him like empty spy holes. Seeing the picture of Ruth and the kids on the top of the bookshelf, where he left it before Christmas, face down, he turns away and with a single click enters the virtual world. He's surrounded with

74

the kind of creative muddle that he loves. It's a source of inspiration. An accumulation of surrounding objects is never a distraction. And now it's also consoling.

Searching through a pile of folders he pulls out Jason's project. His task is to design a multi-storey arts centre for a restricted site, and he's having fun with it. Original thinking, technical know-how confidently used, and probably over-ambitious. Not yet able to fly, but he soon will be, if he listens. Not that he has much time for that. Simon settles into his swivel chair with a sigh and stretches his legs out under the table. He thinks about the time he spotted Jason's application amongst the pile of highly qualified hopefuls for the new posts he'd created. He makes an internal note to slow him down.

Jason has an unusual background in engineering as well as architecture that could be useful one day. However, right now it's not at all clear that he's ready to continue the dash ahead without making mistakes, and mistakes lead to accidents. There are myriads of hazards to avoid in this world of fast-moving technical change. More every month. Jason's ideas can be brilliant. He's prolific and imaginative. And restless. Talking to him is both stimulating and irritating as he seems incapable of keeping still. Besides he's not nearly as interested in checking details as he should be and doesn't like anyone to point this out.

Pushing Jason's folder to one side he turns back to his plans for the Westover Group and jumps in surprise when Hannah arrives with two coffees.

'Ready?'

Simon removes a scattering of papers from the table in the window, and they settle down with their mugs, Westover's logo imprinted on the sides in two shades of blue, looking out over the car park and the icy weather.

Hannah comes straight to the point.

'Simon, you've been upsetting people.'

He stares at her, elbows in, chin up.

'Who? Which people? What are you talking about?' He taps the rim of his coffee mug.

'The three of them in the New Project Group.'

'All of them?'

'It started with Jason. Dissatisfaction spreads fast.'

'Well, he's overconfident. Too big for his boots. Focusing on appearances far more than safety. He needs to work things through on a small scale before going for something bigger. Rein in his ambition. I've told him that already Someone had to.'

'Simon! They say that all you do is criticise. Why don't you soften the message? Why don't you tell them the good stuff too? You make them anxious. Frightened of putting a foot wrong.'

'I don't see why.'

'Clearly not.'

Simon stares straight at her, chin down and teeth clenched. She doesn't flinch.

'Jason is fed up. Talking openly about moving on. He'll get snapped up as soon as he turns round you know.'

Simon fidgets in his chair. He looks out of the snow-flecked window and shivers.

'... and the others?' He hand-strafes his hair.

'Well if he goes they'd most likely follow.'

'Ungrateful if you ask me. This isn't an easy profession. I did the hard slog without help. Lots of us did. Why can't they do the same?'

'They can with encouragement. If you give it. Not everyone can win prizes the way you did.'

He flinches. 'Did ... yes. Well.' He stares at the snowflakes. 'I'd better go and talk to them.'

'Not yet, I think.'

'Why not? Where are we then?'

'They. Things have just started improving. They're in a much better place. That's why you were hearing about it ... But it's early days. Let them get on with it for a bit first.'

'All I've heard is rumours. And laughter. No facts.'

'They've settled down and they work well together. When would you like to take back responsibility for managing them?'

He hesitates. So much else to be getting on with. 'Uhm ...'

Hannah puts her mug down on the table. 'I thought so.' She leans back and looks out of the window. Dead leaves are blowing with the snowflakes over cold, grey London. She explains what has been happening in his absence. He listens, one foot tapping.

Hannah has let the New Project Group, three independent-minded thinkers selected for their exceptional talents but not known for their ability to cooperate, manage themselves. She persuaded them to set up a regular joint meeting and to share their problem-solving. She bypassed their scepticism with the suggestion that Joan, the intern and Bardo a school-leaver on work placement, join the meeting as observers with added responsibilities. Joan would help them with her up-to-date technical wizardry and together she and Bardo would be the note-takers and record-keepers, learning both what and how by degrees. The carrot she offered was access to the new technical stuff stored in the big conference room. There they could be noisy without disturbing others, early in the day, provided no one else needed the room. That meant a big table, leather chairs, a high-end coffee maker and no interruptions.

'And who's been keeping tabs on them?' Simon taps the table with the tip of a finger. 'How do we know what they're up to?'

'Through me. The notes come to me. And it's worked far better than I expected.' She hands him a summary while continuing to provide her own version.

'They say they now have brain-space for the creative stuff. They help each other out. They've stopped hiding their ideas for fear they'll be pinched. Or torn apart before they've had time to develop them. They come out of their meetings late. Still talking and the support team have learned lots too. They're excited to feel part of the front line. No longer moaning about being stuck with routine stuff and hinting at being exploited.' She flicks through the papers on her lap. 'Here's their feedback.'

77

Simon glances at the sheet of comments and ratings. Frowns as his finger jabs the list. His knees knock into the table and make the mugs rattle. His voice rises.

'Look! They say: *It works OK. Helps us to decide where to focus next.* He scans to the bottom of the page. 'What are you on about? Hardly an endorsement of your new arrangement.'

'Look at the ratings.'

He turns the page. Silence follows. They are the highest Simon has ever seen. He sends her a questioning look.

Hannah says: 'I know. They're good. Even though they hate doing them. They'd definitely rather be 3D planning than 2D form-filling.'

Simon's heard enough. He puts the papers on the table and stands up. Not the way he'd have chosen but good to have kept them on board.

'Oh. Well ...'

Hannah interrupts. 'I've emailed you everything, including Jason's progress notes. He's been inventing ways of linking the buildings in his arts centre. Like bridges in the sky. Could be interesting.' She turns as she reaches the door. 'Why don't you come with me to one of their meetings. I think you'd enjoy it.'

Then she's gone.

Simon can't concentrate.

Upsetting people? The echo persists.

He paces round the room. Whatever does she mean? They're grown-ups doing the job they're trained to do. No one said it would be easy. They should be grateful to get an intelligent reaction to their ideas. And an informed one.

Thinking about leaving? That's drastic. What's all the fuss about?

He hopes it's all sorted now and decides to leave Hannah in charge. He would never have created those new posts if he hadn't believed that the Westover Group could be one of the best. They're lucky to be here, he thinks. Eventually they'll learn what to expect.

His office, however, feels less like a sanctuary than usual.

Hannah

Hannah sits at her desk with a notepad in front of her, without writing anything. She's thinking about Simon's ambitious new plans, and whether this is the right time to push ahead with them. She puts the pen down. It's a pity that all that talent comes with such a high degree of insensitivity. He seems to have no notion of what other people need in the current unsettling circumstances. How easily they can be discouraged, and how important it is to keep them in the picture. Keeping an eye on the workings of the New Project Group will be like a Litmus test. It'll show whether he's taken the point and can learn to be more encouraging.

She taps back into her email stream and starts working her way through the usual barrage. There's a message from Marion.

I can't get a response out of Simon. Is he away?

Oh. He's been ignoring her. What's that about? She forwards the email to Simon with a question:

Will you get back to her? Or would you like me to?

Within a few minutes she has the answer.

Tell her I'm busy. Say I'm sorry, OK?

Sorry for what? For not answering? Or: Okay, I'm sorry, and now I'll do ... whatever she's asking? Is he avoiding her in the hope she'll stop bothering him? Hannah frowns and her fingers lie still on her keyboard. Marion is not someone Simon can afford to ignore. Doesn't he realise that a response from me instead of him could sound like a brush-off? There could be more going on here than he's told me. She emails him back.

What's this about? Is there anything I should know?

She doesn't have to wait long for an answer.

No. But don't make her any angrier than she already is.

Ok, Hannah thinks, tactful wording needed here.

Simon is leading us through a reorganization following the crash. He's been especially busy and sends his apologies.

She reads it through. Thinks the apology sounds a big grudging and adds the word '*sincere.*' Hope that does it. She copies Simon in and presses send.

Chapter 12

Ruth

Ruth and Leila made friends through their daughters, Isabel and Meena, and regularly meet in each other's kitchens. Leila runs a rental agency and has a lot to say about deadlines. All her meetings, kitchen ones included, have an end time as well as a start time.

'How's it going?' she asks Ruth.

Leila's a long-term single mother and Ruth feels like a newbie in search of advice. Without judgment.

'One day at a time. Susie can't come back. We couldn't afford her now anyway.'

'How do you manage work?'

'Routine. Every moment counts.'

'Tell me another.'

'Surprising thing is the kids hardly miss Susie. They're doing well, until Simon shifts the schedule. Or feeds them nothing but junk.

'Nightmare behaviour. All the time? Just sometimes?'

'Less than he used to. The children are more relaxed now.'

Leila nods. 'Know where they are … always makes it easier.'

'They contact us whenever they want. Know we're there for them. It seems to be working.'

'Great. Whether or not you separate for good.'

'Right.' Ruth looks out of the window. 'We haven't decided. Christmas was a nightmare. We spent the day together and it was as if he came straight out of a gloom-pit into riot mode. He had the children shouting and dancing round the house to top volume musical schmalz, then slipped straight back into misery mode and left them watching the Wizard of Oz. He goes from all to nothing and back again like a switch-back.'

'Bet that didn't feel funny at the time.'

'Huh?' Ruth sighs and picks herself up. 'He's getting better at tuning in to them. Listening ...'

'How about the way he talks to you?'

'I wish he'd stop telling me about his triumphs ... He never used to boast. It's as if he wants something ...' Ruth stops. 'I'm not sure ...'

'Trying to impress you?'

'Maybe.'

'Odd in someone so successful. Perhaps he wants you back.'

'Yes. But he hasn't realized I never signed up as an admirer.'

'Of course you didn't. A recipe for lifelong inequality if you ask me.'

'I loved him irrespective of successes and prizes. Still do. Or would if he wasn't so totally wound up in himself.'

Ruth isn't ready to talk about her sadness. Or disappointment. Anyway, her time is up. Leila has to go.

It's a new skill Ruth thinks: stepping carefully round emotion-raisers.

A couple of months after separating Ruth is part furious and part desolate.

It's been a turbulent day. Now the children are with Simon and she's waiting for the ripples to subside. She's relegated superficial demands to the background: kitchen stuff, children's clothes, time-tables. No risk of a family version of gridlock. Now she wants to think. What she doesn't want is to grub around for the source of an underlying sense of disturbance. She doesn't want to go there. Navel-gazing is unnecessary. Selfish. Or downright alarming.

She sits at her desk and looks around. The blue of the walls fits with the sky whatever its level of intensity, just as she meant it to. There are books, boxes, folders, files with stick-on labels, open cardboard thingies with diagonal sides, envelopes, an in-tray. Full.

The rank and file look organised. The stand-up desk bought for the sake of health and fitness has been pushed back. It's now a clothes-horse for a discarded sweater with an inside-out sleeve.

Ruth adjusts the backward lean of her chair and looks up at a picture of a lake edged with wind-torn reeds. Ripples show the ducks and moorhens are busy. The light suggests the sun has just left. The real one is about to do the same thing.

Her mind wanders. Talking about the past to Dani as they walked along the canal helped to make sense of now as well as then, but it missed out the good bits. Picnics after school. Cooking scones with friends and eating them still warm. Watching the Marks brothers or the two Ronnies with her parents and laughing though her friends thought they were way out of touch. The things they did together outside.

Ruth suddenly realizes she's air-brushing the memories. Cheating herself by ignoring the reality beneath.

The shame and embarrassment is still there. She thinks of the time when she wore school shoes to the end of year disco. They were brown, polished with lipstick and left dark red marks everywhere. They lived down by the river, far out of town, unable to afford school trips. She didn't have light-coloured trainers because they'd be ruined by mud-coloured high-water marks. Humiliation always ready to pounce. She had no passport. They never went anywhere.

The thought of not having enough money again is terrifying as she thinks about the time when she had none. She clenches her fists, opens them and crunches a sheet of paper into a solid lump. Enough for what? The children. So, they never feel like that.

She leans back, closes her eyes and is confronted with a huge balance sheet. One side is blank. The other shows a zillion lines of outgoings. A muscle ties a knot in her stomach.

She sits up straight. It's not real. It's imaginary. A total exaggeration.

Grainbox is dead and everything is ready for a new business. Plans approved by the accountants and the bank. It's time to ignore the uncertainty gremlins and hang in there – not for the first time, Ruth thinks.

But what if it goes belly up? What if something happens to one of the children and it's not possible to work? What if Simon's business hits a rough patch. What then? Back on the dreadful see-saw of marriage. Constant ups and downs meant the past was never plain sailing for long. Ruth now can see that when Simon was on the up it sent her sliding down. Paying the price for his successes with double the workload. All sorts of disturbing questions race through her head.

The past doesn't just vanish, she realizes. She will have to ask Simon for help even if he doesn't understand. Or sympathise. There's no choice about it. Ruth opens her email and types a new header:

Grainbox Update.

Simon

An audible alert tells Simon a new email has arrived.

Grainbox Update.

He opens it straight away.

> *Hi Simon, Grainbox is a casualty of the crash. Prices for biodegradable packaging material have soared, and I'm winding the business up. I am developing a hub for the distribution of recycled products instead. I've done the research. Spoken to the bank and lined up suppliers in need of an outlet. There's a growing market for things made out of recyclables and I'm in at the beginning.*
>
> *Start-up is risky. But it should be OK in the end. Less travelling. More work from home. Easier for me and better for the children.*

I need to talk about our finances. Rx

They meet for lunch on a Tuesday. Ruth chooses the local Italian with vegetarian options and a good wine list. Little risk of feeling crowded and nobody on home ground. Simon arrives to find her sitting at a table in the window.

'Am I late?' he asks.

'No. Only been here a few minutes.'

They exchange a peck on each cheek.

Simon's heart-rate changes, but that's invisible. Proximity at variance with reality, he thinks. Close but not close. He sits across the table from her.

'You look OK.' He smiles.

'New shirt?' She asks. He has a giveaway horizontal crease across his chest. Odd to see him in pink stripes.

He picks up the menu. 'I'll have the saltimbocca. You? Let's order straight away. I've only got about an hour.'

She orders a butternut squash and spinach risotto and they touch base with the worlds of the children. The food, when it arrives, looks good and smells delicious. Comforting. He sits back.

'You begin.'

'How much do you want to know?' She places a blue folder with a band round the corner on the table. In business mode. 'It's all here. I'm short of money and I need your help.'

'What? How can you be? I make all the mortgage payments.'

'The cost of winding up Grainbox. The new venture is just getting off the ground and there's little coming in.'

'I don't know how I can help.' The quicker he makes this clear the better he thinks. He waves to the waitress and orders a half bottle of red.

'Do you want a drink?'

'No thanks.' She pours water into her glass and sits tall. 'We've been successful and we've been lucky. Thanks to your success and to mine, we've lived in a wonderful place. We've made it beautiful and paid for childcare. We've had holidays when we wanted and where we wanted. I'm grateful for all of it. Things are different now.'

'Lucky? I earned it the hard way you know. It's not been easy.'

'Yes. Hard work for both of us. And I'm still at full stretch. I'm doing school runs, keeping the house, and can't afford another Susie.'

'I have the children two nights a week.'

'One of them is a Friday. No school run or work in the morning ....' She stops. She places her large hands on the table like stabilisers. 'Why do you do that? I think you missed the point.' She speaks with a tight mouth.

'Do what? Did I?'

'Go so fast. It unsettles me. The point is: I need a regular monthly payment. The council tax and the insurance bills alone leave me short. They should be shared. It wasn't a problem before my business got into difficulties, and it won't be for long. Now I'm struggling.'

Simon fills his glass. He looks at her. Not smiling.

Ruth wipes her mouth. Selects a rocket leaf and nibbles at it while she waits.

'It wouldn't be easy. To pay tax and insurance for two places.'

'If we had a legal separation you might have to.'

'Is that a threat? I've told you I don't want that.'

'So how can you help?'

'I'll think about it. I'll ring you.' A direct question has got a direct answer and a direct gaze. He pushes the bones to one side of his plate.

Ruth puts the blue folder away. Wipes her mouth with the napkin and lays it on the table. 'I've said what I need to say. I hope I can get going again quickly.' She sounds calm.

'You're a good business woman. It won't take you long.'

Simon looks at his watch. 'Got to be off.'

'Oh. So times' up?'

'Afraid so.'

Ruth leans back in her chair, her hands in her lap, and watches as he pushes his chair aside and retrieves his wallet. He has the card ready by the time he reaches the front desk and, business done, he turns towards her with the briefest of smiles. As he strides back to work, he waves at her through the window.

She raises one hand in response.

Chapter 13

Simon

Simon walks down the corridor at work slowly after his lunch with Ruth. That wasn't easy he thinks and wonders why she takes her problems so seriously. He can't deal with them for her and she wouldn't want that anyway. She'd be far more likely to call it interference.

On the way to his room, he catches sight of Jason. Ah ...

'Come in for a moment. I've made some notes on your project.' Simon opens the door.

'Oh?'

'Here.' Simon hands it over.

The pages rustle. There are scribbles in the margin, comments and suggestions all over the place, and at the end, in Simon's handwriting, it says: *Great ideas here. Let's talk.*

'Excellent work. Well done.'

'Oh .... Thanks.' Jason looks up. Looks down. 'You like it?'

'Read what I've written. You'll see.'

'Oh ...' Jason turns to go, fingers of one hand twitching.

Simon sits at his desk and takes a long breath in. He holds it and then lets it out slowly. He wriggles his shoulders then taps open his computer and searches for feedback from the New Project Group. He looks closely at the screen and smiles. Finding the funds for them was an excellent decision. Their meetings are extraordinary. They spark each other off and the end result is a constant flow of good ideas. Simon stops in his tracks as he realises how much he now owes to Hannah. A hand moves to his cheek.

Dear Hannah. This is months late. You were right about Jason and about the way I was helping – or not helping – him and the others. The meeting I came to with you was a revelation. Jason's work is steaming ahead now. Thank you. Simon.

He presses send.

The same evening Simon has a drink with Dani after their regular run. Dani laughs at their different attitudes.

'I do this for fun. You're always trying to go faster. Or further. Where's the pleasure gone?

'We couldn't be more different.' Simon shrugs. Completely unruffled.

'If you went a bit slower, I might be able to keep up ...'

'Never!'

They laugh.

'I just had lunch with Ruth.'

'How did it go?'

'OK. She told me about Grainbox failing. And her new plans.'

'She must be worried.'

'She didn't say so.'

'Did you ask?

Simon looks at his hands. 'Don't you love the way our kids keep in touch with each other ...'

Dani interrupts. 'I saw her at the school gate. She didn't look good. Said she was exhausted – and then she made me laugh. She said it was as if she was trying to put down foundations on a bed of wet sand in order to change the weather. But I think she was serious. I think she's scared.'

'How d'you mean?'

'About money. No income. All the things the kids need.'

'But that's rubbish ...'

'Because of her past. Not easy to get rid of that kind of worry.'

'It'll be OK. She knows what she's doing.'

They finish their drinks and get ready to go.

'See you Tuesday, same as usual.' Dani speed-waves some airy inverted commas in Simon's direction. 'Consideration,' he says. 'Think about it. That's what matters. Take others into consideration.'

Simon frowns. Think about what? Running styles? The past? Ruth's business? Dani's ambitionless attitudes?

Simon sits on the sofa in the corner nearest the window with the lights reflected in the river-water below. He taps out Ruth's number. It's late enough for the children to be asleep.

'Hello. I thought we should talk about the money stuff.' He crosses and uncrosses his legs.

'Oh. I didn't expect ... so soon ... could be useful. Hang on a moment.'

He hears a door shutting.

'Back again.'

'Dani said you're desperate. Is that right?'

'Did he? Yes. I suppose it does feel a bit like that.'

'How serious is it?'

'Serious. I've taken advice and put the accountant in the picture. The bank's backing me. They've got my spreadsheets and calculations, but no one can predict how long it will take to break even.'

'I didn't tell you ... I've got to move. Out of this flat. It's been sold. Product-testing time over.'

'Oh.'

'Got a deadline.'

'So, you're in difficulties too. Where will you go?'

'Near to you. But that will cost.'

'Time to sell this house?'

'Not if I can help it. It's my home.'

'Our home.'

'Yes. And I don't want to lose it.'

There's a flashing light on the river path. Dots and dashes behind the trees come and go.

'What does that mean? Are you thinking of coming back here? It's not a good time for that. And this isn't the right reason anyway.'

'I didn't say that.' He opens and closes his hands and straightens up. So many pitfalls to steer round. He puts himself on pause. 'We need to think this through and consider the housing options and the finances together. For both of us.'

'Not sure I can take any more uncertainty.'

'Sorry?' It was hard to hear what she said.

'Perhaps this comes at the right time with both of us having to make changes. What I need to know is how long have I got? How long have we got? Don't just sigh. Tell me how urgent it is. How long will you be able to manage as you are?'

'Yes.'

'What? What does yes mean?'

'Sorry. I was surprised. Not making much sense.' There's a long pause. 'Why don't we do that online? Think the options through online first?'

'Yes.'

'OK.' She pauses again. 'I wasn't expecting ... You sound different.'

'Well, I'm not.'

Simon was glad he rang and glad he listened to Dani.

Simon has a bad night, plagued by visions of threatening female competitors. Of homelessness. Of financial disasters. No app to tap. No drop-down list of solutions to choose from. He looks at the river and even the trees look tired. It takes an increasing amount of effort to hold onto his habitual attitude of certainty. Unsettling doubts creep in and operate like risk alerts.

It's time to sort things somehow or there'll be nowhere to live.

He turns on the radio but doesn't like the talking, so searches for a CD and chooses Debussy. The sunken cathedral with wide spreading rhythms. Good word: englouti. He makes some coffee.

Odd for me to prevaricate, Simon thinks. This place may be beautiful but it's time to get up and go. The children hate sharing a room. Or is it just Isabel? There's nowhere for James to let off steam. He's not safe going out by himself. Simon runs both hands through his hair in frustration and goes straight to his desk without eating breakfast first.

Right, he thinks. Start thinking about finding somewhere to live. He grabs a sheet off his store of rough paper and picks up a pen. What are the options?

1. Move back home.

That may be obvious but it's not an option that Ruth would consider for a second.

2. Sell up and share out the proceeds.

Then we'd both be back to square one, building our separate foundations. Simon's stomach clenches and he puts the pen down with a gasp. Anyway, it can't be done quickly.

3. Find somewhere else. Close to home, school and work.

That sounds okay but it'll be difficult, and expensive in this part of the city. It would be horrible to have to live in a basement. He has no idea what might be available, and suddenly he's hungry. There's nothing he fancies for breakfast in the fridge so he grabs a coat and heads for the bakery round the corner where he finds a freshly made blueberry muffin and a stack of papers just inside the door. He chooses a national and a local and is back home in less than ten minutes.

A scan through the ads in the papers provides a feel for the price ranges in different areas but he can't find anything that looks remotely suitable. The blueberry muffin is turning the paper bag soggy and crumbs fall everywhere as he tries to eat, read and write all at once. The crumbs are soft and sticky and hard to brush off but he ends up with a shortlist of flats on the market. Misleading photographs make a place look twice the size and the paint hardly dry. None of them mention that they're next to the railway or have all-night bars and take-aways directly under the windows. It is impossible to find anything without going out to look.

Simon spends the middle of the day exploring. The children's school is his starting point and he moves in ever increasing circles and squares away from it, moving nearer to the family home first and closer to work last. The walk is a long but an informative one. He discovers some roads to avoid and finds some quieter and more suitable areas as well.

He returns feeling more settled but with no definite plan. The glass and steel refuge provides temporary relief but he knows that will soon end so he goes to his desk to think about next steps and discovers an email from Ruth headed **options**. Unlike her to miss out the capital letter he thinks. A foot-hook swivels the chair beneath him and he slumps down, chin on knuckles, and frowns as he opens the message and reads her list.

1. We go on living separately.

In limbo? Neither together nor free to leave? Too disruptive for the children if it didn't work out? At least she's not talking about divorce.

2. Put the house on the market.

What? That's not her decision. He glances at what she calls *Sums. First attempt.* Then there's a second list, this time without numbers.

Work more from home and rent a smaller office for the business.
Cut back on after-school clubs, music lessons, half-term expe-
ditions etc.

93

> *Let a room. Find a student who'd do some baby-sitting. (That*
> *would mean you collecting your stuff from the spare-room*
> */ study. I need that cleared up anyway. Soon.)*

Simon takes a sharp intake of breath. Nothing's been decided yet.
He reads on:

> *You need to be within walking distance of home and school.*

Of course. No reminder needed. What if there's nothing affordable?
Her email ends with a simple

> *Rx*

He clenches and unclenches his fists. He picks up a fallen sweatshirt
and stuffs a pile of washing in the machine. He collects mugs from
right, left and centre. Plates, forks and glasses too and opens the
dishwasher. He has to empty it before he can restack and switch
on. At least something is getting organized.

That evening he falls asleep on the sofa while Bill Evans plays
himself out.

Chapter 14

Simon

Simon's nights are interrupted by increasingly disturbing dreams, often about his childhood. The last one was horribly realistic. It was supper time after school and he and his parents were eating off thick grey-green Denby-ware plates. A plain water jug was silhouetted against the window. Three chairs faced the kitchen table and three sets of hands spooned out the mash or dealt with a drumstick and peas without gravy as the interminable question and answer session ended in the usual way. 'That's OK then.' 'You did well.'

It made him think about how people used to expect him to know all the answers. Why don't you ask Simon, they would say when they couldn't decide whether to go to the pub. Whether to listen to Mahler or Billie Holiday. Or, more recently, sign the contract. Since school days people had relied on him for good decisions.

All gone now, he thinks. But the inside monitor's still at work. Checking success rates and achievements all the time. Relaying the output back in an indecipherable chatter. It's confusing. Hard to listen to anything else. But there's no need. It's all noise and no meaning.

He stretches and pushes back the duvet. Keep up the effort. Work hard and do well. That's what got you where you are. That's the way to get back their respect. On consideration Simon thinks his plan to do what has worked before is definitely the right one.

He's hard at it when someone knocks on his office door and opens it without waiting for an answer. 'What?'

Hannah comes straight in. She's smiling. He doesn't respond and goes on typing using four fingers of one hand and three of the other with an astonishing degree of accuracy.

'Hi,' he manages. 'Need to finish this sentence before I forget. What do you want?'

'No hurry.' She gives him an accepting wave which he sees but ignores.

She's not leaving. She stands by the window and watches something down below.

'Sorry. That's it. Ready. What are you looking at?' He joins her at the window.

A woman in the car park, wearing a tartan coat takes the rug off a pushchair and the matching tartan hat of a tiny child disappears into the car.

'Idiot.' Hannah says. 'Trying to create someone in her own image. Poor kid.' Simon shivers. Then she presses go on her internal file and she's away.

'I'm so glad you agree. Jason and his lot have really settled down. They're properly anchored now and productivity has doubled. I've had no more hassle from Joan and Bardo. They love having something more demanding to do... .'

He opens his mouth to speak, but she has more to say.

'Thank you for your apology.' She looks straight at him. 'It means a lot to me.'

'Oh. That's all. I thought it must be something important.'

'Simon! This is important.' She speaks slower. 'To both of us. My re-organisation set the ball rolling. Your change of tack with Jason has worked like an accelerator. You did well. We're not going to lose him and there's a different atmosphere in the whole office.'

Simon returns to his desk, sits down and places both hands in his lap. He takes a deep breath in and looks directly at Hannah. The problem is solved and things are working better from everyone's point of view. He smiles. Eyes too.

'Thanks, Hannah. I'm really glad.'

She returns his smile. 'That's OK then. I'll leave you to get on with it.' She turns as she reaches the door. 'Marion says thanks for the apology too. Two of us. On the same day. What's changed?' She vanishes without waiting for an answer.

Simon blinks. She's gone? Amazing. The word 'accelerator' sinks in. And 'You did well.' Three short words make such a difference. It's ridiculous to be so dependent on approval. Perhaps that's what Jason needed too.

He renews his energetic pounding of the keyboard.

Yes, something has changed. Ideas assemble themselves coherently and with ease. He approaches the tangle ahead and for the first time in months has the sense of firing on all cylinders. It's like putting a hand out in the dark straight onto the light switch. Or hitting the groove. An airliner cruising above the clouds or listening to a saxophone in full flight. The tangents work like the sound of children playing nearby when reading the paper. Mop up superfluous activity in brain cells that otherwise threaten to interfere with the job in hand. All because Hannah told me off for upsetting people. Ouch. But she was right.

He's the last to leave the office that evening and takes Jason's folder home with him to be ready for their meeting in the morning.

They meet in the big conference room. Jason's hair is now bright orange.

'Wow! That was brave.' Simon can't pretend he hasn't noticed. It certainly attracts attention, but it makes him look seriously unwell.

Jason doesn't respond. Either he's forgotten how different he looks or he's focusing on getting his plan up on the big screen and that takes a whole minute. He points at the screen with a forefinger and is about to start talking when he turns round, searching.

'Where's the zapper?' He picks up the long pointer instead.

'I was thinking it could go like this, but at a much higher level.' He brandishes the pointer more or less in the right direction.

Simon keeps out of the way and glances up at the screen. He checks the notes he made earlier.

'You'd need a lot of flexibility. How would you build that in?'

'There's a new kind of flexiglass. That could work, possibly. There are other problems too ... Whoops.' Jason loses his balance as he turns. He grabs a chair back.

Jason puts the pointer down and stands still.

'Yes ... I've got a vision of what it could look like but it side-tracks me from the technology. It's hard to think of both at once.'

Simon looks Jason straight in the eye. 'I had the same difficulty.' He pauses. He surprised himself.

'You did?' Jason's movements are now limited to the extremities.

'It still happens. I've got better at running those two threads in tandem. Partly by keeping up to date and partly by starting the other way round. You need to get to know the materials and methods, and their limitations first. It's like a musician working with a new instrument. Or with new amplifiers.'

'So ...?' Jason slumps onto a chair without taking his eyes off Simon's face.

'Understanding what's changed makes it easier to explore those changes and find out what they let you do. Be inventive. New sounds and rhythms and combinations and so on.'

'I'm not a musician.'

'Never mind. Does the idea make sense?'

'Maybe ... like those running shoes with the air-cushions built into the soles that help people run faster.'

'Er ... look ... I'll send you some things to read. Stuff I've written about the challenge of keeping in the front line. About combining ideas from all sorts of places and using them to make something new. Stepping outside your comfort zone.' He stops. 'Safely.'

'I should have read more ...' Jason looks down at his feet.

'Not published yet. Don't worry. One thing though ... it's always different in architecture. Make a mistake and the building might collapse. Make a musical mistake and the only disaster is not being heard. Or being ignored. You'll never be accused of putting lives at risk.' He now has all of Jason's attention. 'I expect the same goes for running shoes.'

'Break a leg …'

They groan. And then laugh.

They get closely down to work on measurements and perspectives and predictions of strains and stresses. Jason makes a list of papers and articles to read, and buildings to look at.

'That was so useful. Can we go on with these meetings?' Jason has closed down the big screen. He gathers his papers.

'Happy to. Your work is interesting. Heaps of potential there.' Simon wonders if he's found someone to rival the prize-winning Arantxa.

'Why orange?'

'Sunset. Seemed worth a try.'

Half a minute later the rest of the New Project Group heard from Jason there's been a light change in Simon. He's totally different. No nit-picking. And he's doing exciting things too if you can get him to talk about them.

The following afternoon Simon collects the children from school to look at another flat. The seventh.

'Coat on James. We're off. Now.'

James, high on the climbing frame, hands himself to the cross bar, grabs it with both hands and swings down monkey-fashion. A friend runs by. He goes to follow, but Isabel grabs his arm.

'We're going. Now.'

'Where?'

Simon gives him his coat. 'Put that on. Another flat to see.' Their school bags hanging over one arm and a paper bag from Joe's bakery in the other hand. 'Here.'

Two hands shoot out. James is still struggling into his coat so Isabel gets there first. With a doughnut in her mouth, she gives the bag to James. He grabs his and drops the bag. It flies away. Isabel chases it down and dumps it in the playground bin.

Simon puts a hand on Isabel's shoulder as she catches her breath. 'You're a help,' he says.

She gives him a straight-mouth smile with a frown attached, looking more like thirteen than nine. 'Uhmm.' Mouth full.

'It's not far. This one's on the ground floor and it's got a garden.'

'And a bedroom each?' Isabel asks. 'I'm not sharing with him anymore.'

'That's what it says.'

This time they're in luck. It's a big house with a hand-written sign leaning against the gate: NO PETS in red capital letters outlined in black. There's a full skip outside and the small patch of gravel in the front has collected the overspill. At the back, the ground floor has been extended into the garden, making a large kitchen-living-diner space and the children disappear to explore and count the rooms while Simon talks to the agent.

For Simon the best thing about it is the light: high ceilings, big windows and the afternoon sun coming into every corner at the back. There's a small garden with decking plus a patch of grass. There is minimal storage space but he feels a load lift when the children come back smiling and drag him off to explain who's going to have which room.

'No promises,' he says. 'I haven't agreed to take the place yet.'

'But you like it, don't you?' Isabel says.

He nods, and he's beset with demands about the stuff they want in their rooms. Tall, thin rooms with picture rails on three walls and none on the partition that now separates them.

Simon fixes a time to talk to the agent, takes one more look round with Isabel in tow, and it's time to go. James runs ahead and back as if on a self-winding dog lead.

'Can we live there, Dad?' Isabel asks.

'Listen,' he says, 'the first thing we need to know is how long it takes to walk to school.'

Isabel's hand fumbles its way into his. He looks down at the shiny brown hair that frames her pale face so beautifully. He clears his throat.

They reach the school in just over 10 minutes without having to wait for the lights to change.

'Under 15 then. That's OK with Mum.'

Isabel runs off to catch up with James.

London seems cleaner today. The river's full to brimming, there's a light wind ruffling the water, and golden pennies are still attached to even the slenderest of the branches of the silver birches. They shiver, and late though it now is (early November), they haven't yet started to fall. No puddles so a safe day for light shoes. A train rattles away in the distance, windows gleaming as the slanting sunlight turns up the dial on the colour chart. Simon screws up his eyes to see through the glare.

The sun slides away slice by slice as he walks along the river path. It's a longer but quieter route and he needs to think before talking to Ruth. Three weeks to moving day and serious business to get through. Flat deposit paid. Beds ordered. Ruth wants the study cleared and there's a small mountain of belongings to be moved from their home.

Not their home. Ruth's home. The house they jointly own but where only she lives now. An image of her standing in the window, the sun making a halo of her hair, interrupts his train of thought. He shudders and buttons his coat right up to the top. She's keeping him at arm's length. Perhaps it'll be easier when her new business takes off. He rounds the bend in the river as the sunset colours fade. A line of ducks slips into the water one behind the other.

Maybe she'll have him back. You never know. He speeds up, arms swinging.

Oh! He's forgotten to bring anything for them. He makes a detour to the deli. The one they often used a year ago but it smells just the same. A mixture of coffee, cinnamon and fresh baking.

Anton smiles at him. 'Haven't seen you for ages. How're you doing?'

'OK thanks.'

He leaves with a bottle of wine and two enormous brownies in a paper bag.

Chapter 15

Ruth

'Careful James.' Ruth shouts as he flings himself headlong down the stairs in his pyjamas.

Ker-clunk. It's a familiar front door.

'Hi Dad. Will you read me a story?'

Their feet pound their way back up the stairs. The heavier ones slower.

Ruth looks up from sorting clothes into wearable and washable. 'Hi there.'

'Hello.' Simon picks up a damp towel from the landing and stuffs it onto the bathroom rail. He reads James's story and Ruth reads to Isabel. Duvets are arranged, rearranged then disarranged for a goodnight hug.

Done. Nothing has interfered with the smooth transition from turbulence to a steady flow and that's as rare as driving all the way home without meeting a single red light. Ruth looks out of the landing window. It's totally quiet. Only a distant hum of evening traffic.

Downstairs, she hunts in the fridge. 'Pasta and salad. OK?'

'Fine.'

Simon opens the bottle. She unscrews a jar of stoned black olives and shakes some into her pasta sauce, twists the lid back on and picks up the parmesan and the grater. Simon lays the table and reaches into the cupboard for the glasses.

It's an odd sort of visitor who knows where everything lives ...

The water's boiling so Ruth adds the salt and tips the pasta in.

They eat at the round white table in the window. She's found an avocado to add to the salad and he's found the old honey jar of her homemade salad dressing. They talk about the children and how well they're accepting their new version of normality.

'The routine makes a huge difference. To me as well as them.' Ruth shines a spotlight in her need for stability. Predictability.

'I suppose I'll get used to it.' Simon says. 'I love their chatter and mess though.'

Pasta eaten, Ruth looks at the paper bag Simon left lying on the table.

'Brownies?' She gives the bag a prod.

He nods.

She opens the bag and pulls one out. Turns the opening his way.

'Stealing.' He grins. He looks at her and helps himself to the other one. 'They'll never know.'

Her mouth is full. Her eyes agree.

They're excellent brownies. Squidgy, with unpredictable walnut crunch.

'So,' Ruth says, rather suddenly, 'Are you going to be able to help? Have you thought about it?'

'Uh-uh. Let me know when you're in difficulties, and I'll be there as back-up. I won't let you go under.'

'Uhm … How do you mean?'

'I'll always bail you out.'

'OK. But how would that work? In practice?'

'What?'

'I need a regular payment. I need to know what's coming in every month. Or I can't keep the kids' activities going. Let alone mine.'

'Send me the figures. I'll work it out for you. It won't take long.'

'I can do that myself Simon. I've been running a business for ten years.'

'I'll tide you over. I'll make a transfer now and you can let me know when it runs out.'

Ruth holds herself in.

'Make it last as long as you can though.'

She pushes her chair back, piles up the plates and takes them away. For a moment she stands by the sink with her back to the table, one hand on the draining board. In the background she can hear the wind getting up, its bluster competing with traffic noise.

'No. I told you. I need to know what's coming ahead of time. Otherwise, how can I keep things running?' It was safer not to catch his eye.

'Yes. And I've said I'll help …'

'But that won't work.' She's breathing fast now.

'Of course it would. Don't be idiotic.'

'Oh!' She wraps both arms round her waist. 'I know what I need Simon. Regularity. Not a handout.' She turns to stare straight into his face.

'What?'

'Stop trying to control me.' It's hard not to yell at him. 'Why do you always want to be in charge?'

'I'm only trying to help.' He stands up. 'That's what you want isn't it?' The fingers of one hand open and close. He takes a step towards her.

Ruth shuts herself down. It's a huge effort.

Silence. They stare at each other without moving.

Ruth breaks through the shock waves. 'Right. That's it. Time you went.'

'Don't worry about it. I'm off.'

He grabs his coat from the hall and leaves without looking back.

Simon

Simon paces around the room like a zoo animal. That's not helpful, so he stops himself with a quick heel-and-toe turn and sits down on the sofa from where he can survey huge swathes of West London but can't see the river with its diverting activity, or the bridge lights reflected in the black water beneath. The view is amorphous in the almost-dark with the horizon obliterated. A faint glow from rows of street lights shines down not up. Whole acres of houses appear squashed together as if covered with a giant sheet of clingfilm that smudges out the details.

The wind is blowing hard out there. Simon shudders. He brushes his hand over his forehead. Images and echoes imprison him in Ruth's kitchen. He can hear the strain in her voice as she delivers a full-on rejection that dumps him in deep water.

How did that happen? He shakes. All at sea.

He tries to find a clear route through the interfering re-runs, but it's impossible to concentrate with the echo in his head of her accusation: Why do you always want to be in charge? It makes him bristle.

Why was she so angry? What could he have done to deserve that?

She's wrong, he thinks. He didn't want to be in charge. Whyever would he? She has a wonderful independent kind of competence. It's one of the lovable things about her. There's no way he wants to compete with that. So why unleash a full-on attack when he's said he'll help?

Simon remembers that even when starting Grainbox she coped better than this.

He'd only been trying to put things right. To solve the problem for her and give her the security she'd lost. He wanted to make it easier to get back together. To get back to being a real family again.

He tells himself to think it through from the beginning.

The evening started well. The children tucked in, a nice supper. Eating the stolen brownies. Then what? The thread back to comprehension snags on distressed voices and half-remembered gestures.

He sighs and goes to make a cup of tea. He picks up a pile of papers and looks at an unopened envelope from the estate agent. He places it sideways on top of the paper pile, jaw-line rigid.

She's exasperating. Impossible to help. Maybe it's because she's always done her own thing and never been controllable. That's how come she's been so successful of course. It would be ridiculous to try to change her. She's great the way she is ... or usually is.

It's a muddle Simon thinks as his thoughts threaten to go round the circle again ...

He rests his elbows on his knees and massages his head with his finger-tips. Music might help. He chooses Yo-Yo Ma playing the Bach cello suites and gradually the flow of the melodies finds a way of competing for his attention. Bit by bit the regularities persuade his brain cells to align themselves sufficiently to stop jittering.

He makes a decision. There are only two things to keep in mind now.

1. I'm not stupid.
2. I'm going to help.

And there's a third: I'm not giving up.

Ok. But no more risk-taking. Best to keep myself to myself. As he turns to pick up his laptop, he resolves to lie low, convinced this is now the best option. He opens his emails and types:

I said I'd help and I will.

He stops to think. Adds a request to see her accounts and presses send.

It's still windy in the morning and sudden gusts thump at the window panes. Simon is warm but his bed feels empty. Which it is, except for him. Everything he looks at speaks of aloneness in a temporary shelter. Everything from the single bedside lamp to the scattering of male clothes, shoes and miscellaneous objects on every available surface including the windowsill where he can see the penknife he confiscated from James and doesn't want to give back. He turns on the radio for company and tunes it in to Radio 3. He's wanting to reduce the cacophony inside his head.

An email with an attachment arrives while he drinks his coffee.

Thanks for saying you will help. Accounts attached. I can get by for the next 3-4 months on my savings if I'm careful. What can you manage? Rx.

She writes as if the explosion never happened, all business and no fury. And she's used the same horrible sign-off, 'Rx'. How come she can ignore last night's disaster? Is she hiding her distress? Trying to make sure of getting the help she needs?

Simon opens the attachment and reads it twice.

What? Why all the fuss? This is not a big problem. Not from the financial point of view. He thumps his knees and groans. She sends me this in the same breath as distancing me? She just put up a no-entry sign on the road that seemed to be leading somewhere …

Simon thinks back slowly over the past few days. He can still hear Hannah's voice when she said: 'You did well.' And Jason was full of inept but heart-felt thanks when he got the good feedback he deserved. Then the right flat turned up. Everything seemed to be going so much better. And last night with Ruth began well too. But suddenly, out of the blue, she was on the attack. Simon grinds his fists into his eye sockets.

It's not reasonable. It doesn't make any sense.

Is she really that worried?

Stop dithering Simon tells himself, and he moves the financial calculations to top slot. His own are easy as the estate agent has emailed all the figures he needs. He rereads Ruth's attachment carefully and sits back in his chair. In his mind's eye he can see Ruth as she was last night, winding her arms round herself as if she might break if she didn't hold herself together.

That's not the Ruth he knows so well. She's always been strong; beautiful, competent, independent. And unflappable. All those messages and timetables pinned up in the kitchen. Able to settle the children down to sleep even on the phone from Spain. Making instant friends with Dani and his family. What's going on?

He scribbles out some sums with a pencil. Online banking next. The arrangements easily made. No family holidays abroad for now. Not a problem. If Grainbox is anything to go by her new business will take off fast.

He responds to Ruth's email with one of his own:

Hope this works.

No sign off.

That should do it. He chucks his pencilled calculations in the bin. Speedily done, and no risk of being abolished in the process. Or wiped off the slate.

He goes out to get an energy boost. Head down and frowning he chooses the deli on the distant corner that work colleagues usually avoid. With a bowl of sweet potato soup and a heavy hunk of rye bread he sits with his back to the window and thinks about what to do. Easy if the problem is practical. Not so easy when it involves families. Or the person you love … the only person you ever have …

He squashes breadcrumbs into a pellet. If you don't have a strategy then where do you start? Decide what you want and get on with it. Prepare for an awkward meeting. Revise for an exam. Design another bridge. Persist until you win through.

But stopping to devise a relationship strategy suggests you're up to no good. Wondering how to get round someone, or how not to let them tumble to what you really want. That's not for Simon. He's never been a manipulator.

Putting in the effort used to work fine but it doesn't seem to work with Ruth. Or not now. He plays leapfrog with the salt and pepper shakers. Things can't go on like this. Up one moment and at risk of being annihilated the next. It's not safe. Best to keep right out of the way or do the wrong thing by mistake and lose the whole family.

His phone rings. It's Ruth. He lets it ring. He listens to her voice as she leaves a message.

Thank you. For your generosity. It makes a big difference.

He gives his head a short rest in both hands and decides not to respond. On consideration he realises that he couldn't trust himself not to say the wrong thing.

Chapter 16

Hannah

Austerity places a serious damper on the Westover office and 6 months later it shows no sign of lifting. Hannah's pleasure in her work is taking a battering.

Simon has lost his shine and he looks a mess. He needs a haircut and a lesson in ironing, and no longer stops to chat, let alone laugh. He's totally focused on spotting signs of progress towards his new targets, trapped in work-mode, and not good at connecting on a personal level. Disappointing. Especially after doing so well with Jason and the New Project Group. Apparently, he's slipped straight back into being oblivious to anyone's concerns but his own.

She wonders whether to say something.

Then the summer of 2010 starts to warm things up and Hannah has a message to deliver to Simon.

'Good news,' she says.

'What?'

'The footbridge over the Thames. The one that won you the prize. It's got the go-ahead.'

'About time too.'

'I thought you'd be pleased.'

'Well, I am. Just not sure whether to believe it.'

'You're so pessimistic. What's happened to you? You used to be the ideas-generator for all of us.'

'Er..uhm ...'

'The economy's unsticking itself. You've made heaps of new contacts. But you've isolated yourself. That could put all of us at risk.'

'That's not true. There are new contracts in the pipeline too…'

'What? Well, why don't we know about them?'

Silence.

'I can't be sure of them yet. I don't want to raise false hopes.'

Enough for now. 'We need to activate the Project Management Group for the Footbridge. I've got time tomorrow. You?'

'Always time for a PMG.'

Hannah's well of patience is not quite bone dry. She knows Simon and Ruth well enough to tell they're in a mess. Neither together nor apart. No wonder he's so awkward. Her well-organized room by the lift keeps things running. Her belief in the exceptional potential of the Westover Group is still alive. She'll do what she can to keep it going.

Simon

The sunlight that reaches Simon's ground-floor kitchen comes and goes as gusts of wind and rain do their best to put an end to summer. Simon sits at the table listening to the radio. Now it's the mixture of child and adult in Dolly Parton's crystal-clear voice. Before that it was Sibelius with mind-wandering images (juxtaposition not explained). It was liberating.

His strategy was working - head down and you keep out of trouble.

He drifts along with the odd choices of music on the radio. Freewheeling for the mind, like stretching unused muscles. He lets go of the super-controller and submits to the unexpected, ready to respond to whatever happens next. His heart and brain in tandem. At least temporarily.

He looks at the garden. That stays the same though it's always changing. Fixed and unfixed. A stationary place with a multitude of variations. Like countless sensations passing through a single body. A mouthful of coffee at precisely the right temperature. The feel of a new pair of shoes. Sounds of traffic and people and music.

Gone as soon as heard. Making up one experience. Never the same as the last time.

It was like changes in the seasons. Even the day of the week changes the pattern. Traffic flows on a Sunday for instance. People making their trajectories matter as they wander, or rush, or submit to impediments and interruptions. Everyone getting on with their lives directed by different wants and wishes. With shifting concerns and varying intensities. Helped or hindered on their way by the stuff that builders and architects have made with them in mind.

The built environment should be the stabilizer for all those variations.

He keeps still. A quickening of ideas and images is beginning. Don't move a muscle or the image will dissolve. Don't miss anything … capture what you can … see what might fit … go for the best … He reaches for his sketch book and pencil carefully so as not to disturb the thought-image production line. He outlines a 3D structure on the 2D page. A bridge of course. Crossing another gap.

He needs to see it from another angle. Would that work? It's hard to figure out yet.

Ideas need to settle in. He should step back and give them time to mature. Let his imagination lead the way. It's like being on a roll of intellectual adrenaline that coordinates every bit of sensitivity. In tune with alterations in the wind and the weather. With the movements of people outside and the flow of music inside. Their similarities and differences.

A rush of excitement makes it hard not to leap up from his chair.

He needs to keep going or he'll turn off the tap by mistake.

Not just thinking but thinking about thinking. Both at once. Impossible to do if you're at risk of being interrupted.

It's a luxury. A bonus. A privilege.

The experience is rare but familiar. Every time the end product comes as a surprise. How can you surprise yourself when you're the one who produced the surprise? Do I or don't I know what I'm doing? He laughs at his own thoughts.

111

Explaining to Ruth the way that he was sometimes taken over by creative brainstorms was so hard. So important. Making sure she knew there would be times when being alone and undisturbed would be his top priority.

'It's all about making links between things. Making the most of a super-surge,' he'd told her.

'What?'

She probably understood.

The end product might be impossible or impractical but it often revealed new possibilities. Like uncovering a secret about things that totally different worlds might share. It's thrilling. The most important thing that ever happens, and you can't do it to order. It can lead to a dead end, but it can also be the source of something wonderful. Something as inspired and as inspirational as the Golden Gate Bridge. Incredible.

The drawing rate slows down as the expert mind takes over. Simon looks hard at his sketches, serious problem-solving at the ready. Now he's wondering about 'how? ... and 'what with?'... and 'where can I find out whether ...?' and 'What will the engineers say?' He makes notes. Faces up to new sets of questions about practicalities like changes in methods, materials and technologies.

Right. Ready for action.

He goes to the office and loses himself in technicalities. Having the beginnings of a structure in mind has revealed a design that demands his full attention.

Designing a bridge involves facing risks. Safety first, of course, but others too: economic, financial, managerial, political. There's the fear of missing something important, like the limitations of new methods or materials barely out of the testing stage. Or forgetting demands from the world of sustainability. The thought of a bridge made entirely of recyclables makes him smile. Ruth would understand.

Thank God for the team. They were hand-picked for their creativity as well as their expertise. He saves today's exciting new work and leaves it to mature on its own. He's given it an electronic anchor to keep it safe.

The excitement of a new project doesn't last. It dies away once everything is theoretically in place. The original conception is subject to endless threats and pressures from engineers and members of the construction industry. From clients and groups of noisy people in surrounding communities, fighting to get their needs met. From the unexpected, like finding a burial chamber when digging begins. Or sudden explosive rifts when the agreed mix of public and private funding is questioned. Beautiful designs can easily be compromised. Architects, seeing the shine taken off their designs, have been known to turn thunderous. Or tearful.

In my case, incredulous and explosive probably, Simon realises.

The Thames Footbridge is finally about to embark on this unpredictable journey. Keeping it on course will be hugely demanding. And there are other projects as well. Teaching, writing, keeping in touch with clients. Running the Westover Group (with Hannah), mentoring, promoting a hub of excellence in bridge design ... He stops.

He could make use of Jason and get him on the Project Management Group for the Thames Footbridge. He'd be stretched, but it's just what he needs. That would release some time for Simon.

Hannah's the key. She's brilliant at coordinating everything and holds us all together. She keeps people communicating and working smoothly in whatever combinations are required. Probably because she allows them to step on her toes when put out rather than on each others ...

He has a word with her but Hannah is doubtful.

'Jason is certainly talented. Exceptionally so. But he's excitable and impulsive. Project management work needs a steady head. And a liking for detail.' Hannah says,

'I reckon this could help him to develop exactly that.'

'Is he ready for that?'

'There's one way to find out ....' He could be. He's a fast learner.

'He'll need careful supervision. Sure, you have time?'

'Er... no...'

Simon is tempted. He wants to work on his new designs but he would like to give Jason a chance. He's talented and ambitious in just the ways that Simon remembers being at his age. His background in engineering as well as architecture is unusual. And useful. His curiosity can be irritating but it's original.

Simon likes the thought of working more closely with Jason even though he tends to cut corners when immersed in a new idea, and he might take risks. That's not OK here. This profession depends on ensuring its products will never endanger their users. But he'll learn. And the combination of their individual talents could be good. Exceptional even.

Hannah makes a suggestion. 'Get Clive Estridge involved. Give Jason double supervision time.'

'Do you think that's necessary?'

Hannah pauses. 'I'm glad to see you're no longer trying to do everything yourself. If we really are taking off again, then you certainly need to share the work. Could be a step in the right direction for you. But for Jason?'

Simon is convinced that Clive Estridge, chief engineer of the Thames Footbridge PMG, is the perfect person to keep an eye on Jason. He has a woolly brown beard big enough to keep him warm in a Siberian wind and it gives him a powerfully authoritative look. He's famous for picking up stragglers and motivating the evasive. With five sons and seven grandkids, he has learned how to quash insubordination when it threatens to get out of control. How will he react to Jason? He'll definitely keep him in line.

Simon sends Clive an email.

Please consider Jason for the PMG. And we could share the job of supervision.

A reply comes straight back.

OK.

Clive Estridge is a plain speaker.

Simon talks to Jason. 'How about joining the Thames Footbridge PMG?'

'What? When? I'm right in the middle of sorting my new design ...'

Simon speaks evenly, so as not to persuade.

'There's a useful opportunity here. To gain practical experience. It's got to come some time. Clive and I would share supervision.'

Surely no one with any serious ambition would refuse such an offer.

Jason stands up. Takes a step back, arms flapping. Unable to keep still.

'I'd love it. I know it's got to happen. I'd have to give something up though. Difficult to see what ...' He sits back down. 'What would I be doing?'

'The team will work that out. There's always lots to be done for new projects. Selecting materials, finding a source for them, technical stuff of all kinds, groundwork at the site, endless checking and financial work...'

They talk about details and timings and agree that he will join the PMG team meetings at once. He'll pick up more responsibilities as soon as he can hand the technical stuff he's been working on to others and Clive has had a chance to think about where his energy and talents will be most useful. Simon knows Clive won't let him take on anything crucial without a proper assessment of his skills and abilities. Without making the lines of responsibility absolutely clear.

That's a relief.

As Jason leaves, Simon tells him to talk the plan through with Hannah.

'OK. But doesn't she already know?'

'Yes, she does. But she keeps an eye on everything. Keeping in touch with her is like listening to the main department engine. You get to learn the sound of smooth running. Miss her out, and you'll find yourself in a tangle.'

'So, I'll keep in touch with you. It's your project. With Clive for the PMG work. With her too?'

'Yes. That's the way.'

Chapter 17

Simon

Persistent summer rain has stopped play and the day out to watch cricket, planned carefully by Dani weeks ago, has been cut short. Anorak hoods and umbrellas are up, and passing buses interfere with conversation.

Walking behind Dani in the rain Simon, mouth zipped shut, doesn't bother to hide his disappointment. He's damp, tense and irritable and not ready for personal communication of any kind. He's worried that his resolution to steer right away from close contact with anyone, including Dani, is about to be challenged.

'Let's get something to eat,' Dani says, as he swerves left into a Thai restaurant.

Simon looks up and down the road before following him. There's no other option. Besides he can see that Dani is determined to save the day and knows perfectly well that this is something he's supposed to enjoy. In silence they wait to be seated, stamping their wet feet on the blue-green non-absorbent tiles. It's not a long wait, and both their heads turn right as an inviting smell of coconut and lemon grass rises and then fades with the draught as the door behind them closes and opens. The padded benches are big enough to be comfortable for people with legs as long as Simon's and they are welcomed with friendly smiles and steaming white cylinders of hot towels to wipe their hands with before they eat. The warmth is all-encompassing.

Behind Dani there's a picture of an elephant that seems to be looking over his shoulder. 'So how are things working out?' he asks.

Simon hesitates and sighs. Then he notices that the elephant and Dani both have their eyes fixed upon him. No wriggle-room here, and somehow that takes the weight out of the question. The thing about Dani is he gets straight to the point. He never did let people off the hook, but he's always had a light touch.

'Same old. Nothing new.'

'Work?'

'Good. Back on course. Thames Footbridge build going ahead at last. Exciting developments in the world of bridges too. It's hard to keep on top of them as there is lots of work in the pipeline, and that's good.' Simon was on safe ground talking about work.

'Children?'

'Much easier now they have their own rooms.' Isabel certainly disappears into hers readily enough. They told me about meeting Maya and Kiri in the park. Simon wonders whether Ruth was there too. His head is busier than his voice. It's hard to focus.

'Yes. I love the way the four of them get on.' Dani pauses. 'Maya's always been good at coping with James ...'

'James is a worry ...' Simon shoves his chopsticks aside and picks up a fork instead. 'That's better.' He goes on. 'His teacher thinks he might have ADHD. He can't concentrate and creates havoc wherever he goes and then the other kids play up. It's hard to know if he's interested in everything or nothing. She's suggested we get him assessed. Ruth is getting it sorted.'

'Tough. He's certainly a handful.'

'You think he needs help?' One of Simon's lightening flashes bats the possibility of real communication straight to the boundary. It can't be much help for James, living with separated parents.

'Maybe. He's so easily distracted. And fearless.' Dani has balanced a heap of rice on his chopsticks and is holding it still in midair. 'When Ruth and I took them to the zoo he kept wandering off. We kept thinking we'd lost him.'

Simon can just see Ruth and Dani in joint parenting roles. His shoulders slump. 'We'll soon see,' he says.

They eat in silence until Dani waves to the waitress and asks for their teapot to be refilled. When he turns back to Simon he starts again.

'You don't seem to be enjoying the running much.'

'Oh? Why not?

'That's what I was wondering.'

Simon stops eating. What's happening? Here's the one person he has always been able to talk to being nice to him and he can't even begin. He has no idea what is making him so uncomfortable.

'Sorry Dani. I've been cutting myself off. It's hard to get going.'

'I should have kept in touch.'

Dani is steady as well as quiet, and Simon is embarrassed. I'm the one who created the distance, not him, he thinks.

'Basically, there's not a lot to report. Ruth's new business is doing OK. Maybe she's told you. I never understood why she got in such a panic. She was totally scared when starting up but she could turn a molehill into a mountain when she's worried. There was no big problem to face this time, but somehow I upset her when I was trying to help, and she went straight into attack. I've been lying low ever since. With everyone.'

'She told me. Not about being angry but about her worries. She said she was haunted by visions of her schooldays.'

'Uh-uh?'

'Worrying that Isabel and James might end up the same way: missing out, feeling excluded and humiliated. Especially after all the stuff you've given them, and the things you did, and the holidays you all had.'

A string of half-thoughts runs through Simon's head before he has even finished his mouthful: I had no idea ... I never thought ... I'm so sorry ... Wish she'd said ... Why didn't she tell me ... What did I miss? ... Why didn't I catch on? He takes two hands to his handle-less cup of green tea and looks at Dani over the rim, ready to listen.

'She told me you came to the rescue. You helped her out. I thought you must have known.'

'I knew without knowing.'

'What?'

'Funny how you can do something right without having any idea why. Why it's right.'

Idiotic not to be able to add up. Maybe it's because daily demands shut everything else out. Unless it's the legacy of past troubles. No one wants to revisit those, especially when they're moving on and busy building their present lives. The past is definitely best left behind. The facts might intrude sometimes, but there's no point in exploring their meaning. It's water under the bridge. Let it go. Put it away in a box labelled 'Insignificant.' Lid shut. No implications remaining. Especially not for now.

Looking up he realises Dani isn't fussed about being kept waiting. He's making a note in one of those dog-eared blue notebooks that he keeps in his shoulder bag. Occupying himself with something else. Looking patient. So is the elephant.

'I'm wondering whatever I've been using my brain for!'

'Me too,' Dani replies, shutting his notebook and pocketing his pen. Ready to down tools for Simon. 'When you're running you look as if you've shut everything else down and out of reach. I envy your concentration, but what about the fun...?' Dani is searching. 'What's happened to enjoying yourself? To letting go? Laughing?'

'Almost forgotten what it feels like!' Simon admits.

Dani looks down. On the wall behind him Simon sees a small pair of piggy eyes in a huge grey body staring at him. Despite himself he has to smile.

'Dani!' His shoulders are starting to shake. 'Turn round. Look behind you.'

And Dani's laughter joins in.

'You know what they say ... ?' Simon is coming alive again.

'There's an elephant in the room ...'

'No Dani, the one about forgetting.'

'Ha!' It's the relief of real laughter.

'Well, I won't forget. Not now.'

'Do you remember the game we used to play with your grand-father's records? The matching game …?'

'… when we'd see who could find the best music to match some-thing completely different? Like a boring school assembly …'

'… or skiving off a cross-country run. Going to the record store instead?'

'… and splashing through puddles to get our shoes dirty but forgetting the socks?'

'… and legs. And you chose *Don't Fence Me In* that time.'

'… and I chose *Mud, Mud, Glorious Mud.*'

'And your grandfather called it a tie and challenged us to eat a whole loaf of bread between us.'

… 'which wasn't a problem at all.'

Simon knows they are back on track. Back in a much warmer place where lightning strikes, hard stares and notebooks are off the menu. Protective devices moth-balled as the armour falls away, banished by being with Dani and memories of his grandfather. Simon glimpses the possibility that you might not have to keep on struggling in order to belong. No need with Dani to trade success for acceptance.

He thinks of Isabel and James. It's totally different for them. They've always been free to be themselves without worrying about not coming up to scratch. Thanks to Ruth.

Simon remembers Dani's fingers waving at him as they left the running track when he mouthed the word: 'Consideration.' Ah. Yes. I think I see what he meant. Get out of yourself. Widen the focus. Consider what makes others tick. Take them into consideration. Discover what that brings into view. He looks up, inquiringly.

'How about you?'

'Managing.'

'Difficult?' Simon's curiosity has been shaken awake.

'Family's amazing. Never thought I'd have one. The only thing I wanted after Sita died. My sister. Maya's still thinking about making houses and Kiri is full of music from top to toe. Always humming. I love the sound of it. Amit's been away a lot.' Dani slows himself down. 'We miss his cooking.'

'But? …' Simon is giving Dani all his attention. Waiting. He looks away when Dani doesn't respond, not sure how to encourage. How not to close him down. He looks at the table.

Dani finds the space he needs. 'I've been wondering what he's up to. Not daring to ask.' His eyes wander round the room.

'Oh?' Simon isn't sure he heard that right. He doesn't want to put a foot wrong. But if you're not sure you need to find out. 'What do you mean?'

Dani looks up and away, briefly. Then he explains. 'He did a presentation back in Malaysia, on organisational management, and met up with an old friend, Malik. A charming snake with a beautiful head of black hair and a shiny expanding briefcase. I'm not sure I can trust him - workwise or otherwise.'

'What's going on?'

'Wish I knew. Amit is far too susceptible to his charm. It could be nothing at all. Or a dodgy deal. It could be worse … for me that is.'

Simon takes that in before he responds. 'Anything I can do?'

'Nothing that I can think of. It's hard to get the balance. I mean the right mix of showing I'm worried and showing I trust him too.'

'I hope it's OK Dani. Hope you'll be OK.'

They paid the bill and are just about to leave when Simon says:

'Let's do something fun … there's a regular Jazz evening at the Golden Lion, near the park. Shall we go?'

'Love to.'

Chapter 18

Simon

Once again spring wrestles with the job of warming up the cold ground. The economy recovers and Simon rediscovers his sociability with the help of Dani and jazz at the Golden Lion. The frost has suddenly been dispelled by unexpectedly glorious weather.

Simon sits silently with Ruth and Dani watching all four of their children take charge of Ruth's kitchen. A hand goes to his chest as he sees Isabel and James enjoying themselves in the home he helped to make and turns round to see Ruth there too. He sits still and straight and pays attention as if he needs to take careful note. His coffee cup is too full to pick up safely. He lets it rest.

Jackets have been dumped anywhere. Vegetables spill out of orange and green supermarket bags over the kitchen table. The room seems to be full of T shirts and long thin arms and sunlight filtering through a haze of constantly mobile hair of many colours. Children with a serious plan in mind reach for what they need, create a cacophony of pans and trays, mixing bowls and cupboard doors, and take their collections to home-base for today. Maya has the stove and nearby worktop. Kiri and Isabel take the far end of the kitchen table, and James the end nearest to Maya and the cooker.

Simon sits by the window with the sun at his back and the smell of wisteria just coming into flower wafting through the open garden doors. He remembers giving that plant to Ruth just after Isabel was born and she was nothing but a warm bundle to hold close while watching Ruth dig a hole, hair glistening with rain drops. She bent down to sprinkle in a handful of bone-meal. A good start in life for a tender plant.

So many changes. It was hard to tune back in. Wiser to keep a safe distance.

Ruth and Dani are deep into one of the quiet conversations that, over the past couple of years has become a specialty of theirs. Their mutual ease is enviable. They don't even question something so elusive, and Simon makes a mind-shift away from his puzzling territory back into the present. Back to remembering that Maya, at only 15, is the one who brought them all together. She sent out a summons. Not an invitation.

'It's our turn. You grown-ups always keep us out of the kitchen. Come to Ruth's for lunch on Sunday and we'll cook for you. She's OK about it. Don't forget.'

Simon crunches a Hobnob but ignores his coffee. He loves the way the children take possession of each other's homes. They seem to operate as a single family.

He does an internal calculation and discovers that all the meals the two families have shared, one for each of the half-term breaks since he and Ruth separated, have been cooked by the grown-ups. It hasn't always gone smoothly. Only Amit can manage a meal for eight at the end of a working week with pleasure. But that, Simon thinks with a touch of envy, is because he's a bit of a wizard. A cook with flair, who can join in with conversations and pour out drinks without turning round to discover a culinary disaster going on behind him. Success doesn't just perch on his shoulders. It wraps right round him. He welcomes it as naturally as a comfort blanket on a cool evening. Nothing elusive about it. He even looks relaxed as he eats. And smiles with unembarrassed pleasure as he accepts compliments from his friends and total silence from the young. He is not here today. Where is he? Simon has no clue. But he has a few fears on Dani's behalf.

After many regular meetings and shared meals, he has no real sense of what Amit does. Or what he thinks.

An hour later Simon discovers nothing but gritty salt inside a flattened peanut packet. Will we ever get a meal? Waiting used to be agony, but today the watching is utterly absorbing. It's good to see the kitchen he designed for Ruth, for a proper family, working so well for a crowd. Maya shakes some nuts into a frying pan and selects a wooden fork to stir them with. Isabel and Kiri invent a rap as they make their fairy cakes look grotesque and inedible. James sits at the table chopping. Loudly. The knife thumps onto the wooden chopping board and carrot chunks bounce away. He can't reach them as he has one leg strapped up and a grubby knee bandage on the other. Playground wounds are keeping him uncharacteristically rooted.

'Help! Maya, help me,' he calls above the rumble of the cooking rap.

'What's the problem?'

'Jumping carrots.'

'You chop. I'll collect. Then do the celery.'

She multitasks like a pro.

There's an enormous platter in the middle of the kitchen table. James is making an edible foundation layer out of the salad packages within reach. Maya keeps the supply coming. Multi-coloured peppers next, then a couple of long thin Chinese radishes she has just peeled.

'Ready for the messy bit?' The feta is slippery but fun to crumble. He won't touch the salmon. He tips a tub of pomegranate pips right in the centre and some strays end in his mouth.

Simon remembers the bedtime battles he had with James when Ruth was away. Cooperation of any kind seemed to be either impossible or a cause for drawn-out negotiation from extreme positions and explosions of childish distress from everyone, irrespective of age. 'You never let me do what I want. I hate you.' At full volume.

There's a sudden shriek. James has twisted his legs as he reached for the olives and everyone jumps to attention. The rappers pause. Ruth and Simon are on full alert but the girls are right there. They straighten him out. There's a box to rest his foot on. Some hugs. Distraction in the form of an avocado to squash and turn into a creamy dip with dashes of tabasco and lemon juice … and the rappers get right into staccato mode:

You wanna eat …

You gonna eat …

All you can reach …

It's out of reach …

'Ouch.'

James thumps out-of-time rhythms. They laugh and vegetable confetti smothers the table and the floor. Maya tips her crispy nuts over the dish. She opens the oven and the smell of hot bread fills the room.

'Ready! Ready when you are.'

'You grown-ups haven't laid the table.'

'I'll get the chairs. Let's eat outside'. Simon leaps to it. The next family meal is about to begin.

Ruth

Ruth and Dani end their conversation.

'What's up with Simon?' Dani asks. 'What's going on?'

Ruth looks closely.

His face, no longer heavy with fatigue and the habit of not responding person-to-person, is alive again. He's allowing himself to be carried along by the stream of activity in the kitchen and seems to be enjoying himself.

'What's happening?' she asks.

'He's changing, I think.'

'How? How do you know?'

'Paying more attention to others? Listening more? More aware, perhaps. Can't say I really know. He's getting more like he was when we first met. More involved.'

'You know him even better than I do!' Ruth laughs. 'I can't help wishing I'd known him then too.'

'Can't have too much of a good thing.' Dani laughs too.

Ruth hesitates. 'My friend Leila's been telling me to start online dating.'

'Are you ready for that? Is that what you want?'

'Well, ask me right now and the answer is definitely not. But I do sometimes wonder …'

Time to eat.

Simon

Simon puts a chair down by the table and stops. How come these children are so aware of each other while they do their own thing? As if they're dancing independently and together all at once. And the end result belongs to all of them. No need to single someone out with a raised glass. No need to apologise for a botched presentation or late delivery. It's just a bit of fun. Fun that spins the turntable of pleasure and leaves good memories behind. It creates the confidence that comes from participating in a mini adventure.

Simon waits for the surge towards the garden door to end so he can collect the glasses and drinks. He reflects on the pageant. Here before him is a stage on which failures and prizes are irrelevant, he thinks, and then remembers with a shudder of embarrassment the time when Hannah had told him how he upset people. In his thoughts he hears Ruth's voice:

'Your thirst for admiration seems totally insatiable. I married you because I love you. Irrespective of successes and prizes.'

Maybe she's right. Maybe it's not about winning after all.

Chapter 19

Simon

Day after day the clouds loom low. Not unusual for February. Simon takes a break and looks through his personal collection of bridge pictures. A bright red ponderous one rises and descends steeply over a canal. An apparently weightless highway like the Orwell bridge in Suffolk soars over a tidal river. Norman Foster's Viaduct at Millau is the best. Or one of them. Its seven white sails are not designed to keep it moving but to stop it going anywhere while the traffic crosses a gigantic valley in a few minutes instead of a few hours. The fascination of creating links is key, whether they join two parts of a shopping mall or a whole archipelago of Scandinavian islands. His dreams of making an addition to architectural history resurface.

Something feels different. A stream of whispers, apparently created spontaneously in his head, used to accompany his working life. They were mostly cautionary messages. Intrusive, obstructive and annoying. Like the expanding foam from an aerosol of shaving cream blanketing everything in range. Messing things up. The whisperers have gone away. It's like noticing the absence of something that you never noticed in the first place. The smell of the weather. How to run downstairs.

Simon's dreams are let off the leash. He imagines bridges with moving walkways. High-level wind-assisted cycle tracks in transparent tunnels. A gigantic supporting tower that works like a tuning fork and turns moving air into musical notes that go up and down with changes in the weather and traffic flows. Not serious but definitely fun.

The playfulness is beguiling. And an introduction to serious thoughts. His office provides everything he needs to combine new ways of thinking with thousands of gigabytes of accumulated knowledge. His own and others. He explores new ways of ensuring strength and safety. Of fixing things together and using sustainable materials. Or a 3D printer to bend things this way and that. Separating spaces according to flow patterns without perpetuating social differences so as to foster inclusion not exclusion ... his vision widens.

Still have to check things out of course. Follow up the 'what ifs' ... Measure interacting flexibilities and everything else. Always something new ... new methods, machines and materials ... new ways of re-using stuff ...

Go for it, he tells himself. See what you can do. Beneath the dreams there may be a nugget of something that could really make a difference. Something to make the world stop and look ... and leave the competition standing.

He looks up and sees the photograph of Ruth and the kids still lying flat on his bookshelf. He picks it up and stares at it. Still there all of you, he says to himself. Not lost yet. He stands it up again.

Ridiculous, he thinks, to have been so dependent on the sustenance of admiration and achievement. Needing to win imposed limits. This feels more like liberation.

He is astonished by the imagination-fest that comes his way. It's too much. Like the discoveries of an adolescent. All over the place. It needs focusing. Taking a moment to consider, Simon realises that it's time to find his own stamp. Or signature. Or vision. Curiosity, he thinks, has taken the scariness out of uncertainty.

The sound of a telephone works its way through the brainwaves. Opening it up he sees Ruth. It's the day she's taking James out of school for his ADHD assessment. They can't have results yet can they?

To his surprise he hears traffic noise and a garbled mix of voices. Then Ruth's voice. Out of breath. Gasping.

129

'Simon! Thank God I've got you …'

'What?' … She's talking to someone else.

'Help.' More traffic noise. More voices. 'There's been an accident. James …'

'What? Where are you? What's happened? Is he OK? …'

'You need to come ….'

He hears a woman's voice saying, 'Sit down. Here …'

'Where? Where are you?'

'The ambulance has just got here … taking him to A&E in Kingston.'

'What's happened to him? Are you OK?'

'Emergency department. Paediatrics.'

'Got that.'

'I'm OK. It's James. He's not conscious. He fell and banged his head.'

'I'm coming. I'm leaving now.' Simon's heart is banging and he can't think straight. The way Ruth is keeping herself together is amazing. 'Hang in there. I'll be with you as soon as I can.' He does a swivel-search looking for what he might need to grab before he goes.

'Oh ….' He hears her swallow. Hears a shaky intake of breath. 'Don't be long Simon.'

He drops the phone onto his desk and runs a hand through his hair. He presses both palms to his temples. Coat. He grabs it off the hook by the door and steps outside. He pats his pocket, no phone. He goes back to pick it up and looks at it as if there's something he's not sure about. He sees it's nearly 3 o'clock. He clicks a file shut on his computer, glances at his diary and draws a blank. He's off. Fast as possible.

Nothing fits together properly for Simon that evening. Sights, sounds, smells and sensations of all kinds swirl around creating a random jumble of impressions. There's a feeling of wanting to hang on to them and not let go until they fall properly into place.

130

But Simon can't force them. One of the doctors said it might take a while for the disturbance to settle down, and it would be good for him and Ruth to rest if they could. But Simon couldn't rest. The images seemed to have a life of their own and obeying the order was beyond the range of available possibilities. He was being swept along in a stream of apparently random images and memories that he couldn't stop.

White sheets close to a white face. A limp white hand falling from a bed. White knuckles grasping a shiny bed rail, the band of a wedding ring on the fourth finger. The need to keep focused. Willing James to open his eyes.

A porter stops what he's doing to point out the way to Paediatrics. 'Oh thanks. That's really helpful. Thanks for stopping. Sorry to interrupt.' … An overflow of words keeps pace with Simon's speeding thoughts and feet.

A feeling of desperation as the guy on reception, who hasn't heard of a James Westover, moves a leisurely hand to pick up his phone, then interrupts the action as a panicky voice behind him intrudes: 'I can't find Dermatology. Wherever is it?' Simon's fingernails bite into his palms.

A nurse, one hand on James' wrist, tracks the bedside monitor with its constantly moving lights and numbers. Suddenly he uses his other hand to prize open James's left eyelid. To Simon, the unseeing eye seems to belong to a stranger. It's the right colour though.

There is endless walking. He can still hear the sounds of leather soles pounding the pavement, and of trainers squeaking along plastic corridors. The click and snap of heavy heels on shiny stairs. He has to circumvent polishers with a surrounding swirl of sweet-smelling air mixed with tangy antiseptic and make way for huge hospital beds on wheels pushed by silent porters who negotiate corners like expert taxi-drivers.

There was such a queue by the lifts that it was best to choose the stairs. Simon asked the way to Ward 6. Another endless corridor loomed up ahead.

He sees Ruth standing with her hands clasped together, staring white-faced at the door, looking out. She wipes a tear from her cheek. Simon rushes towards her and they hug. What will she say? His heart is pounding. Even his finger tips throb.

'So glad you got here.'
  'How is he?'
  'Don't know yet.'
  'What happened?'
  'He stepped off the pavement right in front of a bike. It couldn't stop in time. He was knocked over and hit his head on the pavement.'
  'What have they said?'
  'Just that it's good we got here quick. They are going to do X-rays next. Or a scan I think.' She sounds shaky. 'I should have been watching him. I could see the bike coming ...' She has one hand on her mouth.
  'Don't go there Ruth. It was an accident. You always take care. I've seen you doing it.' He has a hand on each shoulder, holding her far enough away to look straight into her eyes.
  'Thanks.' With an effort she straightens herself up and steps back, from the brink. Ruth is now back in control.

Simon's images and memories bring intense feelings back with them, and gradually they become more coherent. Ruth and he were in a place full of busy people, but still felt isolated. At one moment they sat on green plastic chairs in a waiting room and could hear the answers given by invisible others to questions asked by professionals who spent their lives attending to an interminable stream of ordinary disasters. They think they shouldn't be allowed to hear all that. Simon tries not to listen. Not to decipher the words or to hear exactly what they said. Now he remembers deciding not to say anything about it or complain. They waited together in silence until James was brought back from being bombarded by electronic rays in a darkened room. An ordeal that he knew nothing about.

A nurse holding a list called for Mr and Mrs Westover. She pointed them to the hospital cell where Dr Arendt was waiting for them. He was calm and factual, with a professional kindness that stifled all risk of sympathy. He told them that James didn't have a skull fracture. Simon was holding his breath. Knowing his son's head was still intact he let it go. The words that followed were overwritten by relief and obscured by Simon's internal surge of questions. Then why doesn't he wake up? What's happening? When will we know? How will this affect him?

When he comes back to the present the doctor is still talking. He's explaining to them what will happen next. 'We'll keep him quiet. You can stay. He'll be in Ward 6 in Paediatrics.'

The nursing staff settle James into the cubicle closest to the nursing station. Simon and Ruth wait. Simon is fidgety. She is completely still.

Simon grabs her arm 'What about Isabel? Where is she?'

'I'd arranged for her to go home with Kiri. I didn't know how long J's appointment would take.'

'We should tell her.'

'Yes. I was waiting. Hoping he'd wake up first.'

'I think we shouldn't wait. I'll ring if you like, but wouldn't she rather talk to you?'

Ruth nods and picks up her phone. Simon hears Isabel's voice. 'Mu-um. Stop checking up on me. I'm fine with Maya and Kiri.'

'Listen Isabel …' Ruth takes a deep breath and looks at the floor. 'There's been an accident.' She explains calmly. Isabel is silent. 'I'm in the hospital with James. Dad's here too.'

'I want to see him. When can I come? When will you be home?' Ruth could hear tears from Isabel now, and she wonders how much she has understood and how much they should tell her. She thinks it would be best to wait until things are a bit clearer.

'Soon as possible. Of course you can come. We're going to stay with him for now. He needs to be kept quiet. You can come later. We'll keep in touch. Can I speak to Dani?'

Simon looks at Ruth. It's amazing how she can switch on the organising part of her brain under stress and keep all the threads in play.

'You take it. Please.' She hands her phone to him.

He sees her tears fall and a muscle twitch as she grits her teeth, one hand clenching a clump of tissues. She did the hard bit without hesitating. He puts out a hand that she doesn't see. It's his turn. Not a problem to talk to Dani.

'I'm so sorry, Simon. I've got Isabel right here too. What would you like us to do?'

'We don't know much yet, but I'll ring you again as soon as we do. He's in good hands but probably best to wait for us to ring again.'

They agree the basics. They sound calm. Sensible and under control. Of course Isabel can stay with Kiri. Yes, Dani can bring her up whenever …

'We'll look after her. Keep in touch. We're not going anywhere.'

'Thanks Dani.'

'Thinking of you. All three of you.'

Being occupied helps. Simon turns to Ruth and puts a hand on her arm. 'I'm going to get us a drink. Tea? Coffee?'

'I'm OK.'

'Ruth … we might be here a long time …'

'See if they've got something herbal?'

Simon feels for his wallet as he gets up and hesitates. What if something happens when I'm gone? Better be quick, he thinks. He braces himself for the impact of the world of hospital corridors again, with their mix of busy and worried, and worrying, occupants.

'Don't be long,' he hears Ruth say as he reaches the door. It's the second time today she's said that. He clocks it without implications.

Following signs takes every ounce of Simon's concentration. The corridors are endless. He must have come at least a mile. He shudders. Poor Isabel. Best for her to stay where she is for now. Tea for him. Chamomile for Ruth. Hot water in a paper mug with a small transparent bag attached to the lid. A muffin to share, and a KitKat as well just in case. There wasn't much else to choose from towards the end of the day. The route half-learned as he came, the way back would have been easier to find if there'd been a tray for the cups and there was no need to hurry.

There wasn't any need to hurry.

Simon and Ruth move two chairs close to James's bed and drink tea in a darkened room. Nothing's changed except the staff. The hand-over here is not like a relay. No quick transfer from one person to another. Without warning people vanish behind closed doors for hours, and when they open them all the names and faces have changed. James has a named nurse now. Samira, with kind eyes and a quiet voice.

'How about talking to him again?' she says, after giving serious consideration to James and his monitors.

It's hard to think of anything to say. It's exhausting to keep it up. Ruth is more resilient.

'Hello there J,' she says. 'We're both here with you. Dad and I. Both of us. Can you hear me?' She has taken his hand in hers and is stroking the back of it.

'Look. His eyes are moving.' Samira says. She turns to Simon.

'I'm holding onto your toes James. Maybe not the best way to wake you up, but it might work.'

And it does. James opens his eyes, briefly. A narrow window opens and then shuts again. He stirs. Slightly. His eyelids flutter open again.

'Hello James. We're both here, We're with you.' Simon catches his breath. The power of two parents working together is astonishing. It doesn't feel illusory either.

Then the professionals take over. Observation. Quiet discussion. More torches are shone into his eyes. Hello there. What's your name? The mumble sounds correct. James's fingers are plucking at the sheet when Samira says,

'Hello James. You had a big bang on your head. I'm Samira. Here to look after you in hospital.'

He's coming back. How far will he come? What comes next? Simon looks at his watch again. It's not even 6. He can't believe so little time has gone by since he left the office. A lifetime ago. Another time altogether.

Part 3: Nothing unusual

Spring 2012 to Autumn 2012

Chapter 20

Simon

Six weeks after discharge the adjustment to new realities is certainly not finished. It's not a bit like the straightforward line of progress described at the pre-discharge meeting.

Simon looks up as he hears a low mumble coming from somewhere behind him. Oh dear. Here we go again. An exasperated shriek comes next.

'It won't go!' James sounds as if he's had about as much as anyone can bear. 'Can't do it.' There's a thump on the floor. 'Dad ... where are you? Da-ad.' Vowels lengthen as the crescendo expands.

'I'm right here. In the kitchen. What's the problem?'

Hearing the gulps that precede the flood, Simon pushes aside his new bible: Acquired Brain Injury (ABI) in Childhood and goes to find James. He's been doing well and he looks fine. Just like his normal self. Simon takes a deep breath in as he eases his way into managing another crisis. It's not the first and it won't be the last. James is constantly up and down mood-wise but he's moving in the right direction.

Simon finds him sprawled on the floor of his room, almost dressed. The T-shirt is back to front. Pants on but no trousers or socks, and he's been trying to fit a motley assortment of possessions into his slim green school bag. Too much stuff ... and that includes the threadbare killer whale that has recently recovered its role as first choice comforter.

Kneeling on the floor, with a gentle hand on James's back, Simon tells himself to go slowly. 'What's up, mate?'

There's no response. The crying jag dies away.

'You're almost dressed! That's good.' They're sitting close together now and Simon wipes away the tears with a thumb and reaches for the tissues. 'Are you getting ready for school?'

James grabs the tissue box and uses a fistful as a rapid face-mop that smears tears and snot over his whole face.

'Won't fit.' He aims an angry kick at the killer whale.

'Never mind. We'll work something out. No school this week. Half a day next week, so we've got lots of time to get you ready.'

Silence. James fiddles with Simon's watch strap. 'It's 9.34.'

'Yes. Quite right. You woke up late this morning didn't you? How about breakfast? Aren't you hungry?'

Simon eases James into his trousers sitting on the floor.

'Let's leave the socks. Here's your hoody.' He spreads it out with windmill arms and watches as James struggles into it. Awkwardly. What's new? Getting James dressed is not something Simon's had to give any attention to for ages.

'Off you go to the bathroom. And wash your face too. What do you want for breakfast?'

'Weetabix.' Sniff.

'Again?'

'Uh-uh. And juice.' James swipes his nose with the back of his hand.

'I'll get it out. Don't be long.'

Simon puts the ABI book high on the dresser and reaches for the Weetabix box. He pours himself more coffee. He finds a bowl and a spoon and gets the milk from the fridge. He switches on the radio. Sits and waits. Not for long as James, face partially clean, attacks his cereal as if it's the first full meal he's had in a week. It's tempting to enjoy the peace and quiet while you've got it, but not fair to him. Not good. He sighs.

James pushes the empty bowl across the table. 'What shall we do Dad?'

'What would you like?'

'Can I work on one of your drawings?'

'Course you can.' Simon turns off the radio. Looks up, straight into James's face. 'Wash your face properly first.'

'I already did.'

'Look in the mirror this time. After you've done it.'

'Can we find a picture first?'

'Wash your face first, then we'll find one.'

James slides from his chair and lies on the floor staring up at the ceiling.

Simon ignores him. 'Go on. Off you go,' he says. 'I'll get the file up and you can choose which one to print out.'

'I did it already.'

'Your face? Well, have a look in the mirror.'

James starts drumming on the floor with his heels and tugs at one of Simon's shoe-laces.

'Stop that James! Get up and get going.' He pulls his feet back sharply and nicks a child-sized finger on the way.

James leaps up and thumps his dad on the thigh with both fists. Simon grabs him by one arm and marches him to the bathroom door.

'Enough! In you go. Wash your face.' He pushes him in and flinches as he hears the key turn in the lock. Fists clench and unclench. That child can be exasperating, and trying to keep calm only ratchets up the tension.

What now? Leaning against the wall he hears the water running. He'll probably be OK but anyway I'll know soon enough if he's not.

'Ready when you are.' Simon says loudly and goes to the living room, turns on his computer and starts answering emails. He gets to the end of today's messages and looks up. James is right beside him. He jumps. James laughs.

'I didn't hear you coming.' He puts a hand on his shoulder. 'Let's have a look at you.'

Polished face. Soaking wet hair. You have to laugh.

'Well done.' Simon closes his emails and opens the file of drawings. 'You choose which one to work on.'

James hooks a buttock over the seat of the big chair and gets to work. Simon fetches a tea towel (nearest thing) and gives the wet hair a rough rub. He drops the towel on the floor. Glad Ruth isn't watching.

Where was I? He looks at his watch. What was I meaning to do? It's nearly 11.00. James has printed out a drawing of a bridge crossing a major road. It's seen from different angles and he's lying on the floor amongst a litter of pens, papers, cars and discarded Lego. He colours it bright orange, red and yellow. The road beneath is blue, like a river. He adds some stick-figure pedestrians wearing wellies even though there's no river. Normal? Or not?

It's going to be another long day, Simon thinks.

The main message to hold on to is simple. 'There's no identifiable damage. He should make a complete recovery.' The doctors were reassuring, but how long will it take? How can you know what to expect? There's so much Simon wants to know. Sometimes it's as if he's not gone back to square one but to square three. But not in every way. Crossing back to where he was before doesn't happen smoothly. It's like being on a flight of stairs with uneven steps.

You have to stop and think all the time to work out what's happening. Has he lost it because he's tired or because he can't string the letters together to make the word he wants to write? His feelings are all over the place. Dani asked which computer games he liked and he cried as he couldn't remember their names. That's OK now, but humiliation lurks just below the surface. It's a horrible feeling. Not surprising really if you're thrust back a year, into a place you just left behind. Pushed back into the time before you could get your own breakfast or use an instruction sheet to work out how to build a spitfire from the fiddly bits and pieces jumbled up in a poly bag. It was heart wrenching to witness.

The bible-book has been incredibly useful but it's too general. It has to be probably, because of all the variations, but there's so much else it would be good to know. Why is he so hopeless at getting dressed? Has he been distracted? Is he muddled? Forgotten that pants go before trousers? Or is it that he doesn't want to do what's expected? That would hardly be surprising even before the accident.

Ruth had to show him again and again how to do up his seat belt. Then suddenly he got it. Done. Now, given a chance, he'll eat everything with a spoon instead of using a knife and fork (lazy bugger), and when the psychologist asked him his address he got really upset. Sometimes he picks things up quickly, but sometimes he's stuck. And you have to keep an eye out all the time. Don't want him falling downstairs. Or tripping over the edge of the pavement. It's exhausting. For all of us.

'Your child will need lots of reminders and encouragement, and more sleep than usual.'

Right. Exactly.

But the warning messages aren't clear: 'At first, doing ordinary things can take all his or her attention.' So what? Isn't that like all children? Totally absorbed in whatever, so they don't hear what you say? We were told to keep him quiet when he's concentrating. Noise makes things harder. One thing more and it's one too many.

So three-year old tantrums in someone aged nine are nothing to worry about? Are you serious?

And the more patient and encouraging you can be the more it will help.

Always?

Yes. Tell him he's doing well. Because he is.

Basically, it's like starting all over again. It's not just James who's got new stuff to learn, it's all of us. Remembering, or forgetting to remember, provides a permanent underlying rumble with occasional scary drum rolls. Ruth's far the best at keeping him on an even keel. She always was. There are instructions to rely on, and sheaves of shiny handouts. Notes from meetings. But the children operate on a mix of instinct and impulse. Isabel has adapted quickest of all.

She's amazing. Quiet and steady. She watches him and lets him lead the way. When things go pear-shaped she doesn't bombard him with questions but tries to work out what he wants. Or she leaves him be. She doesn't panic and somehow he gets back on track. How she knows what to do is a mystery.

Yesterday was chaotic. Ruth and Isabel were chatting about rehearsals and play dates and a sleepover with Kiri. The TV flickered and rumbled in the background. James was creating a city with wooden blocks, train tracks and cars on the floor. Suddenly he stood up and swept both arms across everything on the table laid for supper. He waved his arms about, turning to everyone in turn. He couldn't speak. Then he couldn't stop crying. Ruth sat in the window with him for ages.

The booklet warned us: 'It may be difficult for your child to handle more than one thing at once.'

Right. Too much going on. He can't talk to you when he's eating. Or hear what you say when he's drawing a picture. Or read when there's music playing. One thing at a time is enough. Isabel turned off the TV and went to her room to recover in her own way. By herself.

Knowing what he needs is so difficult. He wants to tie up his shoes but he needs help. He wants to do it himself and doesn't want to be helped. We all want to help him but don't know how. And he can't explain. Thank God for the experts. And for good friends like Dani. But it's a lot more complicated than the experts say.

We've been told he'll be OK, but he was always a bit out of control. The ADHD assessment might have made sense of that, but it's been postponed now as the picture is more complicated. It's worrying. So sad. And frustrating.

Everyone caring for James has to learn fast and they need to work well together. You can be overwhelmed and concerned one moment. Caring and sure-footed the next. But you have to keep heading in the same direction. Even if infuriated and resentful. All the usual stuff is pushed off centre. It's like entering a world that has an immediacy that can't be ignored.

Ruth

Ruth opens the door and blinks as she looks round for Simon. His sitting room looks entirely red even though it isn't. There's a

144

brown and red sofa, patches of red and pink in the carpet and scarlet curtains that never quite clear the windows. It's warm in winter, and sombre in summer. The Golden Gate Bridge is there above the desk. Simon sits in a sagging armchair that used once to be yellow. She sits down on the sofa.

'Simon. How would you feel about having James with you a bit more? Could you manage that? And still get your work done?' She reaches for a cushion and stuffs it behind her.

He looks up. 'You're much better at managing him than I am.'

Am I, she wonders. Maybe I used to be, but I'm the one he was with when he got lost in Richmond Park ... not only that ... She can't face thinking about the accident. She's quiet. Glad that Simon hasn't jumped ahead again and reacted like a speed boat.

'I don't think so,' she says.

'What?' Simon pulls in his legs and sits up. 'Sorry. I've lost track ...'

'I'm no better than you are at managing him. Not now he's so much better. And he wants to be with you. It's quieter. You let him do what he wants.' She looks round the room as if searching for something. 'The new business is at a difficult stage. I should be spending heaps of time talking to people. I'll be able to delegate more soon but often I have to ignore him. He gets upset and miserable. And it unsettles him, constantly moving between two houses. Could he stay with you all the time for a bit? Until he's properly back at school?'

Simon looks at his hands. 'I could work in the evenings I suppose.' He's thinking as he goes. 'And early morning if he goes on sleeping late. Could you and Isabel take over in the afternoons? I could work then. You could be here if you like. But I'd need this room.' Simon leans forward in the faded armchair. He looks up and waits.

'That could work. I could take him out in the afternoons. We could go for a walk to collect Isabel from school and come back together. If he sleeps here and Isabel stays with me that could be much better for him. Fewer changes and more stability.' She closes her eyes for a moment. 'It would make a huge difference to me.'

'OK. Let's try it. Glad to be useful. For once.'

Ruth looks up sharply but doesn't respond. She is relieved to have that fixed. Work and child management arranged so both adult lives keep on track.

During the next few weeks, the amorphous collection of family commitments and concerns shifts as loads are rebalanced. Another joint decision provides a stabilizer. To have early supper together before Ruth and Isabel go home.

Simon

It's lucky, Simon thinks, that Hannah knows how everything works. Minutes of meetings ping through the ether, highlighter tool indicating priorities. The usual flood of reminders and updates has been minimised. The New Project Group is on a roll. The Thames footbridge work is going ahead with Clive in charge and he's supervising Jason too. Team leaders and fund-holders can be demanding but there's always the telephone. Teaching and writing commitments are either on hold or done slapdash. Simon still finds time for planning the hub of bridge-building excellence.

Jason rings to ask about James and comes out with a barrage of questions and concerns. Simon suggests he comes to talk things over. He turns up mid-morning with a small carrier bag. His hair is no longer orange, but short on one side, long on the other. A floppy fringe hangs over one eye. How he retains any charm at all is a complete mystery. But he does.

James is fascinated by him and delighted with the array of coloured tubing that he tips out of the carrier bag onto the floor. 'I found my old tubiframes. Bit old now, but I loved them when I was 9.' He joins James on the floor, and they absorb themselves, separately, in the silent business of construction.

'What's yours?' Jason asks.

'It's a house-bridge. For going from room to room without touching the floor.'

'How do you get through the walls?'

'Ladders by the doors, But it's only for children. They're not allowed to put a foot on the ground.'

'Good idea.'

'The ladders roll up. Only children can let them down. Then you have to fix them back up after.'

'Sounds as if you take after your dad.'

They go on working together in silence. Simon is surprised how quickly Jason tunes in to James. He makes two mugs of coffee and hands one to Jason.

'How's the footbridge work? How are you getting on with Clive?' Jason eases himself from the floor to a chair.

'The thing is that Clive's great at organizing things, but he's not up to date.'

'Clive's the best manager we've ever had. He can't do everything. None of us can.'

'OK. But there's not much he lets me do, other than checking calculations. It's totally unchallenging. Boring. There's a heap of stuff that we now know that could be useful here.'

'Da-ad.' James has encountered another insurmountable problem. He's trying not to cry. He kicks his heels on the floor then retreats behind the sofa.

'Here. I'm here.' Simon puts out a hand, but James won't come out. He's losing the battle with his tears.

'Talk on the phone, Jason? Or email me if you need. And thanks for these.' He points to the floor. 'Remember to keep in touch with Hannah as well as Clive.'

Jason hesitates. He stands up and looks around. Half-stifled sobs come from behind the sofa.

'Bye James. You can keep the tubiframes.' He leaves quickly. Simon turns his attention to more urgent matters.

Chapter 21

Simon

Simon sits on the brown and red sofa listening to musical phrases that keep turning this way and that (Arvo Pärt's Spiegel im Spiegel). Life has been busy. Time with James, routine work, and his new ideas have been coming together with more of an individual perspective behind them. The new combination of work and home is proving easier to live with than he expected. Best to enjoy it while it lasts.

He stretches. Leans back pillowing his head in both hands. Can't do any more tonight. Ruth probably could. She switches in and out of things so quickly. She manages to shut down her work files and opens up the kids' stuff straight away. Or the other way round.

It does get easier. It doesn't always take every ounce of available energy to get started. But there's an underlying rumble in the background. What about the Westover version of The Golden Gate Bridge? Does potential seep away if it's left unused? How destabilizing might it be to devote so much time to family life?

Ruth manages it. But her journey always moved on different rails. She travels smoothly along the main track and never lurks in a domestic siding not knowing which way to go. She's still the one who holds everything together and knows how to create a real family. Without her there the children were part mystery, part excitement for Simon, and it was easy for him to ad-lib and play for laughs even though that created a sense of being transparent and a dread of being called out. It was impossible ever to be as important as Ruth. His fear of not mattering had been increasing, he now thinks.

One of the best things now is seeing the kids rag about and be themselves knowing they can talk freely to their parents about whatever. No pressure. No burden for them of hoping to trade their achievements for a small dose of approval. Oddly, it's easier to belong and feel a part of things because it's clear that living separately doesn't mean losing touch. James has helped with that.

Simon admires the language Ruth has for creating closeness. For keeping cross or tired children on side. For landing herself on the same page as them. Isabel will probably be the same, Simon thinks. Ruth said: 'You sound so ornery.' The front wheel of Isabel's new bike was stuck in the hedge. She'd turned bright pink as she struggled to turn it round. 'Not ornery.' Isabel stamped her foot. 'Can't cornery.' She made everyone laugh.

Simon is now certain that, in his disorganized way James is alright too because he knows his parents are there for him, even when they don't know how exactly to help. He had serious nightmares and woke screaming in the night, Simon told Ruth about them and they talked it through together. More than once.

He was incoherent and wordless at first, Simon said. Thrashing about as he tried to escape from some unimaginable terror. Inarticulate and at the mercy of images he couldn't control. His head rolled from one side of the pillow to the other, eyes staring without apparently seeing what was in front of him. If you held on to him he stretched his arms out and arched his back. Was he having re-runs of the accident? Imagining his head hitting the pavement? Reliving the daily distress of falling short? Dressing, reading, explaining, listening, remembering all presenting embarrassing or humiliating problems. Like forgetting his friend Ben's name or knocking over the Jenga tower before it had hardly got started.

What should you do? Simon asked Ruth.

Ruth asked if he'd found anything that worked.

It seemed best to hold him close and keep quiet, Simon told her. Stroke his hair back from his forehead. Speak to him. 'It'll go soon. It's not real. Just a nightmare.'

And when he sounded frightened. 'There's nothing dangerous here. We're quite safe. We're together.'

If the nightmare went on and on rolling around his internal horizons he would stop thrashing about and blink up at you if you turned on the light. Talking to him and getting him to answer was good too. Simon told Ruth about the first time this really worked.

'Dad. Dad ...' he put both arms round Simon's neck when the light woke him up.

'Hello there! I'm here. It's alright.'

When he calmed down and kept still it was hard to know if he was in danger of falling asleep before the nightmare was truly over.

'James?' He didn't reply. Was there life still in it? Would he wake up screaming again in a few moments? Best to deal with it once and for all, Simon thought.

'Up you get. We'll go to the bathroom before you go back to sleep. OK?'

No response.

Getting out of bed was a struggle. He was unsteady if you didn't hold on to him, and it helped to turn on the lights and get him to move about.

'That sounded really scary. What was it all about?'

He shook his head and rubbed an eye with the heel of his hand.

'Jumbles. Colours mixed up. Everywhere.'

'Uh uh.'

'It's going to get me.'

'Look round you. See me there?' Two serious people with similar, sleep-tumbled hair looked back from the bathroom mirror. 'Which is your toothbrush?'

He picked up the green one and looked at me as if I was stupid, Simon told Ruth.

'Right. You're back again.' With his face sponged and the towel rubbed over it he put his arms up for a hug. 'Well done.' Back to bed. James led the way.

'I'll leave the door open. Call me if you want, but I think it's gone now.'

He settled quickly then, tucked in with the killer whale, and it was okay to turn off the lights.

Images of a small body in pain and fear, sounding distraught, replayed themselves over and over in Simon's head that night.

'How do you stop the nightmares coming?' He asked.

'I don't know any more about it than you do.' Ruth said, 'But what you're doing seems to work.'

We're on this part of the journey together. On the same track. Or in the same boat. Tracks don't rock.

Dani

The Golden Lion on Jazz nights is popular and crowded. Dani has made a habit of arriving there early and he heads straight for the table in the corner where he and Simon feel comfortable. Following James's accident, listening to music together provided a kind of solace. It still does. You can't talk through music if you're going to travel along with it and allow it to change the current emotional kaleidoscope. Let it fall into new patterns. As the music plays it begins to shape a channel for two-way traffic between the listeners. When it stops they can dip into that channel and find things to share.

Obvious ones to begin with, like food and drink. The pizza toppings. Later on, as concerns begin to fade, awareness shifts up a notch.

'Getting colder now. Glad they've lit the fire.'

'No one singing today? That's a pity.'

No rush. Just ordinary stuff.

Simon never used to be the first to sound a more personal note, but he's much faster now. 'I'm wondering whether I've missed the boat. If I'm never going to make something truly wonderful.'

'How can you tell?'

'No idea really.' Simon spoke with a straight mouth. 'What about you?'

'I'm in a much smaller boat. Steering others along while I make sure it doesn't get swamped. And going along for the ride too of course.'

Deeper elements rise to the surface during the next songs, if the two-way traffic runs smoothly, and all of them make it easier to move closer.

'You look tired,' Simon says. 'What's up?'

It's unlike Simon to notice that sort of thing, Dani thinks, let alone mention it.

'Amit's away again. I'm doing all the cooking.'

'What else? Are you worrying about the snake with the expanding briefcase? I can't remember his name.'

'Malik.' Dani fiddles with a ridiculous table mat embossed with black and white piano keys. 'Yes, I am. I try not to. But I am.'

'Have you asked him about it?'

'Yes and no. As one does. I ask about their meetings, and he tells me about having a meal together while they go on working. They make plans for more visits.'

'Uh-uh?'

'We're good together, Amit and I. He's brilliant with Maya and Kiri. I don't want to rock the boat.'

'I'm glad.'

They've been helping themselves from the bottle of Portuguese red as they talk and the end result is a conversational to and fro that bypasses tendencies to make judgments.

'Have you met him?'

'Long ago. Not recently. He's in Kuala Lumpur. I don't think I was wrong to call him a snake.'

Simon looks up as he speaks. 'Amit always seems so confident. He takes success in his stride as if it's out there waiting for him to pick it up. I have to keep pegging away with my nose down to get anywhere near where I want to be.'

There is silence for a moment.

'Is he looking for something new d'you think?'

'Amit? He's not one for a work-only life. Never has been. I think that's why he loves cooking. It fits because he's so incredibly sociable. He makes friends everywhere. Wants to touch all bases. Explore everything possible in the only life we'll have.' Dani's fingers play over the piano keys on the mat. 'Including other people.'

'Restless?'

'He urges me on. I do know that's good for me. You know me. I've never been ambitious. But there is something I don't tell him about. Fair enough, it seems to me, to have a secret. Can't live in each other's pockets.'

There's more music. Like a new version of interval training, the gaps between songs now provide assimilation time.

'What kind of restless?'

'Amit? He's always looking for something new. I just never thought that included people. Partners.'

'Uhm. Sounds difficult.'

'Have you found someone else now you're not with Ruth?'

'No. But I don't want to. I hope she'll have me back.' There's a long pause. 'Or really, I suppose, I don't want to look for someone else. It's been good being together more since James's accident.'

'What about her? Has she?'

'Don't think so. Haven't asked. Daren't think about it.'

'Neither do I. I mean where Amit's concerned. I'm scared of what might be on the way. It's hard to think of much else. It puts a huge boulder between us when he comes home. I dread talking about it. I do write though.'

'Is that what you don't tell him about?'

'Uhm ...' Not an easy one to answer, that.

'Sorry. Don't say if you'd rather not.'

'Ur- ummm... I do write. But not just words. I've been writing songs. I love doing it. I would so like to hear one of them for real.'

153

'Oh.' Simon looks up at Dani, smiling. 'Fantastic. Sounds like exactly the right thing for you.' He hesitates. 'How far have you got?'

'That's what the notebooks are for. Been doing it for ages. I gave one to Kiri to sing.'

'Dani you're truly amazing. I bet you're good at it.'

'Not yet!'

'Could you be?'

'Perhaps. Can't tell without hearing. Kiri loved the one she sang. She's got a very low voice. And listening to her told me what needed changing.'

'Go for it, Dani.'

'I might just do that.'

'Seriously?'

'Yup. It's something I've always wanted to do. I want to be heard. To find out if people respond to a song I've written. They don't have to be good ... just good enough to raise an eyebrow. Or a smile.'

'Why don't you talk to someone here? Someone like the band leader. Or one of the singers?'

'Maybe. I'll think about it. No hurry.'

Dani feels that he's been properly listened to. And encouraged. It's so good to have Simon back like he used to be with his grandfather. Understanding. Responsive. Showing he cares. Incredible.

Chapter 22

Simon

It's the second week in June when the mists of early spring mornings dissipate too early to be noticed by all but the most committed of early risers. Coats and sweaters can be left behind. The world feels air-brushed. Reminders of damp mud and wet leaves have disappeared and there's a hint in the air that local gardens are about to put on a show.

Simon follows behind Ruth as they walk upstream along the Thames path. This morning they took James for a review with his consultant. They have delivered him back to school, and they're heading, in their separate kinds of silence, for a pub by the river with a big garden. Simon hopes for a table for two within sight of the water. He shakes the tension out of his shoulders and loosens his collar. A few steps further on he undoes his cuffs and rolls up his sleeves to just below his bony elbows.

There's shade under the overhanging willows and poplars, and an occasional breeze that, Simon notices, makes the light falling on Ruth's sturdy brown sandals flicker and dance as she walks.

Undisclosed wishes, for once, come good. There's an empty table under a tree near the river bank and discovering that the white-painted chairs alongside have back rests as well as cushions Simon leans back, then forward, then back again, ready to accept all manner of support and comfort. Ruth looks at the water for a moment then uses both hands to remove the concertina scrunchie that was holding back her hair and stuffs it in her pocket.

There's an uncertainty, a delicacy, in the moment. How do you start?

'That's such a relief. Do you think so too?' He searches Ruth's face for a signal. She shakes her hair about. Loosens herself into a less restricted mode and looks around at the green lawn and the widely spaced tables beside the water.

'I hardly dare to. But yes. He went through everything so thoroughly. I couldn't think of any other questions to ask. Could you?' She doesn't wait for an answer. 'I thought he'd be less definite. I was worried there was going to be a sting in the tail. A horrible surprise of some kind.' Simon waits for her to go on. 'But nothing. Not even a hint. I'm not sure I believe it yet.'

Standing on the towpath with a loud hailer a coach yells something indecipherable at the pair of women in their scull as they fly past, the eddies made by their oars disappearing into mini whirlpools on the glassy surface behind them. From his side of the table Simon can see him shake his head. Not easy to make yourself heard at a distance. Even when necessary.

There's so much to say. How do you begin?

'He was so certain. *No lasting damage.* That was what he said a couple of months ago too, and this morning he said it again. I didn't believe it then. Now I do.' Simon's hands lie still. 'I've been hanging on to those three words. Trying to keep hoping through all the turmoil. It was never possible to be absolutely sure was it? Now I am.' His smile is completely devoid of tension.

'I keep thinking they might not have had long enough to find out.'

'Uh-uh. But it fits with the test results. And with the way he's getting on at school.'

'What about the ADHD?'

'We'll have to see. He's definitely a lot calmer. Not so many outbursts.'

'I think we did well, Simon. Don't you?'

'Uhmmm' … He looks down, and in a while he looks up again. We did do well. In our separate ways, he thinks. What about the together bit?

He jumps. There's a teenager with a snarling tiger on his chest and enviable eyelashes standing right by his elbow with a couple of paper menus.

'Would you like a drink?'

'Lime and soda for you? Extra ice?' She nods. 'I'll have a Heineken.'

They choose two salads. Avocado and feta for her, spicey chicken for him, and they are delivered almost immediately. Undisguised variations on the theme of lettuce, cucumber and tomato with additions. And sour dough.

Ruth grins. 'Must have been lined up in ranks, waiting to know their names,' she says to the teenager as he leaves. They laugh.

It won't be long before James could be doing that sort of job. Simon blinks at the thought. Hope he didn't think we were laughing at him.

The boy with the alarming T-shirt was not bothered, and Simon settles back into the stripey cushions wondering whether to talk about what the consultant said about their parenting skills. He hesitates. It was completely unexpected to hear those words. You did well. The consultant said he was impressed as he knew they were busy people and not living together. Simon remembers his exact words: 'You got the priorities right for James and that makes a big difference. It's hard to keep that up over the long weeks that follow a crisis like this. Well done.'

Wow. Mostly due to Ruth of course but having James for all those nights was good. It's taking a while to catch on to what it means. Now and to James's future. To the kind of help and support he might, or might not, continue to need.

'I'm glad he stayed with you so much. I think it helped him a lot. And it was good for me too.' Ruth smiles as she looks across at Simon.

'Thanks.' He lets that sink in. Another surprise. Fingers running through his hair release scalp-tension as they go. 'It was good for me too, you know. He shows you the way if you let him. He made me look and listen. And I had all those books and hand-outs and instruction sheets too.'

She smiles across at him. 'It's made a huge difference to him.'

'And I had your example. I could see how you and he worked things out together. Before, I could never understand how that happened. I thought I'd always be out on a limb....' ... Stuck in a siding. Off the main track. Simon keeps these thoughts to himself.

The background roar of jets on their way to land at Heathrow intrudes as one of them lets down its undercarriage.

'Far too low,' says Ruth. 'It shouldn't be allowed.'

The noise fades into the background and it's easier to think. For Simon, links with the past are rising and falling as they begin to make sense in new ways. 'It made me think of how my grandfather was with me. But I'm his dad. Not his granddad.'

He can still hear the difference in the sounds of those two voices from the past: his father's and his grandfather's. It's a difference between expecting and accepting.

'Isn't that what dads should be doing?'

'Well mine never did. You saw him. He was totally uninterested in me. And that's how he always was. Or worse, most of the time.'

'It was as if the only thing he ever noticed was another step on the road to success. Or what he counted as success. It's such a cold road to be on if the only thing that matters is what you achieve. I don't know how you survived.' She delivers her judgement with no hesitation.

Simon looks down. She understands how hard it was. 'I wish you'd known my grandfather better. He loved you.'

Her mouth stays closed as she smiles. 'Dani's told me about him. Maybe there's more of him in you than you realise. Or could be.'

Simon laughs.

'Don't remind me. I know I've still got a long way to go.'

'Look back and remember how far you've come. With James' help of course!'

She's wonderful, Simon thinks. It's impossible not to love her. Suddenly the road home seems a little shorter than once it did. It's tempting to race ahead.

No. Take it slow, he tells himself. She hates it when I go too fast. That's what she said when we had lunch together. He takes a deep breath, lets it out again and changes the subject.

'Tell me about the recyclables. How's it going?'

'Coming good at last.'

Ruth is sitting up straight again, eyes sparkling. Fully alive.

'Glad I made the change away from packaging, though I still think there should be more pressure put on that whole industry. I like thinking about making good use of rubbish. Did Isabel tell you? Her new swimsuit's made of recycled plastic bottles. And it feels soft and silky. It dries almost as soon as she's out of the water.'

'What about the finances?'

She was so worried and that's not even very long ago. Has she done enough research?

'Are there enough outlets? Have you got some good scientists on your team? Or people thinking ahead about how to use other sorts of junk? Like car tyres?'

'Hold on. You go so fast! One thing at a time. Plastic to material first. Then we're working on replacements for plant pots that don't disintegrate when wet. Or only disintegrate once they're planted with the plant. Trust me. I know what I'm doing.'

'Trouble is whatever you go for is likely to be more expensive than the original, isn't it?'

'Possibly. At first. But people think more about their carbon footprints now. And it sells. I'm doing my bit to preserve what we've got.' She pauses as she waves at the trees along the river. 'And reducing the risk of the flood that would destroy us all. It's all about the future. That makes me feel good, even though I'll never know whether we've succeeded. What it'll be like for our children and grandchildren and how they'll manage in a depleted world. I don't suppose any of us will ever be able to sit by this river without jets streaming past overhead.'

'Sight and sound don't match.'

'What?'

'I mean right here. It looks wonderful. But the constant noise of jets is awful. You want to hear some good sounds? Come with me to the Golden Lion on a jazz night. It's amazing. Dani and I go regularly.'

'Simon!' She's silenced at first. Nonplussed. 'But I'd need a babysitter. Or childminder I should say now they're older.'

To Simon that sounds like a lame excuse. 'Ask Maya if she'd do it. She's old enough, isn't she?'

Ruth picks up a leaf that has landed on the table. There's a light breeze and another flicker of moving leaves is spreading a transparent screen over plates and glasses, hands and knees, enclosing them in a network of light and shade.

Gathering speed is automatic. But dangerous. Simon reins himself in again. Not ready to look up.

Ruth's large hands rest in her lap. Her turn to change the subject.

'What's going on with the bridges? I was amazed how much work you managed with James around.'

That's something we have in common, Simon thinks. Being interested in what we do and always ready to talk about it. It's a pity though. His fingers won't keep still. He looks up to see she's waiting.

'It's been good. Easier to see what next. And I've started to think about doing something much bigger than before. It's as if an internal brake has come off. Of its own accord. It's hard to think of anything else. I get so full of ideas I keep forgetting to do some of the other stuff that I ought to be doing. Do you remember Clive Estridge?' She nods. 'He's heading up the Project Management Group for the footbridge, and he's been pursuing me.'

'What about? Do you know why?'

'Not really. Clive's in charge. He'll keep Hannah in the picture. And the inspection team will check things out. It's not urgent.'

'Unlike you to let someone else take control.'

Is she teasing? Simon thought.

'Is that good or bad?' For once, he doesn't know.

160

Ruth picks up the thread. 'That depends. It's OK if the teamwork is top class. I think my teams have much less independence than yours. They're much less confident about taking a lead. Readier to share the decision-making. And the worrying. Don't you worry? You're so used to hanging on to the controls.'

'Home truth? Or professional opinion?'

'Bit of both I guess.' She grins. Not in the least apologetic. Direct without a tinge of aggression.

Where's this going? Simon fidgets in his chair, sensing the intrusion of a familiar interchange that could run the risk of escalating. The breeze has fallen away. The leaves no longer flicker and in the stillness the certainty that was growing within him feels a bit less solid.

'You're right. I would usually keep tabs on everything. It's odd, but I'm finding it easier to leave stuff to others. Let them worry about it instead of me.'

Simon pays the bill. They leave their comfortable chairs on the lawn and wander towards the path along the river.

A different kind of silence surrounds their homeward stroll along the tow path, going much slower than the arrow-shaped boats that slip down-stream beside them, silently, at astonishing speed. No one telling them, this time, how to do it better.

Hope is distracting. Simon buttons up his cuffs. He has opened up his email and sorted roughly through a pile of papers. He takes his phone out of his pocket and places it face up on the desk to his left, as usual. He skims through a list of messages and reads one right through to the end. What was that? Haven't a clue. He pushes back his chair, stretches out his legs and leans his head back into the finger-nest made by both hands allowing images of Ruth to flow by. Her hair unfolding. Her smile. The humorous brand of detachment that makes you sit up and think. Not challenging or critical but fundamentally interesting. And she can be funny. No wonder she has been so successful. Her independence is wonderful to be around. It gathers attention around her so that people forget themselves when with her, and that frees them up to be more themselves. It sounds contradictory but that's how it feels. The big issue is how to win her back. That's what really matters. It's hard to think of anything else.

It doesn't seem to matter to her much. Her version of having everything is more about making a difference now and making a double contribution to the future. Preserving the world as well as furnishing it with more good people.

It's impossible to see how to construct a real version of family life without her. How to forge the links that hold people (rather than bridges) together. Winning her back is like a quest. No mountains to climb or dragons to slay. And nobody could be less like a maiden in distress than Ruth. But how? There don't seem to be any hoops to jump through.

He's interrupted by Hannah.

Hannah

Hannah wonders whether Simon has missed a beat. It would be unusual, but she's worried enough to catch him early one morning.

'About the Thames Footbridge ...'

'Yes?'

'Clive and Jason are at loggerheads ...'

'Oh? I know there's been a snag.'

'Clive thinks the problem is the ground beneath the foundations on the South bank.'

'What?'

Hannah explains. Clive's view is that extensive work is needed to ensure the foundations will support the main structure. Jason thinks newer light-weight materials should reduce the load sufficiently to make extra foundation work unnecessary. It's one of those fights between the old guard and the new entry that engenders a great deal of heat, and the heat makes it hard to look at the findings and the figures with a cool head.

162

'I understand that the jury is out on this one.' Simon says. 'There's not enough information available.'

'So, it's not clear either way. But Jason is completely tactless when it comes to telling Clive what he thinks.'

'You don't trust Jason, do you.' Simon says.

'Well, I know he's talented, but he's young, immature and inexperienced. If you ask me, there's too much at risk here. Surely it would be safest to work on the foundations despite the extra cost. Think what it would do to us if something went wrong.'

'You can never be 100% certain,' Simon says. 'I need to see the figures. And talk to Clive. I think Jason could be right but we need to recalculate the risks. Find out exactly what we're facing. When's the next inspection due?'

'I'll find out.'

They leave it there.

Hannah's still worried. Why, she asks herself, has Simon not picked up on this before? It's not like him to be careless.

Chapter 23

Simon

Simon waits for Dani to finish talking to someone called Melissa. It seems like forever. Only an hour ago the Golden Lion was quiet as they took possession of the corner table with a sideways view of the make-shift stage. Now the place is buzzing and a double bass is propped against the wall.

It's a ragged old man of an instrument. Somewhat bulgy, but it has a comfortable brown appearance and that odd thin neck that makes you think of a bird. Grander than a chicken. More like an ostrich. Floppy brown feathers and a tiny head with sticky-out bits that looks straight ahead even when the legs below are running away with themselves. Drumsticks on speed. That bird couldn't fly with the others if it tried! It stays totally grounded while real birds soar up and away hoping for thermals that will lift them even higher. It doesn't stop the old bird being delighted when they come down to his level though, when they choose to join him. He's definitely male, and he's hard to keep up with when he sprints off …

'Oh!' Simon looks up suddenly.

'Did I make you jump? Sorry.' Dani re-enters Simon's world. Startlingly unexpected. 'Whatever were you thinking?'

'I was miles away! Trying to keep up with an ostrich on the run. Music playing its part in my life again. So, what happened? What did she say?'

'I need a drink. I'll tell you in a second. D'you want another?'

He comes back with a couple of full mugs hooked round the fingers of one hand. Two packets of crisps and one of dry-roast peanuts squashed together in the other. Simon helps him unload. Dani opens the packets and drops them on the table. The place is filling up and, between mouthfuls, he can talk without being overheard.

'She'd listened to my songs again and again. Kiri was singing and we recorded five of them on her phone. It's far better than mine. I'm not much use on her keyboard, but I kept the pace going OK.' Dani feeds in a handful of nuts one at a time. 'Melissa said the accompaniment wasn't up to much but the tunes were good. And she loved the lyrics.' Nuts washed down. 'Kiri's voice sent her into another world altogether. She wants to hear her sing. Wants her to meet Joe.' He waves at the stage. 'The leader of this band. She asked if she could send the songs to him.'

'Wow. What did you say?'

'Well Kiri's not fourteen till November. I said I'd talk to her. What do you think?'

'No way. Far too young. Wait a bit. Besides you don't want to run the risk of straining her voice. It won't have matured yet.' He's quick, sure and definite and totally ignoring the possibility of taking the wind out of Dani's sails. 'Besides, she'll have school the next morning.'

Dani is stopped in his tracks. He reaches for his glass. 'Uhm uhm ....' His fingers twine round each other. 'Oh dear. You could be right. I'll think what to say. To Melissa as well as Kiri.'

'Anyway, aren't they your songs? Isn't this for you? Kiri can always sing them at home. Or when she's older. If that's what she wants.'

'Yes, yes.' Unlike Dani to go up and down so fast. 'What I'm really excited about is the lyrics. I want them to be heard. To find out how people respond when they hear them.' He stops and chews at his lip. 'I'm a bit shocked the excitement could lead me astray so easily.' He draws himself in, elbows into ribs. 'There's something really seductive about opening up possibilities for young people. It's what I mainly do. But you've got to be sure it's what they want. And the right time for them too. I thought that was all I really wanted. Except for a family. But maybe not.'

'Maybe this is your time for once.'

The musicians start tuning up. The bass treads carefully, giving the others space. Then there's a call to assembly and they take off, underpinned by a steady beat. Simon leans closer to make himself heard.

'OK? Ready to go for it on your own?'

'Yup. Terrified but yes.'

'It's your time, Dani. Take it.'

Dani thinks about it.

'Are you and Amit OK?'

'Possibly. Could be.' Dani doesn't sound certain. 'He steps back in at home as if there's nothing to worry about. He obviously loves being with us and gathering the family round a table again. His cooking is sublime. I wonder if that's just the way he is. Sociable, friendly. And loving too. He has an extraordinary ability to make everyone think he's wonderful. Which as far as I'm concerned, he is. But where does that leave me?'

'That's hard. He's so prolific. Charming and hard to resist.' Simon's hand brushes briefly against Dani's sleeve. He wonders how to show his concern for Dani. For the whole family. Amit might be taking risks, but that would be so stupid. Think of the damage.

A faint strip of golden orange hangs low above the rooftops as they leave the Golden Lion in the late summer night, and occasional plane trees are billowing high in the distance. They stride, precisely in step, down the slope towards the bus routes, sounding like a single person. Is it time for another get together Simon asks himself. Are we ready for that? The children are. But what about us grown-ups? Too much separateness? Not enough certainty? Why not? It could be good for Dani and Amit perhaps. They reach the main road and stop at the crossing. As they break step Simon turns to Dani.

'How about all of us getting together for a picnic in the park? When the Olympics end. What do you think?'

'Good idea. I'll find out if Amit's going to be home then. He missed the lunch at Ruth's.'

'I'll do it. I'll put something together.'

They go their different ways.

How did that happen? A head full of worries about however he will manage it gives Simon a rough ride all the way home.

He shoves the papers along the sofa, unearths a flattened cushion and a teaspoon and puts a smeary plate and two empty mugs out of reach. He turns round like a dog creating a comfortable place to lie down and drops into his habitual corner. It's hard to get settled. It's disorienting, finding out more about people. You've got to be prepared for surprises. Like with Dani. And it's an effort. No one can tune into everything at once.

Still. It can't be that difficult to organise a post-olympics picnic and it's definitely his turn to get everyone together.

Got everything? If not it's too late now. Simon turns to see three adults and their variably co-operative children, now aged between 10 and 16, lugging heavy loads of cool boxes and rugs up a slight rise and into the shade made by a group of 12 young oak trees in the park. A notice says they were planted in 1993 to celebrate joining the EU so they're still in their adolescence, and in the middle of a summer day there's a spot of sunlight right in the centre where the shade can't yet reach. Isabel chose the place. It's one of her favourites. And Simon likes the idea that trees planted to symbolise commonalities in the face of difference should provide a home base for the afternoon. He's made sure that they're early enough to take full possession.

Plenty of others are also out and about. There's room for everyone to take advantage of the school holidays and new-found interests in impossibly demanding sports. Young ones with sacksful of energy. Older, stiffer ones soothing themselves with a hand to the small of the back or placed comfortably on a protruding stomach. The open grassland around them has become a danger zone to toddlers as balls are whacked about with no sense of direction, and a bunch of enthusiasts are marking out a running track using a pair of cherry trees as winning posts. Dogs are there too, yelled at with ridiculous names like Jasmine or Bonzo when they chase someone else's ball instead of their own.

As they enter the park James stops by the notice that he must have passed many times before without bothering to find out what it says.

'Why should we thank Charles the first?' he asks.

'It used to be his hunting ground. Then he gave his park to the city. For everyone to use.'

'Where did he hunt then?'

'No idea.'

James runs on. 'He must have been very rich,' he shouts over his shoulder.

Kiri and Isabel lag behind. Despite being loaded with backpacks and carrier bags their energy is directed towards the give and take of intimate conversation which seems to be about everything under the sun and includes occasional bursts of laughter or a tune from one or both. When they need to listen they stop and face each other, arms waving like portable punctuation. They seem to have a special line in non sequiturs. Unless it's a secret code.

'No. Stupid. Like this.' She hums and taps a toe.

'Amit said I couldn't.'

'Damit.' They drop the bags for a high five and a laugh.

'Well funny.'

'Drop the weights and crash out.'

'Catapult from the end of a pole-vault.'

'I dreamt about being on the parallel bars. Flying. I'd love to try.'

'Lose and cry. Win and cry. What's the point?'

'Well dense.'

'Come along you two. You've got all the nibbles in those bags. We need to get started.' Simon's forehead wrinkles and his fingers twitch. He nearly trips as he reaches to move a bag of fruit and choc bix out of the sun. Ruth and Dani are weighting the corners of a checked table cloth (red and white like those in the ads for walking holidays) with bags of food and drinks. Amit picks up one of the bags and adds it to his own treasure store by a nearby tree trunk.

'We need that Amit. To stop the cloth blowing about.' Dani speaks without looking up. His smile arrives late.

'Find something else. This is my stuff for later.'

'What?'

But Amit sounds relaxed and good-humoured. He is not in the least disturbed. 'Here. Why don't you use these?' He hands over a waterproof bag of cans speckled with drops of water.

That works, and it's not long before everyone has a drink and the cloth is spread with crisp bags, nuts, a dimpled plastic tray of mushy-looking dips, a large tub of oily anchovies, cheesy Wotsits, drumsticks, samosas and more. Simon removes the lid from a plastic box of veggie sticks. Ruth explores her backpack and comes up with a handful of plastic forks. She dumps them beside a pile of paper plates printed all over with cornflowers. A giant kitchen roll makes an unreachable centrepiece.

'Isn't there any bread?'

'Did you bring the coke?'

'This salsa is hot, hot, hot.'

'Must be Amit's.'

'I can't reach. Can we have some dips over here?'

'I've made a cold hot dog. Look!'

Simon doesn't know which way to turn. He looks hassled.

Amit laughs. 'Good to be together again. If you can't reach it just run round. Or yell for it. Only don't stand on the table. Hey. Mind my drink.' He's put the lid on a cool box and is using it as a seat. Others copy. There's more than enough to eat and it's going to be OK.

Simon lets himself off the hook. He's done his bit. It's up to them now. He listens to the rhythm of the chatter and responds to its spontaneous rise and fall with a smile that turns on an internal light. The sound of friends of all ages enjoying being together again needs no conducting. Just tune in. He looks round to find Amit beside him, completely relaxed and apparently just as happy as he sounded. That man has a real talent for enjoying himself. It's catching. Simon hopes that's he's stopped upsetting Dani.

'You sound good! How's things going?'

Amit looks up with a grin. 'Really well. Amazing how things have picked up since the crash. Eastern markets are just ready to take off, and I've been helping smaller businesses get off the ground. Really exciting – though there's far more to do than I can manage.'

'Expanding?'

'You know when things happen fast there comes a point when the structure falls apart if you don't keep an eye on it.'

'How d'you mean?'

'It's as if there's no more oil in the system. Nothing to oil the wheels of communication. Left hand so busy that its brain's full.' They laugh together. 'Can't take in any more. It's like yelling at a pilot in the sky to tell him it's his turn to land. Completely useless. That's the bit I'm good at. I've learned how to spot the weak points, and now I'm training others at the same time as my plane's taking off. It could be risky but it's really interesting. And fun. I love it.'

'Sounds wild. No wonder you're away a lot.'

'Too much. But nothing lasts forever.'

'Oh.'

'I'll be back. This is where I belong.'

'So glad.'

Ruth interrupts. 'Simon. Look at James.' He seems to have infiltrated another party. The one with the running track.

'Watch the flag.' A woman with curly black hair and patchwork trousers is waving her orange scarf in a hand held high above her head. 'It's a false start if you go before it drops.'

And when she does, they're off to the cherry tree posts, where James falls over. Was he first? No. Second, but he's through to the next heat. Isabel and Kiri, standing on the sidelines, are invited to join in and accept. Dani and Ruth respond to the request for helpers and organise a starting line. Someone else sets up a long jump as more children gather round, and a huge purple box of Heroes appears from nowhere. You can't have sports without prizes. These are liberally distributed for effort as well as success (and occasionally for disappointment). There are cheers for a winner. James helps himself to Heroes. Simon smiles and looks round for Ruth. She's busy now, enjoying herself. She doesn't see him waving.

Maya is watching. Amit is on his phone and Simon turns to Maya with a big smile.

'Dani told me you did really well in your exams. Well done you.'

'Thanks.'

'What next?'

'Uhm ...' She's playing with one of the plastic forks.

'Arts or sciences?'

'Both. That's the trouble.'

'Trouble?'

No response.

'Do you know what you want to do in the end?'

She mumbles, hand in front of mouth and her glossy black hair tumbling forward.

'Take your time. There's no need to think about that yet is there.'

She pulls the sleeves of her plain grey T-shirt right over both hands and fumbles them into a knot in her lap. She doesn't look up. Simon is puzzled. She was confident enough to organise the lunch party in Ruth's kitchen when Amit was away. What's happened? He doesn't know much about teenage girls. Is this what it's like for them being 16?

'No.' That's all. She glances up with an astonishing pair of light grey eyes. Simon blinks.

Rescue comes from a passing group of girls and boys. 'Maya! You coming?'

'Hi Nadia. Wait for me.'

He watches as she unfolds, revealing a pair of skin-tight silver leggings and a flash of ankle bracelet dangling over the top of shiny purple boots. She turns to him, grins, then with a diminutive wave she runs off, transforming en route into her usual self. A lively and talkative young woman. She's welcomed with a burst of chatter.

'Don't disappear without telling us.' Amit shouts after her. 'Have you got your phone?'

'Yup,' she responds over a shoulder. 'No worries' she shouts as an afterthought and then she's gone.

Amit looks up at Simon. 'Might you be able to help her?'

'What? Does she need help?'

'She's got to find somewhere for a couple of weeks' work experience. End of year 10 stuff. You know she's always been interested in making houses. She's thinking about doing architecture at uni. She's worked out which subjects she ought to focus on next, but she's got no idea really of what it might be like and what it might involve.'

'She should have asked.'

'I know. She's definitely going through an odd stage. It makes me feel I shouldn't have been away so much. I gave her an iPad for her birthday and she's always got her nose in one device or another.' He goes on in fits and starts. 'She never used to be like that. I miss the way we all used to talk, but you've got to let her go. Find her way. Make new friends. Can you help? She's always admired you, you know.'

'Has she?' Simon is surprised. Is Amit in persuasive mode? Or was that flattery? We've had some before. Students on work-experience. It's not easy to find a way of occupying them without a lot of input from someone who's too busy already. I'll talk to Hannah. She'll know. She's our chief administrator. She's the one who keeps tabs on everything.'

'Thanks Simon.'

'Tell her to email me with the dates and anything else I need to know. Can't promise, but if she's interested, I'd be happy to help her on the way.'

The afternoon comes to a late and a warm end. Everyone helps to make sure that there's not a sign of human occupation left under the circle of oaks. James comes back from the cherry trees with a collection of crumpled Heroes wrappers. The grass is littered with paper plates, crumbs, plastic cutlery and a soggy platter that supported Amit's surprise contribution.

Suddenly everyone speaks at once. 'When did you make that?' 'How did you do it?' 'What was in the middle?' 'Is there any left?'

Amit shakes his head, surrounded with curious admirers. Isabel and Kiri skip around on the spot without a trace of self-consciousness.

'Did you like it?'

'Yeah.'

'Monstrous.'

'Amazing.'

'Well good.'

Inside the bags and boxes that Amit had left resting against the tree trunk there's nothing left but ice packs and pools of water that he sloshes onto the grass. He'd made rainbow ice-cream and inside each multi-coloured scoop was an edible, exploding fizzy sherbet button. He refused to let on how he'd managed to put one in each scoop. Wizards don't tell their secrets. What's more the rainbow ice-cream came with percussive Malaysian music from Amit's phone. So, there was dancing and waving of arms as well as flying drips and multi-coloured splashes.

Simon has relaxed enough to abandon any attempt at organising or controlling anything. There's something extraordinary about Amit's ability to share his pleasures. And he has so many. Nothing he doesn't enjoy. It's contagious but Simon hopes he doesn't go too far. It would be so hard for Dani.

Simon and Ruth walk back down the hill together. She stops to adjust her load of backpack, cool box and multiple plastic bags including one full of rubbish.

'Leave some of that there if you like. I'll come back and fetch it.' He has both hands completely loaded too, and a rug hangs loose over one shoulder.

'I'm fine. I can manage.' She waits to catch her breath. 'That was great. They all had such a good time, don't you think?'

'Yes. And you?'

'Me too.' She doesn't look up but reaches out to gather up her load. She shakes her hair out of her face as she stands back up again. He watches. No hands free. He plants a gentle kiss on her cheek.

She takes a step back. Unbalanced by the load?

They walk on side by side.

'I was worried about it, but then suddenly there was nothing more for me to do. Everyone there. We'd got everything. Or it was too late to bother about if we hadn't.' It was good to share his relief.

'You certainly put the effort in. And let us all get on with enjoying it. It was good.'

Simon is confused. Of course, he knows that hopes rise and fall. That they can vanish suddenly, as untraceable as the source of the wind. He's tired and puzzled by the contrasts that leave his childhood in deep shade and shine today's sun on the connections between two families and their four children. Without Dani, he thinks, I'd have fallen into a deep hole. Into the gap between my parents and my grandfather. A chasm that grew deeper every year.

Cars are loaded up, hugs are distributed, and they go their separate ways. Simon to one home. Ruth and the children to the other.

Chapter 24

Simon gets to work early and takes the stairs two at a time. He walks straight into Hannah's office. It's never too early for Hannah. She finishes her coffee and places the paper mug, right way up, lid secured, into the waste-basket.

'Hi Hannah. How're you doing? Got a moment?'

'Morning. You sound good.' She continues reading a note. *Answer by 11.0 please in big red letters on the back.* 'Shan't be a minute.'

He waits. Hannah's office is immaculately tidy and devoid of bright colours. Gentle without being dull. Super-efficient but not in-your-face annoying.

Pin boards cover the walls. Shelves beneath for wipers and tubs of pins and pens. The upfront information is accessible on her computer too but Hannah likes to be active. Passivity was never her style. She keeps her place in the note she's reading with a thumb as she looks at a chart.

Simon picks up an orange pen. 'What are these for?'

'Queries, deadlines, dates to be fixed. Unfinished business and uncertainties. I update everything before I go home. Turn as much orange into black as I can. So, I can see where I am at a glance. Everything's right in front of me as well as on the computer.' She pauses. 'It's quicker and uses energy you don't have to pay for.'

'Brilliant.'

'Just one?' She gives him a quizzical look.

'What?'

175

'Moment. You only asked for one …' She rescues her orange pen and returns it to base. 'I've got a meeting in a few minutes. How long do you need?'

It's odd to be so easily distracted by someone else's working habits. 'Could you make use of a spare pair of hands?'

She nods.

'My old friend Dani's daughter is looking for work experience. Maya. She's 16. She's always been interested in building things and might do architecture at university. She wouldn't be any trouble.'

Hannah looks at him.

'She's interested and she's bright.'

'Oh?'

Try again. He clears his throat. 'It would be good to attract more young women into this world full of men with big egos.'

'Hmph! You're telling me. When? How long for?'

'Two weeks.' He pulls out an envelope. 'She sent me this from her school. It has to be quite soon.'

'You know we stopped providing work experience during the crash. Bardo was the last. No one had time to organise or supervise them.'

It would be good to help Maya but she does seem to be going through an odd phase. You never know how it could turn out. Better not to slip into persuading, he thinks.

Hannah thinks about it. 'We could start again. I could use some admin help, and she could do some shadowing. You got anything she could do? Meetings she could sit in on? Information searches? Checking figures?'

'Maybe…' The thought of organizing someone of school age produces an inward groan.

Looking at her desk Hannah says: 'You could get her to tidy your room perhaps.'

'Not funny Hannah. She needs to learn about real life architecture not domestic chores.' He takes an audible breath.

176

'OK. The request has to come through the school. Or it would look like an inside job.' She turns a pen round with three fingers and a thumb. 'If the school contacts me, I'll see what I can do. No promises.'

Great. Simon goes away feeling hopeful.

Jason next. How to take advantage of his talents. Or help him make the most of them. He's settled down. Or grown up. And he's exceptionally gifted. It's rare to feel at home in engineering as well as architecture. Time to find out whether he could break through the convention that channels people one way or the other. The feeling of wanting to do everything is utterly familiar.

Jason has acquired some good research habits. He has a tendency go on a bit about new high strength steels, but his ideas are interesting and his enthusiasm is infectious.

'That's not new you know,' Simon said when Jason told him about niobium.

Jason wasn't fazed. 'I know. But the techniques for adding it are. They make it stronger, and stiffer and more formable.' Then he went off at a tangent … 'and concrete reinforced with natural fibres is much lighter too. There are all sorts of trials going on. My favourite's called Hempcrete.' That made him laugh.

They share a serious interest in new materials. Simon has done his research, thinking more clearly than Jason about the economic advantages of shorter construction times and less waste. About how to use the new materials when building bridges.

Frank O'Ghery's museums in Seattle and Bilbao provide a source of inspiration for both of them. Encased in thousands of variably shaped titanium sheets, they change colour according to the weather and variations in the light. Jason gets carried away with the complexity of these buildings and the intricate ways in which segments of them interlock. Simon is more single-minded in his search for anything specific to bridge design. He loves the way variations in colour, with time of day for instance, can make a solid building appear weightless.

The new materials, advanced computer modelling and techniques developed for the aerospace industry have released many designers, including Simon, from four-square modelling and 2D sketches. But computers generate far more than any one person can see how to construct. Technical developments never stop.

Jason and I could make a good team, Simon thinks. Collaboration between different generations ... We both like thinking outside the box ... There'd be risks of course. Does Jason ever listen? He usually seems to have more than one stream of consciousness to choose between. He flips between topics as if a wayward breeze was blowing this way and that through the open window of his brain. But he learns fast.

Last time they met, Jason had just heard about a new fiberglass being used in Brazil. Ideal for constructing buildings with continuous curves, wall to roof. 'It's translucent.' Jason said joyfully, hopping from foot to foot. 'It lights the building up inside and it glows as the light falls. It could be wonderful for a bridge over water.'

The number of new possibilities in the world of bridge design is expanding, intriguing, and a bit alarming. There's no point in having fly-weight, corrosion-proof beams able to withstand mega-tons of pressure and strain if you can't give them the stability and flexibility they need as traffic weight (or the probability of tornados) increases. Bridge-building, as well as the average temperature, is accelerating through a period of fundamental change. Collaboration is the way to go.

The telephone interrupts.

'Simon. Hello. About Jason. He's hard to control and to keep an eye on. Does he know what he's doing?' Clive, the plain speaker, has raised his usual directness up more than one notch.

'Yes. No. I don't know... I mean yes, I can see why. And no, I've never been able to control him. Is there a problem?'

'No. Or not yet. When he's on site he behaves as if he's completely unaware of what's required. Not technical stuff. But ordinary behaviour, like walking into workstations. Interrupting people.'

'I'd better talk to him.'

'Yes please. And remind him when you do, to read the rules of site-working again. He's so impatient it worries me.'

Simon sighs. It was good to have someone like Clive in charge. Definitely the right person to keep an eye on Jason. He's so fixated on the new stuff that he loses touch with the lessons drummed into him during training. Either that or it still takes all his energy and brain-space to move between the theoretical and the practical. Hannah thinks he's careless, which he certainly isn't when it comes to research. More inadvertent than careless, if there's a difference. And he's exciting to work with.

But the situation with Clive is disturbing.

'Always remember you don't know what you don't know.' Clive's voice from way back. Unforgettable. Or unfathomable.

Yes. But how can you know what you don't know? It sounds as pointless as a hope with a guess attached especially if the guess is completely clueless. No more realistic than a wish.

Jason's hairstyle has slipped down his priority list. Perhaps he's been too busy to bother. Instead of the shock value of a new shape or colour he's developed a flick-back that starts with his chin. It stops his fringe obscuring his vision and producing an inevitable slide into a personal twilight. The flick-back goes with his usual arm-waving version of emphasis. Default output of energy on the rise.

'We need to be getting on faster, Simon. Clive's so slow.'

It was not easy for Simon to tell the difference between Jason's impatience and his enthusiasm. It could well be worrying.

He decided it would be best to slow him up. 'Well he's responsible for making sure everything's done right. That it's structurally sound and safe. He has to satisfy the inspectors and watch the budget. He also needs to co-ordinate different teams. You can't expect him to …'

'But there are so many delays. It must be possible to go faster…'

'Slow down Jason. Sit down a minute.'

Simon gives him a lecture on the main parameters and extra costs. Attitudes of stakeholders and clients and keeping team leaders informed and including them in the decision-making. The impossibility of going it alone when dealing with a big public project. The overriding need for safety. Jason listens in silence, head lowered, hair falling over his eyes. Simon hopes he's listening.

'Right. I get it. But all Clive lets me do is endless checking. I spend days repeating calculations. He won't let me do anything else. I make sure the figures are correct then double check that everything's done to specification. Over and over.'

'Do you understand the importance of doing exactly what's been specified? What we agreed to do? Not changing anything? We're still in recovery. The whole country is. We can't take the risk of making a mistake. Of any kind.'

'Right.' A long pause. 'You're right. But it's so frustrating.'

It's tempting to go through all of it again. Simon wonders if Jason is properly on board. At least he sat still while he listened. That's unusual enough.

Jason's mind is now elsewhere. 'Have you seen the paper on the Brandanger Bridge in Norway?'

Maybe he wasn't listening. Simon does know about "the world's most slender arched bridge." Intriguing solutions to technical problems were found during its construction.

'Did you read about their new method for assessing its structural capacity?' Jason asks.

'Conventional methods of measuring reliability weren't any use to them ...'

'There are so many variables to measure. So many elements that could reach breaking point, each of which could be over-stressed in different ways, or different combinations of ways. I've gone through all the design criteria in their paper. Did you see? They used a new kind of simulation that enabled them to assess the reliability of a complex system ...'

Simon interrupts: '... they needed to. Network arch bridges have inclined hangers. Instead of hanging down from the arch to support the platform, inclined hangers make multiple intersections with each other as they cross. In a network. They worked out how to optimise the hanger slopes.'

'And that allowed them to reduce the weight of the steel used by almost 50%.'

'Amazing.'

'And it looks good.'

Jason's arms are flapping again. They face each other with satisfied smiles. It's fascinating and technically beyond the comprehension of many even in this specialised field. Their discussions stray across borders. Between architecture and engineering and they take in elements of mathematics and digital technology as they go. Simon can only admire Jason's ability to continue mastering new skills.

Jason leaves with an upward chin-flick in the doorway. Simon remembers he forgot to schedule their next meeting. He wonders what else he might have forgotten.

Chapter 25

Hannah

By mid-September the afterglow of the Olympics has faded and Hannah is angry. Thousands of children will now collect a lifetime of debt when they go to college and the size of the burden on the young and disadvantaged is not fair. She has no doubts about re-starting work experience and tells the school she is happy to accept Maya.

'What do you need from me?' Hannah asks on her first day. 'Do you know?'

'To find out what architects do? All about what goes on? Fill in the school forms?'

Everything and nothing. Do all her sentences sound like questions?

Hannah likes Maya. She's attentive and asks intelligent questions. She's not embarrassed to hide her ignorance and ready to listen. She probably could lighten my load. But that's not what this is about. Hannah works out a plan with Simon.

'Maya's obviously interested. I'm going to have to find people she can shadow or I'll spend the next two weeks fielding her questions.'

'You set up a timetable and I'll answer the questions. Meet with her daily before she goes home and help her to make sense of what she's learning.'

'Good idea.'

'It's an opportunity for us too.' Simon says. 'To attract people with potential into the profession. We might even be able to get more out of them. In their holidays.'

Not surprising, Hannah thinks, to want to make use of cheap labour – nor indeed that Simon's apparently unaware of how it sounds to be so up front about it.

Maya makes herself useful. She's a quick learner, and more organized than most, though that isn't what she looks like. She's abandoned the school uniform and found her own variation on the challenging versions of attractiveness that make parents bite their lips. Her long thin legs in skin-tight black jeggings end in scruffy thick-soled boots. Brown, with laces and shiny toe-caps. She wears pitch-black tops reaching almost to her midriff and sweatshirts with sleeves longer than her arms. When she puts on her short leather jacket it's hard not to laugh at the mixture of lengths and wonder how she keeps warm. She flings a crumpled scarf round her neck, extracts handfuls of shiny black hair from inside her collar, and stuffs the scarf ends back inside. With the sleeve-ends bunched in her fists and she's ready to face anything. Weather-proof down to her hips but permeable from there to the top of her boots.

Simon

Simon looks forward to his 4.30 meetings with Maya. She has to leave on the dot of 5, log-book signed. She likes to sit on the floor which she dares to do in Simon's office but not in Hannah's. That's where he finds her when he comes back a bit late during her first week.

He's told her to help herself to his books as long as she writes down what she's borrowed. She's chosen British Bridge Building: Architecture and Engineering and is thumbing through the illustrations. Better rescue her from that one.

'Hello. That's a bit of a mouthful isn't it?'

She blushes. 'Just looking. Amazing pics.'

'So. Good day?' She nods. 'Any questions?'

'There's so much more to it than I'd realised. Can't believe I'd ever manage all that.' Her voice has lost its usual lively undertow.

He looks at her attentively and thinks she looks lost. She's surprisingly uncertain how to go on. Maybe she needs time to think.

'Feeling daunted?'

She turns a page before she looks up. 'Uh uh. A little.'

Odd, he thinks, how motoring on doesn't get you there quicker. Simon has discovered that when he slows himself down, he finds out more, not less. He wonders whether he's used the right word.

'Daunted? ... Or disappointed?'

What's going on? Simon asks himself. He watches her hands twist the long sleeves together. It would be a pity to put her off. He sits down so as to give her, at floor-level, his full attention. 'Listen. It happens bit by bit. All the learning, so as not to give students indigestion or discourage them. Look at the boards in Hannah's office. Have you noticed how they're labelled?'

'Uh ...no.'

'Well. There's one for each of the expert teams, as well as one for each project. You don't have to know it all. Just know who does what, and how it fits together.' He watches for a reaction. 'And where to find what you need.'

'But ... I didn't realise it was so complicated.' She looks away.

Simon is puzzled. 'You've only signed up for two weeks. No need to think of the thousands of miles, or days ahead if you decide to go on with it. Tell me what you did today.'

Maya hesitates. She avoids eye contact.

What's that about? Simon opens both hands while he waits. This, he says to himself, is what Dani meant about taking other people into consideration. He's right. It makes all the difference.

'I couldn't understand what they said. The New Project Group. Jason showed me the digital technology they were using, and I couldn't follow. I asked lots of questions ...'

'Sounds like you!'

'... but I got left behind. The more they said the more muddled I got. They ended telling me this was just the beginning.'

184

A hand hides her face. 'I'm good at all that stuff at school. I've got all sorts of devices and apps and things. Amit's always happy to pay for them. But this ...,' she comes to a halt and bites her lip.

'Did you ask when they learned all that?'

Maya shakes her head, unable to speak. She holds herself together with an effort.

That's not meant to happen. What now?

'Well for me it didn't begin till well after my training.' Simon turns to his desk to provide some thinking time. When he turns back he says, 'For them it started long ago. At school and at university.' He sees she's listening. 'The technology didn't exist when I began. You already know far more than I did at 16.' She looks down. 'It's like climbing a mountain. If you look up the path may seem endless. Look back and you can see how far you've come. After only a few minutes you can look right over the treetops even though there's still a mountain ahead.'

Her hair has fallen over her face but her fingers are no longer entangled in those sleeves. They stray over the big book on the floor. She traces the trajectory of two bridges across the Firth of Forth as if leaving Edinburgh to walk in the hills beyond, carried from one bit of firm ground to another and over a bridge like the Golden Gate.

'Do you like what you see there?'

'Yeah.' She nods.

'So, what's the take-home message today?'

'So far to go!'

'Does that matter?'

'Well ...'

'It's OK to put that in your log you know.' Simon is warm and encouraging and Maya smiles.

He has a bit more to say. 'I'm still learning. I don't think it ever stops! Look at all this.' He waves at the piles of books and papers on his desk and floor. 'Tell me what you're doing tomorrow. I've forgotten.'

'Helping Hannah in the office.'

'Good. That's practical stuff. Useful background and less challenging. She's a brilliant organiser and knows what everyone's up to. So, keep asking questions.'

Simon lets the silence grow before he adds, 'Look at her notice boards too.'

She passes him her log-book to sign.

'Feeling better?'

'Uh-uh.' Another nod.

'Still interested in the long haul?'

'Think so. With houses not bridges.'

'Fine. Good to find your own path.' Maybe she'll be a groundling, Simon thinks. Not into flying across a void. It's no matter. 'I'm here if you need me.'

Maya bends to collect the book from the floor and turns to put it back where it belongs, eyes averted. She is flushed but definitely happier.

'Thanks.'

'See you tomorrow. Remember this is an introduction. It's for fun. Not a test.'

She looks up at him. Nods and vanishes.

Simon rolls his pen round in his fingers. He puts it on his desk and turns to the window. He hopes she feels better. It's a pity to discourage her at this stage. She's been interested so long, and she's certainly bright enough. It's good to help young people into this complicated world. To feel you could light up a few sparks. To do this for Maya would be great. And for Dani's sake.

Simon gives her time every day to encourage her. In the last of their meetings, she asks him which subjects to focus on now and which universities to try for later. He hopes she might discover a passion for bridges, but that goes unsaid.

'Any chance of holiday work?' she asks at their last meeting. 'Paid or unpaid?'

'Ask Hannah. You can tell her I said so.'

'I'd love to do more. It would be great to put that on my personal statement.'

'Your uni application? Let me know if there's anything else you need.'

Hannah

Hannah organises a small gathering of new friends during the afternoon break on Maya's last day. She sends round a card to be signed. It gets to Simon last and he scribbles a quick message.

> *Thank you, Maya.*
> *You've done well, and we've enjoyed having you here. Come back when you can. Good luck.*
> *Simon.*

Hannah has gathered together most of the people Maya has had contact with and she's surprised that Simon doesn't turn up. However, it's a short event and it's not long before she brings it to an end.

'You've been a great help to us, Maya,' she says. 'You're the first person we've had on work placement for ages, and you've shown us just how useful placements can be. To us as well as you. We've discovered that you're clever, energetic, willing to do anything including making the coffee you never drink, and you pick up what's needed even when doing something completely new. Well done.'

There are smiles and nods of agreement all round.

'Come and visit us. We can find plenty to keep you occupied if you need a break from revising.'

'We'll let the technical ogres know you're coming. Keep them locked up while you're around,' Jason says.

'You never know. I might get used to them one day.' Maya laughs and glances at the door.

'I'm wondering what's happened to Simon,' Hannah says. 'Must have got caught up with something. So, I'll say goodbye from all of us, including him. And thank you too.' She hands Maya the card that everyone has signed.

Maya opens it and reads the messages with a serious look on her face. She can't say anything audible in the face of so much attention - and appreciation. She nods, smiles, looks away and then pulls her sleeves over her hands again.

The next morning Hannah discovers that Simon missed the party by mistake. He was busy and didn't look at the time but dashed straight out to collect James from school. It was a pity not to say goodbye. Careless and inconsiderate is what Hannah thinks.

Simon

The next month is an unusually productive one for Simon. He works on clarifying the Westover brand and this time he talks about it with everyone. Architects, engineers, specialists in construction, or in technicalities, or electronics. Or programming and digital technology. The New Project Group. Everyone. He develops a reputation for being approachable as well as interesting. Hannah is not the only one who notices the difference.

'I want to hear what you think.' he says. 'About whether we should focus solely on bridge design.'

The general view is that it would be a risk and wouldn't make best use of the expertise available.

'So how do we define ourselves?'

The difficulty is that the Westover Group has more arms and legs than an octopus. It's hard to define as it reaches out in so many directions. Is it too many, so that it's hard to define its unique personality? Or is it enough to spread the risk?

Hannah stops the process of discussion disappearing into the ether.

'Simon, we're doing well. Enquiries from new clients are on the up. The group is attracting more and more attention. So don't rock the boat.'

They agree to go on as they are. This gives Simon time to work on his hub of excellence in bridge-building. It's a vote of confidence that opens up a longer perspective for him and when he reads an announcement about an international competition in Brazil he responds at once. Of course. It's an opportunity to create something exceptional. It could be exactly the right thing at the right moment.

He dreams of creating a game changer and resolves not to race ahead of the current technology. He decides to work closely with the engineering team from the earliest possible moment. It's important not to design something that no one knows how to construct and end up at the head of a fiasco like the Sydney Opera House with huge delays and a massive hike in costs. He needs to keep focused.

Simon's attention is demanded elsewhere when Clive rings. He doesn't beat about the bush. 'There's been an accident on site.'

Simon heart thumps. 'No! What?' Shit. He moves the phone into his right hand. 'Are you OK? Anyone hurt? What happened?' The other hand sweeps over his forehead and into the air beyond.

'Yes. Two of the construction crew. One had a bang on the head and he's been taken off in an ambulance, unconscious. The other is badly bruised and is still being checked over by paramedics to make sure he's OK to go home. Everyone is shocked.'

'No! You really OK? How much damage? What a disaster …'

There's a hum of machinery in the background and the sound of Clive taking a deep breath. Just like the phone call from Ruth about James, Simon thinks. On repeat. He pauses. 'Dreadful. I'm so sorry. What do you need? What can I do?'

'Got to make sure everything's safe. Get people off site. Call the Incident Contact Centre and the Health and Safety Exec. Take pics and find out what they need. I need to stop by the hospital and close things down. It'll take time. Where will you be?'

'I'm not going anywhere. How can I help?'

'Tell everyone. I need Jason to re-check the figures on the support system for the tower on the South bank. That's where the problem was. The platform started to twist and sent things crashing down.

Lucky no one else was hurt. Get copies of those calculations and anything else he signed off on.'

'Jason?'

'Yes. He was the last to check the calculations. I asked him to double-check them. He checked the foundations after the concrete was poured.'

Simon's heart sinks. Jason? What has he done? Or not done? Has he made some stupid mistake? He scowls. Shit, shit, shit! Was Hannah right? He should never have asked Clive to take him on…

'Right away. Keep in touch. Let me know if you need anything else. Or Hannah.'

'Thanks.' He's gone.

Simon strides out of his room to Hannah's and walks in without knocking.

She drops what she was doing as soon as she hears the word accident. She gets up, reaches the filing cabinet behind her, pulls open the top drawer and takes out a green folder. The immediacy of her response is both reassuring and astonishing.

'Here. Look through this. Clive has his own copy.'

Site Accidents: Essential procedures.

'I'll find out if there are any recent updates from HSE.'

'Good.'

'They're good, Health and Safety. Often fussy, but helpful in a real crisis.' Hannah's right. Simon knew he could rely on her.

'I'll keep in touch with Clive,' Simon says. Best to keep lines of communication simple. 'Let me know if there's anything urgent to tell him.'

Simon thinks, next stop Jason. He finds him in the room he shares, checking more calculations right this minute. Many faces turn towards Simon as he opens the door. Jason glances up, then back at his screen, keeping one finger on the page in front of him and his chair tipped forward. Urgency held at bay, Simon asks him to come to his office.

'Now?'

'Yes.'

The two back legs of Jason's chair thump back onto the floor. He uses both hands to push himself to his feet. He follows Simon out of the room in silence. Simon sits at his desk and waves Jason into a chair nearby.

'There's been an accident. On the Thames Footbridge site.'

'No! How? What's happened?'

'Two people hurt. The support system for the South tower started to twist. The platform collapsed and I don't know yet what went with it.'

Jason gasps. His pale face gets paler.

'How? What caused it?'

'Too early to say. But Clive wants all the calculations re-checked. And anything else that you signed off on.'

'Oh? Yes. Of course.'

'Send them to me too. Everything you think might be relevant.' As Simon looks up he realises that Jason is holding his breath.

'Size of the damage not yet known. Let's hope it's not a total disaster.'

'Who's hurt? Is Clive OK?' Jason twists his hands together. 'No!' He stamps one foot then the other. 'How come? That's awful.' As he lets his breath go, he seems to deflate. 'Terrible.' He looks at Simon. 'The calculations were fine. I double checked them. Twice. Once to be sure, and then Clive asked me to do it again. Yesterday.' Jason seemed not to know where to look, or how to keep still. 'What now? What happens next?'

'Clive will do an incident report and the site will be closed. We'll all have to account for whatever we're responsible for, including me. Then there'll be inspections, more reports, endless delays and accelerating costs. Discussions with everyone including clients....' Simon looks down at his desk.

'Is this the first?' Jason seems to have sorted out his breathing.

'First what?'

'Accident. That you've been involved with.'

'No. Minor accidents are common. Less than they used to be and site-training is better too. Did they give you the safety booklet? Did you do the safety training?' Simon should have asked before.

'Yes. Online. It was good.'

'I've never been involved with a major accident. Don't know if this is one of those yet.'

But it could be, he thinks. It could be a total disaster for us and send the whole show down the tubes.

The silence is not a comfortable one. Jason stares out of the window and traces the arm of his chair with one finger.

He's worried, Simon can tell.

As Jason's supervisor Simon knows that the responsibility lies with him, not with Jason. But they all need to face the facts. The sooner the better. There's no way to protect Jason from that. Better together than separately. More open and probably the best way to make sure that information is shared.

'There'll be lots of things to consider. The way the work was organised and managed. Its supervision. Then there's the machinery and equipment they were using. Whether the site was kept tidy or had got messed up. And more. The experience and training of the construction crew. Safety systems on site. We're not the only ones in the firing line.'

'It's bad though.' Jason is almost inaudible. 'I'll start the re-checks right away.'

'Good. Don't spend too long on them or you'll end up multiplying the doubts. Someone else will have to check them anyway. Why don't you find the things Clive needs and send copies to Hannah as well as me. Then take a break.'

'You'll tell me when you hear how the guy in hospital is, won't you?'

'Of course. And it's OK to talk about it. We should let everyone know.'

As he leaves Jason looks as if that's the last thing he wants to do.

It's dreadful news to be imparting, and it takes far too long. Simon contacts all the internal team leaders, the clients, local councillors and the neighbourhood action group. They've banded together in strong support of something they've been wanting for years and want to know immediately how long a delay to expect. Everyone has to live with uncertainty today, and as soon as more information is available, he will talk to all of them again.

When everyone's been put in the picture, alone in his office, Simon is filled with unanswered questions and turns the analysis onto himself. Is there something I missed? When did Jason and I last go through his work in detail? I don't remember. I know how he feels. A finger has been pointed at him. No way to deny it. But I'm the one who got him there. I'm the main supervisor.

So much that it's impossible to know for sure. There's chattering in the corridor and Simon gets up to close the door.

'This ends everything.' It's the voice of the lead technologist. 'Nobody's going to trust us now.'

Other voices chime in:

'… everyone's extra aware of risks as austerity continues …'

'… it'll put an end to the flow of new stuff for us…'

'… shouldn't have been so ambitious. Or grandiose …'

'… total disaster from top to bottom …'

Simon shuts his door quietly and leans against it in shock. Taking immediate action was instinctive. It kept thoughts about the ultimate consequences at bay and now they crowd in on him. Could this end everything?

It's a destructive realization and he daren't give the front of his mind access to it. He tries to gather the threads from details of Jason's work and the notes he made during supervision. He searches for the right folder. He remembers how enjoyable those meetings had recently been. So much to talk and think about when you can share ideas about new possibilities and developments. Where's that folder gone? He asks himself. Stuffed with the notes made while talking. Ahh … here? Not that. A pile of papers and letters falls to the floor. He steps round them and pulls a blue folder out from the back of the desk. Got it. He goes to the window and sits in the chair by the table to open it. There's quite a lot of scribbles. Coherent notes are sparse to the point of being incomprehensible to anyone else. Another problem to face? He sits still. It's taking time properly to digest the news. It's a while before he's ready to move. Could this really end it all?

He puts the file back on the desk and reactivates his screen just as the phone rings again.

'Clive here. News from the hospital. He's not too bad. They'll keep him in for observations overnight and think about discharge in the morning.'

'Phew,' Simon's shoulders slip down a notch. He stretches his arms out sideways and shakes his head.

'It's a huge relief. Now to think about why it happened. What's the cause.'

'Thanks for ringing Clive. I spoke to Jason. He's gathering everything together now.'

'Good. Speak again tomorrow.'

'OK, but you can get me any time before then on my mobile if you need to.'

They end the call.

Simon tells Jason and they share the relief. He turns to leave but stops when Jason says. 'I can't stop thinking about what I might have missed.' He sounds much younger than he looks.

'Try not to worry.' Simon sees the signs of distress. What can he do to help? 'I know that will be hard, but if all's well with the calculations and the things you signed off on then you're off the hook.' It feels a bit lame.

Simon worries about his end of the paper trail. Or electronic one. About whether, in his recent bout of creative distraction, absorbed in his own ideas and no longer worrying about James, there were things he forgot to do. Questions he didn't answer. He busies himself by bringing more order into the papers on his desk, fearful of what he might find as he excavates. No disaster there. He moves stuff about the Brazilian competition to the table in the window and creates a clear separation between the creative and the practical with everything else sorted into appropriate piles. He begins to feel more in control.

A scan through the emails in his inbox reveals a large number of unanswered messages. Mostly stuff about other people's projects. Keeping him informed, but not things to take action on unless something goes wrong. He finds Clive's old messages asking him to make contact. Definitely a response delay there, and that was when Jason and Clive were at cross purposes. Disagreements between them were increasing. Then it went silent. Why? But that was all about using new methods and materials. Nothing about the tower on the South bank and its foundations. Did I miss something? The same questions that Jason must be asking. The thought of total disaster intrudes again.

Simon bends to pick up the scattered mail. Most of it ends in the waste bin. He opens a small envelope to find a picture of the Double Helix bridge in Singapore shining with purple and silver lights on a dark night. He knows it from professional papers and magazines. It's extraordinary. He turns it over.

I'm sorry I didn't see you to say goodbye. It means a lot to me that you gave me so much time. I shan't forget it. Thanks for believing in me. See you soon. Love Maya xxx.

PS. There's a town planning conference at UCL at the end of the month. They're offering architecture students the chance to act as stewards. Would you sign my application form?

When did this come? He shudders and says to himself, 'What have I missed?'

Chapter 26

Simon

Simon's bed feels hot and scratchy. It's hours to go before sunrise. He swipes a hand over his face. It makes no impression on the images of falling scaffolding that are going through his mind. Men wearing safety helmets and hi viz jackets scatter. A support system rips apart and underneath it someone wearing a mask staggers out of a dust cloud carrying a giant drill. He hears the sound of tearing metal and a splash. Something falls into deep water. Suddenly he's wideawake.

Immense extra costs … People seriously hurt … What about damages? What did Jason miss? I should never have asked Clive to take him on. I should have listened to Hannah. He rubs his eyes, turns the pillow over and pulls the duvet straight. His brain-races and the image-echoes continue.

Outrage at the prospect of massive personal loss searches for a target. Jason. He's excitable and doesn't trust Clive. He wants to go his own way and he disobeys the rules.

Simon tells himself to shut that door immediately. He knows he has to step up and handle it. He's in the front line because that's where he put himself. No one else put him there. And no one can put the clock back. If there's blame it can wait. The only option is to do what has to be done step by step, starting with HSE.

Everything has to be reported to them, including near misses. The majority of accidents aren't new. The same things keep happening. Health and Safety no longer insist on pointing the finger. They focus on finding out what went wrong. They tell us that safety is a priority for everyone, from beginning to end, regardless of their place in the system or level of experience. If accidents are inevitable, everyone has to be aware of the possibility. All you can do is try to make them less likely and limit the damage.

But the list of safety procedures keeps growing, and far too many of them include idiocies like insisting on a bin for used tissues beside every workstation. Or extra people on site to keep an eye on those with dangerous tools in their hands. They've got absorbed in the detail and lost sight of the bigger picture.

Simon grunts. It's not fair. It's not even light yet and he is running on empty.

HSE has had a change of attitude Simon thinks, and they're right about not blaming people. It's pointless and has no effect on the number of accidents. Or, costs. It's better to normalise mistakes and accept they'll happen and put the effort into prevention. It makes it easier to report accidents and to acknowledge they're inevitable.

But the flow of worries is no respecter of reason and post hoc questioning trundles on in the back of Simon's mind bringing with it a worrying list of 'if only's.' … if only he hadn't pushed Jason forward. If only he hadn't been so distracted. If only he'd answered Clive's messages …

A pink tinge edges its way round the blinds.

He can't do anything useful from here.

Simon rushes up the stairs to his office and has to catch his breath when he gets there. He shakes his head.

'Simon! You look done in.' It's Hannah coming out of the lift behind him with her usual paper mug. Brown coffee. Red-brown Costa logo. Corrugated insulation cuff. Lid to prevent spills. Wonderfully familiar.

'Bad night. See you later.'

'We'll sort it. Don't worry.' She disappears round into her room unwinding a pale blue scarf as she goes.

Predictable and reliable, from Simon's point of view.

Simon decides to put everyone properly in the picture at once before they construct webs of imaginary causes and effects. Or attribute, responsibility according to the level of belief, or trust, or respect, they have for their colleagues. It's always a risk when architects and engineers work together. Engineers do the calculations and make things work. Architects spend their lives in a dreamworld of imaginings, then smile when given the praise. And the prize. Now's the time to stand together.

He asks Hannah to summon everyone to the big meeting room. First, he repeats the facts about what happened. One of the work platforms on the south tower collapsed without warning. Two people were hurt. Both are recovering well. Not a lot more.

Causes as yet unknown. He tries to diffuse the automatic blame game by explaining the requirements and attitudes of HSE. Worries start to niggle but he shuts the lid on them. The age-old habit of compartmentalizing slips smoothly into place.

'Any questions?'

None. Just serious faces and a sense of thoughtfulness.

'Take your time. It would be useful to hear about it if you have information or ideas about how this might have happened. Any time. Email me. Or drop by the office. Whatever suits.'

Questions, when they come, are about the state of those who were injured and the amount of damage. Also, probable costs and delays. He doesn't know all the answers but he takes it slow and gives it as long as it takes.

'I've kept a note of the queries and will keep an eye on the group email for regular bulletins. Hannah will put up a notice board for updates and answers when we have them. Anything else?'

Silence.

'OK.' He hesitates, his gaze wandering over attentive faces. Time to draw their fire and unearth their doubts. 'Ultimately, I'm responsible for this project. I'm ready to hear anything, from anyone, at any time. I'm sure we will find out what went wrong. Then we'll need ideas, working together, about how to prevent such things happening again.'

Everyone gets back to work.

Jason has kept quiet during the meeting and Simon noticed how this, or something else perhaps, created space around him.

'Thanks Simon,' he says as he leaves. He's hardly audible and looks as if he hasn't slept.

A video of the damage to structural work on the South bank is soon available on everyone's screens. It was taken from an expensive helicopter. Simon runs it through repeatedly. He can see little damage to the partly-built footbridge and a lot more to the support system for the high-level work-stations. But it's an overview taken from high up.

The guy with the head injury should be OK but he is being kept in for another 24 hours just in case. Speculation about what might be learned from this accident is impossible to resist, even without hard data. It's too soon to do more than guess.

Simon collects another coffee and hears that someone thinks they've found a mistake in the calculations. He starts his own search through the figures. The ones that Jason has distributed. He has the skills of an architect but lacks the super-speed of an engineer. He's always been happier in the image-based realm of design than in the calculation-based one of engineering. It's frustrating and intrusive worries grab his attention. Should he do something to lift the burden of perceived responsibility from Jason? He loses his place in the checking and has to start again.

He's nearly got to the end when the phone rings. Shit. Dani? Whatever could he want? He tries to ignore the noise but it goes on.

'Dani, it's not a good time. Sorry. I'll ring you back. Soon as I can.'

'No Simon. This is important. We need to talk. Now.'

Simon keeps his place in the figures he's checking. He's half listening. Dani sounds odd. Not like himself. He's breathing oddly.

'Simon this is dreadful news. For all of us. Maya. She's gone.'

'What?' Simon's hand rises automatically to his head. 'Where? Is she OK? Oh, I'm so sorry. When did you last see her? How are you?'

'You're the one with questions to answer. Not me.'

'What's happened to her?'

'Happened to her? Done to her you mean.'

'She was wonderful.' Simon is appalled. The kindest, most considerate person he knows sounds distraught and he's rung to make an accusation?

'How could you?' A pause. 'How dare you.' He sounds colder now. Intense but trying to keep control. 'She's only sixteen.'

Simon hears a gulp. Dani blows his nose.

He pushes his chair back swivels round from his desk and again his hand goes to his head. He's looking straight into the sun and half blinded. He blinks.

'What? What are you saying?'

'You know perfectly well.'

'No, I don't.'

'She thought you cared.'

'I do. I'd always help Maya. Like you helped James.'

'Not that way.'

'What on earth do you mean? What's happened?'

'Amit read your message on her iPad. *Of-course I care*, you'd written. *Come round after school and we'll sort it.* She'd left it open on the kitchen table. Now she's gone.'

'When? Where? When'll she be back?' Simon is getting more and more confused.

'Gone to stay with Nadia. In Acton. She told us to leave her alone and said she'll get back in touch when she's ready. She told us not to contact her.'

'That's awful. It doesn't make any sense. Why?'

'Apparently you weren't there or couldn't see her when she turned up after school. She was told not to bother you and to come back in a day or two. Something like that.'

'What? When did she come?' He frowns. His knuckles on the edge of his desk were bone white. 'The place was in turmoil yesterday. There was an accident … I'm still dealing with the consequences…' He pauses. Dani is silent.

'Are you talking about yesterday? Did she come here yesterday?'

'You should know.'

'But I don't …. Dani, what are you saying? What are you suggesting?'

'You should know better than to take advantage of someone so young …'

'Take advantage? How?'

'You tell me.'

'It never crossed my mind.'

'You misled her Simon. You should have been more careful.' Simon hears him swallow. He goes on. 'You're twenty years older than her. Amit's told the school and made a formal complaint to your ethical committee. Your professional affairs board. Whatever it's called.' A long silence. 'I don't want to see you. Stay away.'

The telephone goes dead.

Simon is shocked into total stillness.

Incomprehension turns to horror as the fall-out dawns on him. This will affect everything. Work. Status. Reputation. The team. The Westover Group. His plans and theirs. Family life. Friends. The children. Ruth … The combined after-effects of the accident and the accusations are like the jolts that upset the carriages when a train comes to an abrupt halt. The impact increasing as one crashes into another. Each into the next.

Within the hour Hannah comes to say she's had a call from the head of Maya's school.

'She's had a complaint about you, Simon, about Maya. She's put future placements on hold.'

'Dani rang me.' He's expressionless. 'Hannah, I didn't do anything …'

'I don't see how you could have. I'd have known if you had, given the time we both spent organizing and supporting her.'

'What did the head say?'

'Nothing specific.' Hannah looks down and then up again. 'She said, "I'm not asking for information now." But she's taking it seriously.'

'Oh?'

'She told me she'd already spoken to Maya's parents and looked at her logbook. She's going to talk to Maya as soon as she can.'

Simon is pacing round the room. Hannah hasn't sat down.

'Horrific,' she says. 'A total surprise. Outrageous. Completely out of the blue. As if the accident wasn't enough to be dealing with…' She's turning this way and that as she watches him. Then she stops, shaking her head.

Simon is still pacing.

She goes on: 'Maya's not back at school, but the head of safe-guarding is fixing to meet with her.'

Simon stops suddenly and looks at her with his mouth open. 'What did you say to the head?'

'That I couldn't believe anything untoward happened. And she said, "At this stage none of us can be sure. Further action depends on what we find out. From Maya and from others." Nothing else. She promised to keep me informed and ended the call.'

In the afternoon Simon receives a visit from Mathew James, head of ethics, accompanied by Hannah. He's a comfortable looking man with bright red cheeks that match the swirls on his Art Nouveau tie, and he wears a soft tweed jacket. He's known as a good lecturer on training courses and a good listener.

Simon gives him nothing to listen to.

'You understand that the parents of Maya, a schoolgirl on work experience with you, have made a serious complaint about you?'

'Yes. Her father rang me.' He makes no movement at all. 'Earlier this afternoon. He's an old friend.'

'The rules are these: You have to leave the premises and cannot return without permission. We will start enquiries immediately. Be as quick as possible.'

'You mean now? Leave right now?'

'Yes, as soon as we have completed the formalities.'

'How long for?' Simon asks. 'When can I come back? Can I collect the papers I need?' He looks around and remembers Maya's post card. Where is it? Maybe I took it home. He can't remember. He daren't speak.

'That depends on what we find.' Simon's heart rate accelerates. He can't hear himself think.

Things then happen fast, quietly, and politely, with a momentum of their own. Procedures first explained then immediately executed. Their life-changing effects ignored. Simon is blank with shock as he provides the passwords for his computer and gives up his keys. He asks Hannah to witness the handover. HSE together with Hannah and Clive will deal with the consequences of the accident to the Thames Footbridge. For that he will provide whatever input is needed, at a distance. He will be kept fully informed. Hannah will deal with his mail.

He looks up to see Mathew holding a pen. The paper on the desk between them has to be signed by both of them. Simon signs first. His hands are shaking, but the signature is fine.

Procedures completed Simon stares at Mathew in silence, without moving a muscle. It's a moment that to him seems both endless and cuttingly brief.

Part 4: All things considered

Autumn 2012 to Christmas 2013

Chapter 27

Simon

Time passes. Or it doesn't. With no possibility of rest. Simon is unable to eat or keep still. When he closes his eyes it's like falling and waiting for impact. The damage as yet undefined. Injuries are clearer during daylight. Reruns of fragmented memories intrude. Dani's voice sounds strange as he shouts down the phone. Flash-through images show a mess of papers on the floor. A worn patch on a trouser knee. An empty coffee mug, white with a red bridge on it, on his desk, to the right of the computer. All completely normal. The voice of Mathew James from Ethics is absurdly soothing.

The pieces don't link up into a coherent story. Each element is trapped in its own present tense as if still running and caught in an ever-circulating eddy. The whole experience seems to be cut loose from everything organized and regular.

It's hard to stop moving. Simon paces about and forgets to eat. He turns on the TV for the noise-value then falls asleep on the sofa. He wakes at 2.53am and it's still flickering. When he gets to bed, he's pursued by shouts of imaginary accusers. 'Go on. Admit it. Stop pretending you don't know what we're talking about. You're a monster. You've hurt an innocent young woman. Badly ...' He places his hands over his ears but is unable to block the exponential increase in volume.

Simon is so tired it's hard to walk straight.

Obsessions develop out of nowhere. Thoughts about the falsity – the total bizarreness - of Dani's accusation, 'She's only 16.' The echo rises and falls night and day. Dani's voice collapsing as he says it. The cadence endlessly repeated. Hours and hours of pointless, unstoppable, rumination. Going over and over everything in an effort to recall exactly what he spoke about with Maya. But the tape has degraded and rewind doesn't help. The search for clarity fails every time.

The unfairness is outrageous. Wrong. Simon's punches the air, meeting nothing. None of his thoughts lessen the confusion.

He talks to himself. Nothing had been further from his mind than hurting Maya. Or misleading her. He just offered a helping hand. Nothing more. Hannah knew that. Surely Dani did too.

Simon tries to stop his ruminations by writing his thoughts down: *I don't know how this came about but it's not my fault.* It makes no difference.

Obsessive actions follow the ruminations. He reads everything twice. Sometimes three times to make sure he's missed nothing and remembers everything important. The two disasters become entangled. He turns over a sheet of paper about the Thames Footbridge and checks it through. He puts it down to the right and looks at the next one. His mind wanders to an image of handing over his keys. He reads the footbridge paper again. When he finishes the bottom sheet is now on top. His certainty lasts a millisecond. Doubts and what-ifs re-start the process. But this is about Maya. Not about the bridge.

Taking responsibility for the bridge accident isn't a problem, even without knowing what went wrong. Responsibility for Maya's disappearance? For taking advantage of her? That's unreal.

He comes to a shuddering halt. Everything tells him interactions with Maya were benign. Nothing harmful on any horizon.

'No!' he shouts. 'Can't be. What's happening?' But there is no one to hear.

Sounds of pain and incomprehension multiply as echoes of Dani's distress join in. He bends over and groans. His stomach is as hard as a fist. Excruciating.

He thinks about a family bereft and he cries. Maya missing. An unhappy child hiding with her friend in Acton. Family friendships fractured. Two families blasted apart, the care and affection between them banished. Broken within and without. Separated by a misunderstanding. The malevolence of doubts seems real. Start to question intentions and that opens a void. Distrust leaps right in as if it was ready and waiting.

Reality is on hold for everyone. Isabel, the good friend of Kiri, is left stranded. Uncomprehending. Her white face and bewildered look is heartrending. She refuses hugs and sits silent at the kitchen table while she eats. He puts a hand on her shoulder and she turns her head away. Thoughts of interrupting the childrens' habits of meeting after school, texting idiotic jokes, looking out for each other, and of breaking links they've come to value, make him weep. Multiple uncertainties interfere with the ways in which four children naturally interacted with each other and with their parents.

Why? How did this come about? What happened? How can I put things right? What next? The questions go round and round in Simon's head.

It's all too much so he tries to refocus. To focus on something else.

How do you do that? What on? He looks at his sketch books and designs for future bridges, but they seem meaningless. It's as if he can't see them properly.

Papers for the competition in Brazil are irrelevant. Impossible even to look in their direction. Inspiration lost. Destroyed by a different kind of game-changer. Together with future prospects and plans.

Simon's head and shoulders sway side to side. His arms swing loose again occasionally but inside the tension persists even when collecting the children from school or walking along the river path. His feet shuffle through damp November leaves. There's no escape.

After 4 or 5 days he hears his grandfather's voice. 'Hang in there boy. You'll be OK,' He takes himself to stand face to face with the Golden Gate Bridge. He tries to tug himself back into today's reality. But you don't know what a picture hides. There were accidents there too. Eleven people died during its construction. In 1937 they were glad there were only 11 of them and 10 of those lost their lives together, in one horrendous accident. They fell 220 feet into icy water when a platform was being moved. The scaffolding twisted and turned before it collapsed. Accusations and blame followed.

Blame isn't fair, Simon thinks and puts his foot down hard. And it won't be until all of those involved accept a share of responsibility. Which he already has. For the accident.

But that doesn't stop him being bombarded with unanswerable questions about how to put things right, What if that's not possible? What might happen next?

James didn't know, or didn't understand Dani's accusations, but he knew about the bridge accident and he could tell something was seriously wrong. One evening he snuggled up close on the sofa with a notebook in which he'd collected measurements. The weight of a shoe, a bike, a mini, a fire engine. Lengths: the Weetabix box, his desk, his room, the route to school. Dozens more. His markers, and he tested himself by guessing the in-betweens. His own weight. And Dad's.

'Dad? How tall are you?'

'What?'

'6 foot 2. Or 3. Or I was.'

'What's that in meters?

'Oh. Two. Almost exact, I think. Why?'

'I'm into measuring now. To be sure.'

'Sure of what?'

'So, I know where I am.'

'That's good.'

And it is good. He's taking stock of the world in his way. James has won through to his version of normality. That's all the winning he needs. The feel of the small body warm beside him on the sofa, and the tug of childish interests brings with it a second glimpse of comfort.

Simon rings Dani. His call is refused so he sends a text:

There's been a terrible mistake. A misunderstanding. Can we talk?

210

No. The reply comes back.

He shudders and cries and torments his eye sockets with the heels of his hands. His knees, ankles and heels are as rigid as the floor. But he doesn't give up.

Dani eventually agrees to a call, provided Amit is in and Kiri is out.

'Think again,' he says. 'If you did nothing wrong why did Maya leave?'

'I have no idea. What did she tell you?'

No answer.

'Why did you, or rather Amit, contact the school? Didn't you know what that would mean for me?'

'She won't speak to us. She won't meet. She's out of touch.' Dani blows his nose. 'We've read what she'd written on her iPad. She left it in the kitchen.'

'What did it say?'

'Amit will tell you. I can't bear to read it. He's making more sense than I am.'

Amit begins quietly. 'We're shocked. We're worried and confused.' There was a long pause. 'I'll tell you what we found.' Another pause. 'We need to know what you've done. What you were up to.' 'Urr ... here.' He begins again.

'Simon, listen to this. Just listen. I'll tell it as we found it.'

'OK.'

Simon's stomach churns as he listens. He pulls at his hair. He hears about how her interest in making houses seems to have morphed into a teenage crush fed by fantasies about Simon's aloneness. Ruth's refusal to go on living with him. They don't know when it started. It could have been a while back.

'Seeing you with James, helping him so much, made her feelings stronger,' Amit says.

More detail. 'She wrote about being mesmerized by the intensity of your attention. How your interest and kindness confirmed her feelings. Magnified them. She thought you felt the same way. "I couldn't stop shaking," she wrote.'

'She started to write as if she was writing to you: "I walked the long way home, trying to calm down, the sound of your voice in my ears. I don't know how to look normal to you any more."

'She wrote about your daily meetings. The sense of your eyes fixed on her as she sat on the floor. Wanting to know how her day had gone. Said she hardly dared to look up. She said you told her a hopeful story, of being able to see over the treetops as she started her uphill journey towards ...'

'Then it stops.' Amit says.

Total silence. What?

'She wrote: "He really cares. I know he does." She wrote that many times. Then there was a list: "He notices how I feel. He wants me to do well. He says he'll always help. He's opened up his whole room to me. He thinks I could do this if I really want to." And then she had the message from you on her leaving card: *I'm here if you need me.* Amit pauses. "He cares about me. I know he does."

'What have you got to say for yourself Simon?' Amit pauses. Briefly. 'No. I don't want to hear. There's more for you to listen to first.'

Simon is speechless.

'Because you let her down. You missed her goodbye party. We asked what upset her that day but she wouldn't say. She said she was tired and sad the placement had finished. That she didn't want to eat. She wanted to be alone. Then you didn't sign her form for the stewarding event. She didn't know what to do, but she needed your signature so she brought it to your office and Hannah said you were busy. She was sent away. That's the day she left.'

'But there'd been an accident. It had only just happened.' Simon stands and turns round and back. He holds the phone to one ear then passes it across to the other thinking that he couldn't be hearing this right. He keeps still. Spare fist clenched.

Simon thinks about how to separate fact from fiction. What it sounds like, or can be made to sound like, from what it means.

How do I begin? He bends forward as if the answer might be hiding at floor level.

'I didn't do anything wrong. There's no way I would hurt your daughter. It horrifies me that you think I did.'

Silence.

He tells himself to breathe and makes a supreme effort to speak calmly. 'I hear what you say. But what she wrote about was only in her head. Nothing happened between us.'

'But you encouraged her. You were playing with her.'

'No, I was not. Not for a single moment.'

'We need to see her. To talk to her. How can we know what to believe?'

Simon loses the battle and shouts. 'Amit! Stop... . Listen to me ...'

His shouts are fiercely interrupted. But they don't stop Simon.

'You're both mad. How can you believe the fantasies of a 16 year old girl and not listen to me? Dani's known me since we were kids. Think again. And tell him to do so too.'

'That's it.' Amit cuts the link.

Trying to reach Maya is out of the question but images of what might be happening to her keep coming to mind, bringing even more questions with them. He asks himself how he could possibly not have noticed. Poor, loveable, child. It's dreadful to think that he could have hurt her. Unthinkable. Will her friends look after her? How will she come back from this? What's she thinking about, out there without her family? Supposing she's the cause of distress and division and destruction. What a load to bear when you're only 16. And what might be going on in the small house nearby which shelters the rest of Dani's family?

After breakfast Simon stays perched on a kitchen stool with his elbows on the counter. He switches on the radio but can't concentrate. He can't decide what to do. The doorbell rings but he ignores it. Whoever is there persists. He tucks in his shirt and forces himself up. It's Jason.

'Oh! It's you. Hello.' Simon wonders what he wants and whether he knows about Maya. A hand brushes over his unshaven chin.

'OK to come in?' Jason asks. 'How are you?'

'How do I look?' Simon doesn't sound welcoming, but he opens the door and Jason follows him back to the kitchen.

The visit turns out to be strangely consoling. It's soon clear that Jason knows nothing about Dani's accusations or about Maya.

Jason struggles to find the right words, as if there's something understandable to him about feeling helpless. But he doesn't give up.

'Everything you say is met with looks that activate someone else's internal weighing machine.' Jason spreads his arms out wide.

'What?'

'Which side will it fall. Credible? Or not?'

'Uh-uh.' Simon looks directly at him. Listens intently.

'For or against. No neutral anymore. Just endless doubts.' Jason takes a deep breath. 'No way of opening minds once doubts take over.' He turns round and faces front again. He shakes his head and his hair flops up and down.

'As if there's no way of crossing the gap ...' Simon pauses. 'As if people can't connect properly.'

'Yes.'

'Have you felt like that?'

'Uh uh. Often.'

'I'm sorry Jason ... And about the accident on the footbridge site?'

'Uhmmm - yes. Clive thinks I could be to blame. Others too probably but nothing's clear. Anyway, how can I be sure?'

Yes. And I didn't do anything, Simon thinks. It never crossed my mind. 'There's a helplessness about it, isn't there,' he says.

'There is,' Jason agrees.

'Try not to worry. Ultimately, I'm the one responsible, not you,' Simon tells him, and watches him walk away.

Later, Simon listens to Ravi Shankar, hoping for a gap in the clouds, and he gets a glimpse of clear sky. He thinks that all he can do is be himself. Open. No disguises. Locate a source of credibility. A support to use when reaching across a gulf. A set of stepping stones back to friendship. How do you transform scepticism back into trust? Can you? Could he do that with Ruth? These are serious thoughts he needs time to consider. It would be good to talk to her properly without others around. There was a time when she'd have weighed in with support, no questions asked.

Ruth

The house is quiet. Simon won't be back with the children till bedtime and being together might do them all good now he's so much better with them than he used to be. It's been impossible to talk to him in this crisis time as the children have always been around. Perhaps that's what he wants. But it's obvious that he's shaken. He looks distraught, as if he's hardly slept.

With time on her own this evening all Ruth can do is wander from room to room unable to settle to anything. She picks clothes up off the floor, switches on the washing machine, tidies the kitchen, and goes to her desk. But she can't think which of the demands coming her way she should respond to first. Suddenly she realises she's not just wretched and worried, she's furious with Dani and Amit. They're wrong. Simon was and is and always will be completely trustworthy with the children. More likely to stand much too far back from personal boundaries than cross over them when he shouldn't. Now everyone's distress has put misunderstandings on a hair trigger. No wonder it's been so hard to catch Simon on his own.

When, at last, she hears them outside she opens the door to meet them. 'Come in for a moment?' she says to Simon.

215

He hesitates, but James gives him a tug and they wander into the kitchen at their different paces, Simon last.

The kids are old enough to put themselves to bed now. Downstairs hugs have to do for tonight and they go quietly upstairs while Ruth looks for a bottle of wine. She collects two glasses and offers Simon the corkscrew, but he's not looking. He's standing not far from the door.

She opens the bottle, pours two drinks and sits down.

'I believe you,' she says. 'I know you wanted to do the best for Maya.'

She waits.

'Thanks.'

There's a long silence as she can't work out how to go on. 'Why don't you sit down?'

He takes the chair opposite.

'This is dreadful. A disaster for all of us.' Her hands shift over the table as if sorting their way through this and then that.

'I've always known you get totally absorbed in what you're doing. When you get fixed on something it's as if you can't see anything else. You look driven. Out of touch with other things. Compelled to keep going.' She's not judgmental. She wants to understand. She has the sense that something, she doesn't know what, must have been misconstrued. 'But there must have been something ....'

'What?'

'Something you were unaware of. Something you did ...'

'What? You can't believe I'd do anything to harm one of Dani's children, do you?'

'Not intentionally.'

'No way. What are you implying?' He bites his lip. 'That's incredible Ruth. You, of all people.' Simon stares at her. 'That hurts.'

He pushes himself up, knocking over the chair and shaking the table. A glass falls and Ruth jerks her legs away from the wine spill.

'I know you'd never hurt Maya, or any of them, on purpose. They're like part of our family.' She reaches for a cloth.

'I can't believe I'm hearing this.'

She looks at him with her mouth open.

'What are you saying?' He asks. He's backing away from her. 'Whatever do you mean?' His voice is on the rise.

Ruth reaches for the kitchen door and pushes it shut.

'Quiet. Or we'll have the children down again.' She chucks the cloth onto the table.

'Oh! Pity to disturb them! Sorry for the inconvenience.'

The front door slams.

Chapter 28

Simon

Anger is less confusing than misery. It clears the mind.

How dare they?

They know nothing.

They don't listen. Can't even hear.

Idiots with minds closed by their own assumptions.

Totally inflexible.

And there's nothing to be done about it.

Others can sort it.

A puppet's hand controlled unpredictably by a mind on speed clutches at his stomach without warning. A physical wrench that demonstrates the power of thoughts about false accusations. About not being believed.

Simon throws the basics into a case and taps out a text to Ruth.

I'm off. Will keep in touch with I and J.

He stares at his phone and decides not to say sorry. He flings stuff into his car and speeds past the children's school before realizing he has no idea where he's going. He hasn't a clue. The impetus came from behind not in front and it's been steaming him up ever since he slammed the door on Ruth. How dare she! She can't think beyond the mindless belief that there's no smoke without fire. He stares into space with gritted teeth and sucks in his cheeks. Do it randomly and sort it later. Right at the first lights, left at the second. There's the river ahead. Safer the other side. No reason. He crosses over the water. A safe bridge ... Hrr-umph. By now the anger is burning hot and he's twitching. They shouldn't jump to conclusions. They should have listened. They're completely wrong.

Two disasters on one bad day and a winner is turned into a loser! People may well be asking themselves right now what kind of bedrock lies beneath. Well, the past's best left undisturbed. He refuses to excavate. It would only multiply doubts and uncertainties.

He thumps the steering wheel. Then hangs on to it hard, and sees streets and people rush by. Instead of increasing the turmoil the rapid movement starts to absorb surplus energy from brain cells in clamour-mode. But it takes a while.

When it's easier to concentrate he turns on Radio 3. Turns up the volume and snaps it off again. He is not ready for listening.

The sun rises reluctantly in late November. This grey morning has little intention of sparking into life. After a long stretch of motorway, he stops to fill the car and empty his bladder. Inside the door there's a stack of new maps. Good. He buys one and sits at a green plastic table moored inside a picket fence.

A picket fence? What a bizarre choice. Made by interior designers no doubt. Or construction engineers. No self-respecting architect would combine the glint and shine of indoor consumerism with unvarnished reminders of old-fashioned gardens. Intended, no doubt, to keep untethered motorists from knocking into the tables as they exercise their driving legs. Totally inadequate when faced with pent-up 7-year-olds needing to let off steam. Or chattering teenagers oblivious to their surroundings. Or zimmer frames. Whoever were they trying to satisfy?

Simon frowns. People never make the decisions they should. Not anywhere he thinks, with one fist placed on each side of his empty plate and a full coffee cup in front of him. He flips the pages of the map, then leans back and stares at it. So many edges. So much sea. Useful boundaries when you're free-wheeling.

A triple-layer breakfast sandwich has left a deposit of wet dough in his mouth, coating every tooth and filling the gaps between with glue. There's a pound-coin sized shortbread in his saucer. The grittiness of it together with a few coffee rinses clears away the mouth-sludge. That feels better, and it's easier to think straight. What now? Simon shrugs his shoulders. A finger chances on the Humber estuary. Why not look at bridges that cross the blue? Look for gaps to cross. Start South-West and take it from there.

Within half an hour he's given up on signs to Nottingham and is heading for Bristol. By lunch time he's parking by the river Avon. He's going to walk over the Clifton Suspension Bridge. Absorb the details and think about how it was made. He hopes it will be sufficiently impressive to create a distraction. To transport him elsewhere. Exactly what it was intended for.

He isn't expecting to be surprised by the reality. By the footfall feel of it. It's astonishing. Bold and original in planning and in construction. Riveting. He groans inaudibly, pun not intended. A light mist lessens the shock of the depth beneath his feet. It suspends him in mid-air as if in a dream. For the first time since Dani and Amit's assault he pays proper attention to something outside himself. It's beautiful. Grand. He takes a deep breath of damp river air and walks right across the gorge. And back.

A walk over a bridge seems to have prodded his curiosity back into the real world. On to the Avonmouth Bridge next. One bridge opened in 1864. The other in 1974. That's over 100 years he realises, measuring things the way that James now does. Though being sure isn't going to make anything safe. Bridges just keep things moving. Passive components in the business of connecting things up.

This time the walk is a nightmare fuelled by engine roars and the poisonous air of motorway traffic. He can't breathe freely or think clearly. Seen from a distance the Avonmouth Bridge is grand and beautiful too but it pushes people aside with its noise and stink. It cuts them off from each other with an onslaught of gigantic container lorries nose to tail, competing to get where they want to be as fast as they can. Battering pedestrians with their wind blasts.

It's impossible to satisfy everyone.

He retraces his steps in search of fresh air and imagines a trajectory made up of all the bridges built in the years between the two he's just visited. A trajectory of discoveries and innovations that illustrates the developments of a whole century. What next? Don't think about it. Not now. It'll only bring a host of new problems in its wake.

Time to take stock instead.

He drives back up river and finds a guest house with a view over the woods beneath the Suspension Bridge. In a room with an armchair, small table and a reading lamp in the bow window he feels more grounded. The room is yellow and pink but he'll be sleeping most of the time he's in it. He gazes out of the window and shifts the chair to get a better perspective. He turns his phone back on.

There's a flood of messages. Repeated ones from James and Jason. One each from Hannah and Ruth. None from Dani. Or Isabel. James gets first response.

Dad where are you? Answer me. That one's from James.

Simon doesn't feel ready to speak so he decides to text instead.

I'm in Bristol.

How far's that?

Bit over 100 miles.

Simon's phone pings. *Where exactly?*

By the Suspension Bridge. Look it up.

Simon looks down on the woods. He doesn't have to wait long for a reply.

114.3 miles. From my bridge to yours. Can I stay with you tonight?

Too far away.

Clearly James is fine now he's in contact again. Perhaps the three of them will settle down better without me. Simon grits his teeth.

Hannah next. About the stuff she's submitted to HSE for the accident enquiry. They've fixed a date for a meeting next week and want to be sure he can be there. Monday. From 10.30.

That seems quick, Simon thinks. Why so little warning?

I'll be there, he taps out the text, and as soon as he's pressed send he groans. He's not allowed to enter the building without permission from ethics.

Not allowed. Could you ask Mathew James. Ethics Committee.

I'll let you know.

What does Hannah mean by that? That she'll ask them? Or what they say? And anyway, what do they want from me? Do they want me there or don't they? They're going to have to make up their minds in the end. Simon is damned if he'll help.

He scans down his inbox. An info-stream on the footbridge accident has been accumulating messages for days and now contains thousands of words. He decides to work on it where he is. Something about the damp air and the river view is acting like insulation. Staying put might keep his mind from straying across to personal horrors with all their emotional baggage and uncertainties.

Jason's messages tell him about the checks on everything he signed off on; calculations, data tables, foundations, plans etc. They've been double-checked by Clive and by an independent expert from HSE. No one found any errors. Jason's gone through endless worksheets and talked to the construction engineers. Now he's speculating about the cause of the accident and exploring possibilities. He wants to take Simon through every step of his journey. He still feels under suspicion. Not trusted. He's widened his search to hunt for papers about similar accidents … The messages go on and on. Simon starts skimming.

No problems then. It's looking good.

What about the foundations? I'm checking them too. Jason must have been waiting for a reply.

OK. Keep me posted. You're probably in the clear now. Jason's persistence has become intrusive. Irritating.

He looks at the last text he sent. Bother. I've probably landed myself with another barrage of texts about the foundations. Simon stares out of the window and sighs. There's something about Jason that is simultaneously super-sensitive and totally impervious. He's on hyperalert for accusations and terrified of being blamed. Fair enough. And he's always having ups downs in his relationships at work. Why? Maybe he really is a genius, though sometimes he seems more like James. Not even much older.

He moves on to the thousands of words to digest before the HSE meeting. It's turgid stuff and repetitive. He switches on the radio and listens to the early evening jazz chosen by listeners. There's too much talking and no coherent thread linking the songs. Someone asks for 'Your Feets Too Big' in memory of her dead brother. Simon thinks it's a dreadful choice. He turns it off. There's another ping from his phone. Isabel.

What's she want? Why's she been holding back? Who's she been speculating with? He stops to think for a moment before opening her message.

Maya's come home

What? What a relief. How is she? Is she OK? And Dani and Amit? How are they? What did she say? A myriad of thoughts race by in a single instant. Immediately he censors everything he wants to say. It's ridiculous. It makes him furious. Intolerable to have been put in such a position.

He can't think how to reply. A child of close friends has returned home and he can't tell his daughter how he feels about it. Or be with them. Or show his relief. Instead, he has to turn his mind to crafting a statement that will be repeated and measured for undertones and acceptability. Eff it! He slams a hand down on the table top. Be careful what you do next, he says to himself. Calm down ... Take it slow ...

In the bathroom he splashes cold water over his face. And shirt. And the floor. The towel is too small and too thin. There's nowhere to hang it. He flings it over the shower rail.

He sits in the armchair, phone in one hand, elbow on the arm of the chair, chin resting on the other hand. He stares out of the window, into the dark. The wood beneath the bridge has disappeared. He taps out a message.

Thanks for letting me know. I'm so glad.

He has no idea what Isabel knows or thinks. No one has told him who's said what to whom and he hasn't asked. He's pleased to know Maya's home. Glad she has shown she won't or can't, maintain the separation. Poor child. She must be confused too, and embarrassed. Though that probably depends on what she thinks everyone else thinks. And on what they say. Or do.

A response from Isabel comes immediately. *She might stay*

Good. Simon replies.

Kiri's coming home with me

Sleep well everyone.

Oh my God. That's all that Simon can say to himself. The relief is huge, but he's sure there will be repercussions of one kind or another.

He's late going down for the meal he arranged to have earlier. It doesn't matter. There's lasagna and salad, fish and chips or cottage pie and peas. Half a dozen people in the dining room and an empty table rather too close to the door. Nothing matters. The cottage pie is warming and welcome. He has a glass of wine with it and takes a refill back upstairs.

Someone must have come into his room while he was eating. The curtains are closed and the bedspread folded. He wonders what they might have looked at before he realises that everything he might not want others to find is on the device that goes everywhere with him, in his pocket.

Simon can't face the message from Ruth.

He sits in the chair by the window, his heart-rate slowly rising. Contacting Ruth will put an end to the possibility of sleep. Something will go wrong or one of us will get upset. Or both. It would be better to wait for the morning. He searches for some music to listen to on the radio. He can't find any but there's a football match instead. He doesn't even watch it to the end. He finds himself drifting off and puts himself to bed.

Hardly surprising that he's awake again at 5.30. What did Ruth say? Simon is caught in a flood of worries about what she's thinking. Her words come straight back: loud and clear. 'There must have been something you did ...' That's the end of his sleep. He turns on the light, opens his phone, puts it down on the bedside table and gets a drink of water. His hands shake as he opens his phone. He sits on the bed and swallows. His heart is thumping and it's hard to think straight. He takes a deep breath and searches for her message.

I meant it Simon. But I didn't mean you meant any harm. I still believe you.

That doesn't fit, he thinks. Not with saying there must have been something he did. Does she really think he would do anything, ever, to hurt any of the children? That includes all four of them. How could she?

Is she really that detached? Worrying about whether raised voices would wake the children rather than about the main issue ...

His mind runs on and back and all over the place, picking up fragments of earlier conversations and joining them up together in his own way.

She told him what a difference it made when he cared for James. She started him thinking about what James needed instead of getting stuck on what he needed for himself. Helped him to think about how to be more right for others. Stopped him obsessing about winning. Or worrying about how others thought he was doing. She made him feel more part of what was going on instead of standing watching like a bystander. That made a huge difference, including with Maya. Maybe that's how things went wrong.

What does all that mean?

That she's not sure. That she believes he might have done something wrong. That maybe she wants to be rid of him but doesn't want to hit him when he's down.

There's a big question to ask Ruth, and Simon dreads the answer.

Are you saying you want to be rid of me? Is that what you mean?

He presses send. He has a shower, goes down to breakfast and asks if the room is free until Sunday. His phone pings as he walks back up the stairs. It's Hannah.

Mathew James says OK to the meeting. No to returning your keys.

Bugger that. Simon thinks. At least there's something needs doing. He switches off his phone and gets down to work on the footbridge papers.

As he wakes the next morning he reaches, without thinking, for his phone. He turns it on. There's a message from Ruth.

No. That's not what I meant. Not at all.

He stares at it, his heart hammering. He can't afford any distractions now. He turns off the phone and, without a similar button to press, excludes personal matters from his mind altogether for the time being. There's lot else to be getting on with.

Chapter 29

Simon

Simon, Clive and Jason hide from the world of perpetual drizzle outside and work all weekend, separately, through their files and notes. They circulate texts, emails and questions. They search for any information that could be relevant but find nothing. They ban speculation and share their relief. They hide any remaining doubts and agree there's no need to meet.

Simon has more than one ordeal to face on Monday and he dreads them both. First there's the challenge of being in the office without access to his room. On temporary release. No access to a bolt hole. Second, there's the detailed exploration of the accident, including its causes and consequences. The outcome could threaten everything he's worked for. His team, construction of the Thames Footbridge and the Westover Group. His reputation. His future.

He gets there early and stops inside the main door. It smells familiar. Polish mixed with fresh coffee. There's a sound he didn't know he'd missed. It's the quiet shuffling sound of people settling down to work. He sees the closed door of his office.

'Um – oh.' He heads to the meeting room.

Hannah has set it up well and she's distributing fresh notepads round the table.

'Hello.'

'Morning Simon.' She looks at him. 'How are you?'

'It's odd... ... odd to be here like this ....'

'OK?'

'Uh uh.' He straightens up. He's damned if he'll let this destroy him, or his project. That's well worth saving. He just needs to find out what went wrong. 'Good to see you.' He manages a smile.

'And you Simon.' She looks at him. Nods.

Others start to arrive. The team from HSE, independent experts, representatives of the client, insurers, the engineers and more than one construction company. Hannah's made room for all of them.

Simon puts his papers down on the far side of the table and stands with the points of his fingers probing its surface. He resolves to shut out everything else so as to focus on this. There's no need to get phased.

Even Jason is on time. He stumbles as he enters the room. Heads turn. A stranger's hand reaches out just in time to prevent his laptop from falling. He manages an appreciative nod. The meeting gets going without delay, led by Reg Fellows from HSE who has a reputation for scrupulous attention to detail and a liking for being in control. His manner is quiet. His attitude is welcoming and Simon settles down a fraction, one hand resting by his papers. He exchanges a serious look with Jason, now alongside.

'He's not as spikey as he looks.' Simon's words are lost in the surrounding buzz. Jason stops staring at Reg.

Reg's hair is thinning and to Simon he looks as if he hasn't filled in the spare outline of the adolescent he was half a century ago. He calls the meeting to order, and the long agenda, circulated only last night, appears on the big screen.

There are endless preliminaries, introductions, explanations of procedures and thanks to the Westover team for responding quickly to requests. More thanks for the use of the room and to Hannah for organizing everything. They get down to business. Simon's jaw tightens. He stifles a yawn and wishes he hadn't skipped breakfast. He helps himself to more coffee and passes the jug along. He's not the only one in need.

The next hour familiarizes everyone with the intricacies of the footbridge project. Plans, contracts, order of construction, division of labour, lines of responsibility, reports from the site inspector and so on. It's tedious, but eventually Reg is satisfied that everyone is on the same page. He asks Clive to explain where the work had got to immediately before the accident.

Simon is relieved there is nothing new so far. He shifts in his chair, ready to listen carefully. He has always enjoyed Clive's economical style. Not a word wasted. No signs of doubt or uncertainty. He carries everyone with him, covers all bases, and his listeners are left with no questions to ask. A model of good control.

They need a breather. Someone asks for a window to be opened and Reg suggests a break for lunch. It's a relief to move. Jason flutters everywhere, as fidgety as a bird in a hurry to migrate. Simon wanders round the room, smiling vaguely and avoiding all but the most superficial of conversations. The serious side of the business is yet to come. This could be the lull before the storm. Sandwiches are hard to swallow at the best of times. He forces a couple down and watches Reg working the room with tact and occasional semi-serious smiles. Reg eats one sandwich fast, then reaches for a glass of water. It's not long before he calls everyone back to work.

'Time to think about the accident itself,' he says, loud and clear. He takes his place at the head of the table and places a hand on the heap of papers in front of him.

Clive continues as if there had been no interruption, with a list of who was on site and what they were doing immediately before the accident. He refers everyone to the documents before them. Pages clearly numbered. Simon follows the story point by point, moving a finger down the list as he goes. Others fumble, lose track and seek help from their neighbours. Simon frowns. Clive goes straight on. He shows a series of pictures and draws attention to crucial details. Fragments of the fallen platform. Piles of materials ready to be used. Tools and equipment abandoned in a hurry. Someone asks if anything was moved before the pictures were taken.

'Probably.' He replies.

Simon goes rigid and scans the scene of the accident. Then Clive reminds them that the first priority was to account for everyone. To find and attend to the injured and the shocked. There was a wait for the paramedics. Everyone was moved away from the danger zone, up to the portacabin used as a canteen. There had been a certain amount of milling about after the initial shock, but it didn't last long, and no one left the site until much later.

'As soon as possible I went with one of the construction supervisors to make a safety assessment and find out the scale of the damage. These are the pictures I took then.' Clive goes on.

'The place looks a mess.' One of the underwriters reflects out loud. 'Was it always like that?'

'No. It was well organised and tidy. See the inspectors' reports. They're in Section 5.'

'So, you're saying the site was well managed?'

'Yes. It's the mess made by the accident that you can see.'

They watch the video made from the helicopter. From that height the sense of underlying organization is immediately apparent. The mess is limited to the site of the accident. Everything else seems under control.

There are many questions for Clive. More and less technical, more and less relevant.

'Was there rubble there before the accident? Someone asked.

'What was the load-bearing capacity of the temporary platform? What was the weight of the materials on the platform?'

'Was there a fixed route in and out of each work station?'

Simon shifts around and wonders what they could have missed? Why don't they know what went wrong? Jason's fingers trace invisible patterns on the table as if searching for a hidden clue.

When everyone is satisfied Reg says. 'I understand you to be saying, Clive, that the mess is a consequence of the accident and not a cause. Am I right?'

'Yes.'

'So, if everyone's ready we should move on to consider its cause. Or causes.' There was no sound of dissent. Simon sits still as a stone.

Reg picks up the page in front of him and places it face-down on the growing pile to his right. He clears his throat and waits an extra second before he begins.

'You may be wondering,' he starts slowly, 'why we have called this meeting so soon. I know our reputation. I know people expect these affairs to drag on for months.'

Simon nods and others follow suit. There are a few grimaces too.

'People talk about the delays,' Reg goes on. 'And they remember them. And delays are damaging, especially to those who could be, or think they could be, responsible.' Jason looks up. Simon doesn't. 'The quicker we can be, the sooner everyone can move on.' He pauses briefly. 'It keeps costs down too.' He checks that he has everyone's attention. 'I shall summarise our findings. This information has not been circulated in advance, but I will email a summary to all of you later today.'

Simon is totally focused. Jason's legs under the table are keeping time with the fluttering of his fingers above it.

Reg reminds them that the most common causes of accidents are people, machines, systems and materials. This means there are numerous possibilities to be excluded as well as clues to follow up. Then he plunges, again, into interminable details.

Simon pulls his legs in beneath his chair. Does this man know how it feels to drag this out? He thinks.

But Reg is in his element. His details come in three main categories: factors concerning those working on the site: their training, familiarity with the tools, equipment and machinery used; factors to do with the preparation, organization, management and safety of the site, including the disposal of rubbish, and factors concerning construction processes. It seems that he might go on forever. Shoulders slump and Simon's mind wanders. It's irritating, he thinks. Can't they see how important this is?

Reg raises his voice and slows down the speech-rate. He's demonstrated the thoroughness of his team and is ready to present his conclusions.

'We found nothing.'

He's conducting a personal drama Simon realises. It's not about us, or the agony of waiting for the finger to be pointed. He's doing what he likes to do, regardless of what's at stake for others.

'Nothing of any relevance or significance,' Reg says. 'Small stuff like machines needing a service or people taking a short cut to a work station, but nothing that could have contributed to this accident. We wondered what we might have missed. We went through it again...'

Bet you did. Endlessly. So? ... Simon keeps his impatience hidden.

'Then I was contacted by a manager from Mainstay, the contractor responsible for the working towers and platforms on the site. He told me that a new supplier of theirs, manufacturers of the joining parts for scaffolds, elbow joints, clamps, swivel couplers, scaffold locks and so on, had been using a sub-standard steel component. More fragile and less durable.' He pauses for effect. 'It only takes a small deformation in joints at critical locations for a tower such as the one used here to collapse.'

Are we exonerated? Free? This time Simon can't keep quiet.

'Would that be enough? He asks, 'Deformation of a few scaffold connectors?'

'You're right to ask.' Reg nods in Simon's direction. 'Examination of the litter, - the mess you saw in Clive's pictures, strongly suggests that this is what happened here.'

Reg raises a hand to quell a growing murmur.

'A case for legal action against Mainstay's scaffolding supplier is being prepared by them. You at Westover will decide what action you wish to take, and I will send you copies of our evidence: the evidence for what did not happen and the evidence for what, most probably, did happen. This part of the enquiry is over.' Reg places a hand flat on the top of his papers. At last he has finished.

Now Jason sits silent and still and Simon leaps to his feet, their usual roles reversed. With one hand Simon sweeps his hair back from his forehead and he's ready to take charge. He looks across at Clive who raises a hand to give him the floor.

'Thank you, Reg. Thank you for your quick response, and for your attention to detail. An awful lot of detail.' He hears the beginnings of a laugh and, quickly, continues. 'Your openness, and consideration of the consequences of such an accident on a growing business like ours, and on those who share responsibility for decision-making as well as for mistakes, makes a big difference. To us and to our clients. As you said, delays are expensive. Thanks for putting us in the picture so soon.'

There's an explosion of noise and movement in the room that no one tries to control, then they start to gather up their belongings. Clive shakes Simon by the hand. 'I'm glad. And it makes sense too.' Stepping to one side, he adds, quietly, 'Jason is good with figures. I realise he didn't make mistakes. But I want him off the Project Management Group. Immediately. OK?

'I'll talk to him.' Simon's turn for straight talking.

'He's not ready for this kind of work. And he can't deal with stress. Not just major stress, but the ups and downs of ordinary practical work. Keep him in the office. Close to you. I don't want to work with him again.' Clive pauses. 'And I think we should keep lines of responsibility clearer in the future. Especially when sharing supervision.'

'Yes.' Simon looks at him sharply. He remembers Clive's messages but he doesn't remember responding to them. He resolves to apologise.

The long meeting has ended. Simon and Jason now sit in a corner seat at right angles to each other. They've been running and re-running through the events of the day. Pint glasses have been refilled and empty plates removed. A dull red-brown candle burns between them. Outside it's pitch dark. Simon rests against the padded strip of maroon leather stuck to the wall behind him. Jason leans forward, arms on the table.

'The best thing is being let off the hook,' says Jason. 'And it's happened so fast that it's hard to take in. I can hardly believe it. It might have been a total disaster.'

'I know. But there'll still be lots of delays you know.'

'Oh?'

'Reg wouldn't have said what he did if he wasn't sure, but lawyers will get independent experts onto the site. It'll be closed for a while.'

Jason looks puzzled.

Simon looks thoughtful. It would be dreadful to fall out with someone he respects as much as Clive, but their opinions of Jason are fundamentally different, and it's impossible to tell who's right. Jason certainly gets carried away with ideas and loses track of the practical side of things. But few people excel at the thinking and the doing. And Jason's combination of talents could make him an excellent collaborator. Despite Hannah's doubts about him, he's still exceptional. Simon knows he should have a serious conversation with Jason.

'Listen,' he says. 'You and Clive ... you clearly don't get on. You've been at cross purposes ever since you joined the PMG. What's that about?'

'He doesn't trust me.'

'Do you trust him?'

'What? He's just not interested in new possibilities. In innovating, trying out new methods and being creative.'

'That's not fair. Is that his job?'

'Well ... I don't see why not ...'

'Jason what you need to know is that he wants you off the team. Straight away.'

'Oh! Does he?' He looks down. Swallows as he takes it in. 'I suppose I'm not really surprised.'

'Nor am I. It's the right decision.'

'Shit.' He pulls in his chin. Simon waits.

'Maybe I should move on.'

'What?'

'I've been head-hunted. By someone from Arantxa Villela's team.'

'Have you? The woman who won the competition for the Portuguese bridge?'

'Yes. I haven't replied yet.'

'She's good, you know.'

Simon is tired, but not too tired to realise that he might still be a loser today. It's not often you get the chance to work with a future star. Oddities set aside. As Jason's boss, he also has responsibilities towards him. He decides to speak up.

'News of your talents has spread Jason, and I'm not surprised. You seem to like challenges. And keeping up with technical developments. You're a rare beast, with your interest in engineering as well as architecture. Right?'

'Ur …? What are you getting at …?'

'And you like to cross boundaries. Step over gaps that would defeat most people. How about collaborating? Would you like to help me develop a design for the Brazilian competition?'

'Seriously?'

'Uh-uh.' Simon answers quickly. 'You have a real flair for computer modelling and I need someone with your talents and interests. And with your engineering background. Things move on so fast.' He stops. They look at each other.

Jason looks down. After a moment he looks up again.

'No need to answer now. Take your time. Think it through and talk to others as well.'

Jason nods and spreads his fingers wide onto the tabletop. 'Thanks Simon.' He turns a beer mat over as if he expected to find something underneath it. 'Thank you very much.' His eyes are still fixed on the table as he replies.

Simon picks up his glass and drains it clear. 'I enjoy working with you. I think we could work well together. Find out what Arantxa is offering first and let me know after Christmas. In the New Year.'

Jason nods. 'OK. I'll do that.'

They're quiet. So much to assimilate.

Simon stirs himself. 'I'm tired. Time to go.' But no one moves.

Jason looks as if he might, all at once, fall deeply asleep. He speaks while looking at his hands.

'It's odd you know,' he says. 'I knew my calculations were OK, but I still felt blamed. It still felt as if I must be responsible. It wasn't just that Clive didn't trust me. It was inside me too.'

'How so?' That's hard to deal with, Simon thinks. Tough.

'Well ... I think it's about feeling responsible for all sorts of things you never intended. Things that happen for other reasons. Like some of the things that went on at home. Things I did. Or didn't do. Blaming myself for not having stopped things happening. For not having realised what was going on. It leaves you feeling there must have been something you could have done. Something you should have done.'

Simon listens. He doesn't ask for details.

Jason goes on: 'As if I deserved to be blamed even if I hadn't done anything. There was something about being blamed that felt right.'

'I'm not sure I know what you mean. How could that make sense?'

A quick blink, and Jason closes his mouth.

Simon reaches for his jacket and pats it down, feeling for his wallet. 'It's late Jason. Let's bring today to a close. Sleep on it.' He pays the bill. They find coats and scarves and stop for a moment on the pavement outside. A cold wind is blowing.

Simon looks at Jason. There's something troubling about him. There's probably more to know. But they are both exhausted. And the problem-solving hasn't yet finished.

'Sleep well.' He says. 'There's no one holding you responsible for what happened. Enjoy the relief while it lasts.' He turns to walk away, and then turns back. 'It would be a pleasure to work with you Jason, if that's what you decide you want.'

Jason smiles, seriously. 'Thanks Simon. Good night.'

They walk their separate ways.

Alone again. In his mind's eye Simon sees the Golden Gate Bridge. So solidly supported at both ends. He's not there yet. Some of the things he most values are still at risk. His internal scanner provides the list.

Ruth. Troubled and uncertain.

Dani. A friend lost. His childhood companion and supporter. Gone.

The purple bridge of Maya's postcard, still glowing in the dark. Another gaping chasm to cross.

He looks out over the spaced-out lights of London at night. There's a network somewhere in the background, with lights on it that blink when parts of it connect. But the circuits can't be complete. Large areas of obscurity remain. There's unfinished business yet to be sorted.

Chapter 30

Simon

To Isabel and James, the weekends they spend with Simon in his flat, with their separate bedrooms, easy access to their school friends and his relaxed attitude to meals and mealtimes, have become an ordinary part of their lives. Things go on in their usual way.

'Let's go,' James yells.

'Who said you could take my hoody? Give it back.' Isabel tweaks the hood from behind and jerks his head.

'Stop that. You'll hurt him.' Simon grabs Isabel's arm.

'You know it's mine Dad.' She twists free and delivers the cold stare of a 14 year-old. 'That's. Not. Fair. Don't blame me.' She tramps off and slams her door shut.

Cool it, Simon tells himself.

He's stuck. Generally stuck and doesn't know how to resolve matters with Dani. Or with Ruth. Or Maya. The footbridge build is on hold as the legal consequences of the accident are on slow release. Still, there's no excuse for losing it.

Simon and James leave Isabel behind and go shopping. James isn't bothered and silence is not a problem.

Isabel's right, Simon thinks. It's not fair to be wrongly accused. Blamed for consequences you never intended. It makes you feel you've done something wrong when you haven't.

When they get home, he finds James's sweatshirt (no hood), exchanges it for Isabel's hoody and knocks on her door.

'You're right. That wasn't fair. I'm sorry.' He waits thirty seconds until she opens the door.

'Here.' He hands her the hoody.

Stand off? She chucks it behind her and looks up at him, eyebrow-frown on the melt.

'Hug?'

She accepts a squeeze. Her arms creep round his waist and she hangs on tight. He's forgiven, that's a relief.

'Did you get any ice-cream?'

'It's February.'

'So?'

'Cookie dough and caramel.'

An early spring weekend with the children goes better and almost trouble free. Doing nothing much, together. No pressure. Ruth collects them and they go off home with her. He loads the dishwasher, wipes the surfaces and looks in the fridge. A lump of cheddar. A glass of wine would be good with that, Simon thinks. The telephone buzzes.

'Simon! Good moment?'

It's Amit.

Oh my God. What's happened? Why now? He's on full alert.

'Uh-uh. Only me here. No one else.'

'We've got the report from the school. From the head of safeguarding. About Maya.'

'Uh-uh.'

Simon looks this way and that. He crosses the kitchen to sit at the table and holds the phone as if it might explode if he hit the wrong button. A cloud of white petals from the cherry tree in next door's garden blows onto the grass like melt-proofed spring snow. Are problems re-emerging, he asks himself, or are they about to vanish?

'She was slow to talk. That's why it's taken so long.'

'Uh-uh.' Simon's mouth is dry and he can't swallow. He shakes his head. He's damned if he going to say anything. He's not going to help Amit out. As he waits he thinks; anyway, why you? Why not Dani?

240

'They're quite clear. We think she'll be OK.'

'Uh-uh.' And me? Has that crossed your mind?

'I'll read you some of it. About what she told them. About how they tried to make sure what she said was true, and whether there were things she wasn't saying. Whether she felt safe to talk. It goes on a bit.'

Get on with it, Amit.

'Here we are: They say she never told you how she felt. Didn't dare. But she thought you knew. Because you were kind. Because you took the time to meet her every day. Said you'd do what you could to help her. All that. The main point in their conclusion is…. Wait, I'll find it.'

Simon can hear pages flipping over. Do you have any idea what you're doing to me, Amit? Keeping me on tenterhooks, and flooding me with uncertainty? He uncrosses his legs, sits on the edge of the chair. Then he crosses them the other way.

'Here. Got it. The conclusion puts a lot of weight on this: *He never touched me. He never tried to touch me.*'

You bet I didn't. It never occurred to me. How dare any of you think I might have done …

Amit's voice intrudes, and he's speeded up. He talks about Maya being back at school and not always at home. Simon can't take it any more. He puts the phone on the table and buries his face in both hands. Amit talks on. He picks up the phone again and interrupts.

'Amit stop! Can you read that bit again?' There is no response. 'Her actual words. What she said to them. In their conclusion.'

'What? Oh. The report explains how they decided what happened. The facts. They realised saying this was important to Maya but they were uncertain whether it was true or whether she wanted to protect you. So, they went on talking with her until they were quite sure it was true. Hang on I'll find it.'

Again, Simon has to wait.

'Here. It's in quotes. "He never touched me. He never tried to touch me." They're definite. All agreed.'

Simon closes his eyes. He sees Maya sitting on the floor, hiding behind her hair. Poor child. She got caught up, for the first time probably, in feelings she didn't know how to handle. He thinks she was brave to hold on to the facts. To try to put things right.

'What happens next?'

'The report does the rounds. It goes to the head teacher and Maya's head of year. To Mathew James from your professional affairs board. He'll be in touch with you. And with Hannah. They will take steps to wind things up.'

'How long will that take?' Simon grits his teeth. 'I damn well hope you believe it,' he mutters. 'Where's Dani? Can I talk to him?'

'He says he'll talk when he can. Not yet.'

'Tell him to ring me. Go on.' He knows we have to talk. What's stopping him? 'He can't cut me off just like that. He can't still think it's my fault ...'

'Ur ... Yes ... no ... I'm not sure ...'

'What? What are you saying? I need an explanation. You owe me an explanation. You both do. You jumped to conclusions and acted on them without checking things out. You both did.'

What about an apology ...? Simon can't help thinking.

'... Tell him this from me ...' he slows down for emphasis. 'They've locked me out. I'm not allowed into my office. I have to make do with emails and messages from Hannah. I can't meet my team or lead my Group. I need to talk to him.'

'I can't make him ....' Amit's voice trails off.

What's that about? Aren't you talking to each other? Do you enjoy keeping me dangling? Yes again, questions swirl around in Simon's head.

'Yes, you could. If you wanted to ...,' he splutters. 'And tell him I'm not going to give up trying. He's my oldest friend. If there's anyone who knows me it's him.'

'Of course he knows you. You and your dangerous habit of ignoring people's feelings.' Amit is angry too.

242

'Thanks for that.' Simon cuts the call dead. He drops his phone on the table and slams out of the front door without a coat. He walks along the river with a dizzying sense of grey water flowing by on his right. He passes under two bridges without glancing at them. He comes to a bench and sits. It begins to rain but he stays put.

He's wet through and shivering when he gets home. He runs the bath hot and deep. He lies with his feet on the shelf by the taps and the water up to his chin and finally the internal tumult begins to subside.

Simon thinks aloud, 'So that's what Dani and Amit think. Maybe Ruth thinks the same.'

Perhaps that's why the good news about Maya doesn't make things better.

He hunts at the back of a cupboard for the bottle of gin. It's not there. No tonic either. He slumps into the faded yellow armchair with a glass of wine and reverts to type. He shuts down all internal compartments except for two. One for work. Another for the children.

The next morning, breakfast is interrupted by text messages and a call from Hannah.

'Simon it's me. Have you heard from Mathew?'

'Just this minute. He only needs an official message from the Professional Affairs Board and I can come back.'

'How are you doing?'

'Well … it would help to get to my office.'

'I've got your keys right here. Waiting for you.'

'Thanks so much, Hannah.'

The waiting is over. Simon can return to his office.

When at last he unlocks his office door he switches into automatic. Without looking he dumps his coat on the usual chair, puts a heap of bags down on the glass table in the window and switches on the computer.

He needs a new password. Shit!

He looks round, then opens and shuts a desk drawer. He sits in his chair and swivels right and left. The out-of-date photograph of Ruth and the children is gathering dust on the bookshelf. The kids smiling up at Ruth in the sun. It was just before Isabel started school and James is wearing the red wellies he refused to take off even in mid-summer. It seemed like a lifetime ago. Don't go there, he tells himself. Get sorted.

An untethered feeling makes it hard to concentrate. He looks up. He touches base mentally with a heap of files. A row of journals on the bookshelf. The waste bin. Empty. It's like re-loading his internal hard-drive. Things that familiarity had made unnoticeable seem different. He straightens a picture of a bridge under construction and tips the one beside it to the left. He looks along his collection. Each picture chosen with care. Each a reminder of the effort that goes into bridge-building. A row of successful balancing acts.

Where to begin? He goes to collect a coffee.

It feels good just to be here. He's ready to develop interesting possibilities and respond to new ideas. To lead a functioning team and share with them a commitment to something important and valuable.

Then Hannah appears. 'There's a lot of stuff for your diary. Good time to talk about it?'

Seeing the time fill up tells him to be careful. He needs to ring-fence design time. Keep the creativity centre-stage.

'Thanks Hannah. Especially for keeping me in touch with essentials. And for your discretion.' He grins. 'One thing I've learned is that things keep ticking over without me.'

She laughs. 'Maybe you'll give up a bit of control then!'

'Mind my own business. No bad thing.'

She lays a hand on the edge of Simon's desk and looks steadily at him in his chair behind it. She smiles.

'You should know Simon that people don't know why you've not been coming in.'

'I have been wondering ... '

'Of course. But they've been focusing on the aftermath of the bridge accident, and they know about James too. And you've kept in touch well.'

244

That fits with what Jason said, Simon thinks. Problems linked to Maya and her placement didn't seem to occur to him.

'There's been speculation of course. But they know you're working on new stuff. Defining our aims. Keeping us in the front line. The Brazilian competition entry too. That seems to have been enough.'

He wonders if there was speculation, and if so, how she dealt with it.

'There's so much to thank you for,' he says. 'Your sensitivity as well as all your efficiency. I must have given you a huge amount of extra work.'

She moves away.

'Hannah, can I ask you something?'

She turns round. 'Sure.'

'What do you think went wrong? I don't think I did any more to help Maya than you did. And we spoke about all of it. Daily.'

'I never for a moment thought you'd done anything.'

The first time anyone has said that! He looks up. She has more to say.

'Maya was great, but she's young. Idealistic. And I know you, Simon. You could be easy to idealise. But you might miss the signals.'

They stay still for a moment. Then get on with the work

Simon rings Dani again. Another person who knows me well, he thinks. In his heart of hearts, he must know he's wrong. That the accusation was false.

There was no answer.

He refuses to give up. Regularly, mid-week, when the children are with Ruth, he tries Dani's number, again and again.

It's half term and Saturday morning and the days start to feel longer. A shriek of laughter comes from Isabel's room. Then singing. Isabel and Kiri's friendship has survived and it sounds as if they're recording something. The shrieking starts when they listen to the playback. A phrase in Kiri's deep voice is answered by Isabel's less confident one. Then they sing something together. A chorus? The cycle continues: song, playback, shrieks. Listening from the kitchen Simon loses track of what's being said on Record Review (about Beethoven's Tempest sonata. The one that takes you all the way through waves and waves of turbulent emotion). He switches it off and leafs through the Saturday paper surrounded by breakfast debris.

Isabel and Kiri burst through the door.

They find a pizza in the fridge and perch on kitchen stools playing finger-dance games until it's done.

'That sounded great. What are you two up to?'

Isabel uses the bread knife to divide up the pizza. They look at each other and laugh. Holding an unstable triangle in tomato-stained fingers, Kiri stretches out an elastic band of cheese, stuffs it in her mouth and swallows without chewing. 'It's a surprise for Dad,' she says.

Simon remembers about Dani's song-writing. About Kiri's voice and his wish to hear her sing his songs.

'Did you like it?' That's what they both want to know.

'Love it. You need more practice on the bit you sing together,' he says. They show him a whatever face.

Kiri's voice is amazing. Isabel's not in the same league. But she's OK.

Only the next day Simon is getting dressed, listening to the radio, when he's stopped in his tracks by the most beautiful sound. A familiar one, but the voice is new to him. He stands still, with a hand vaguely searching for a shirt button, and wonders at the temerity of the composer. And of the singer. It's Barbra Streisand singing Schumann's Mondnacht, or Moonlit Night in German. And for him, just now, its melody moves in a most satisfying way given that he has no idea what the words mean. How can that happen? He thinks of Dani, and the courage that it takes to write a song. To make music. To attempt a resolution.

His next text to Dani is different. He attaches a link to Streisand's version of Mondnacht. Omits every vestige of pleading or complaint.

Listen to this! I loved it.

246

A one-word answer comes back: *Wow!*

Simon stares for a long time at the word before he responds. *How's the song writing?*

And Dani responds to the invitation. *Good. Enjoyable.*

Brief messages now pass between them. About practicalities like sleepovers, and pick-ups. Sometimes with musical attachments.

Kiri's going to be late. Choir practice. I'll drop her off about 7.

They went to Ruth's after school. Haven't seen them here.

Simon and Dani haven't met since Maya left home more than six months ago. Simon still goes to the running track but Dani has given up. Maya has been home more than a school term. Bit by bit they construct a platform of safe topics beneath them and relegate chasms and mountain passes to the background. By June the ground has warmed up sufficiently to give Simon courage. He throws out a lifeline.

Hi Dani. I and K busy tonight. Meet at the Golden Lion?

Jazz night. Why not. Dani replies.

See you there.

OK.

Dani has picked up the end of the rope.

Simon still smarts from the false accusations. He's determined to do whatever it takes to recover this friendship. He doesn't dare hope for much, so he gets to the pub early, picks up a pint and retreats to their usual table hoping to gather his wits while he's waiting.

Time isn't on his side. Dani opens the door and Simon gasps. He's changed. He's thinner and lost more hair. His arms and legs are spikier. He wonders if he is not well. But his head's up and there's a

247

bounce in his step which is a pleasure to see. Simon is astonished by the friendliness with which he's greeted. Everyone seems to know him and welcome him. Simon can't keep the smile from his face.

Dani looks round and catches his eye. He returns the smile. Simon stands up and Dani holds out both hands as he walks towards him. It's a double hand hug. Better than a handshake, and not as good as a real hug. It doesn't last long enough for Simon.

'Simon.' That's all Dani says.

'Hello Dani.' Could two words ever be so simple and so serious? Simon thinks. It's a full moment before he adds: 'What will you have to drink?'

Simon collects a Heineken. Dani is distracted by Joe, the bandleader. Watching them Simon can see the conversation rise and fall as others join in. Dani appears to be surrounded by friends. How come? He collects some nuts as well as the drinks and has just put them down on the table when Dani joins him.

'How are you Dani'

'Fine. On the up in fact. And it's good to see you.'

'Oh, yes it is. I mean to see you! I've missed our meetings.'

'Well. Here you are again!' Dani turns. One of the musicians touched him on the shoulder as he passed by.

'Everyone seems to know you. How come?'

'The song writing. Melissa and Joe, the band leader, have been working on them with me.'

'Oh! Was it one of yours that I heard Isabel and Kiri singing?'

'No idea.'

Simon sits up. He remembers Kiri said it was a surprise for Dani. Have I broken their secret? He needs to change the subject just in case. 'Kiri's voice is amazing.' He needs to get straight to the point and face up to it. Simon remembers another conversation over a meal. One during which Dani's generosity was at its most accessible.

'Dani, there's an elephant in the room.'

Dani looks behind him.

They both laugh.

248

Not for long. Simon hesitates. It's best to get straight to the point and say what needs to be said. 'Do you really think I took advantage of Maya?'

Dani is serious. 'No. I don't. She's sure of that. And I am too.'

'Thanks for that.' He sits still with his hands in his lap. 'Tell me what you've been thinking. Why you cut me off ...'

'It's complicated. Understanding what happened.'

'I wanted to help Maya. She's talented. She could do it if she really wants to.'

'Yes, but ...'

Don't you dare yes-but me. Simon bites his tongue. With every ounce of strength, he dampens his internal accelerator. He gives all his attention to his friend and waits for him to continue.

Dani is slow. More careful than uncertain. 'You've changed Simon. Or rather you haven't changed at all. You're more like the real you. The one I knew was there all along. The one who's attention everyone wants not because you always come out top but because you're interesting. And interested. Curious about them. Never critical.' He pauses. 'And you know so much.'

Simon looks up. He drinks it in. He begins to doubt. He knows Dani so well. Kindness comes first with him. But that's never stopped him being direct and honest in the next breath. He's right.

'Do you realise the effect you have on people?'

'What are you saying?' Simon's left hand twitches.

'You didn't mean any harm. But harm happened. Did you have no idea how you affected her? You noticed who she was ... Maya ... but you didn't notice how she felt.'

'Yes, I did. When she was feeling overwhelmed, I cheered her up. Helped her take a wider look at things. It helped.' Simon pauses. 'That's exactly how you used to help me. We've both done that for our children too.'

'What I meant was that you didn't notice how Maya felt about you. Your kindness just increased her feelings for you.'

'How was I to know?'

'Noticing the effect on someone of what you do? Being aware of your power? Of what you mean to them?'

Simon can feel the tension in his jaw. His cheeks ache. He grits his teeth.

'Or might mean, given the difference in your ages.'

Simon leans right back with his eyes half-closed. His mouth shut in a hard straight line. 'Ruth said something like that There must have been something you did. Both of you blamed me.'

Dani is still taking care with his words. 'I didn't say that was what you intended. You needn't feel blamed.'

'And that's supposed to make a difference?'

'I am sorry. Sorry I couldn't see that sooner. I was shaken by the possibility of losing the family. I was worried about Amit and Malik. I thought I might lose everything. And all because of something you did.'

'OK. You were in difficulties too. Both of us making assumptions about what might be going on between others. But you can't blame your reaction to me on Amit. What you did to me might have cost me everything. Job. Family. Everything.'

He was being factual. Only slightly bitter.

Dani nods. He pauses. 'I'm so glad it didn't.'

The jazz takes over. Two steps forward and one step back, Simon thinks. They are in touch again but he is still somehow at fault. You can't tell people not to feel what they feel. It doesn't make any sense.

They listened to the music until the lights were dimmed and instruments packed away.

Simon is not clear what it all means. There is too much to digest. 'What about meeting again, Dani?' A question not an invitation.

'Next jazz night?' Dani replies.

'Back to our old routine?'

'Yes. That would be good.'

It could be good. Maybe it will be.

They walk side by side down the hill in step.

Chapter 31

Simon

Simon and Ruth have no option but to work together, but there's a cloud of unfinished business between them that, Simon fears, threatens to drench him if he makes a wrong move. Ruth said she doesn't want to get rid of him. But he doesn't know what she does want. He avoids thinking about it. The children pass between them on a regular shuffle creating pathways and grooves that get easier to travel along as things run smoothly. Simon thinks it's best not to rock the boat. His head is full of echoes of the important but superficial ways in which they now communicate.

Ruth: He's lost his phone. Got a spare?

Simon: Working late on Thursday. Can you pick up and feed?

Ruth: Have you got her red trousers?

Simon: No... . don't think so. Oh. Yes. They were in the washing machine.

Ruth: Isabel meeting with Kiri after school. Pick up by 7 OK?

When it comes to the summer holidays Ruth rents a cottage in the hills beyond Hereford, near the watery landscape she loved as a child. They taste smoked eel (Ruth and Isabel hate it), go canoeing on the river Wye and stay up late. Then it's Simon's turn. He knows his two weeks come next but he buries himself in work with a restorative kind of exclusivity. At the last minute he borrows Ruth's idea and searches for a country cottage. He takes the children to a tiny house close to a huge beach in Norfolk where they brave the east winds, get muddy catching crabs with bacon rind on fishing lines and fill the house with sand. They come back freckled, wind-blasted, and a bit relieved to be home, school about to restart. The children get haircuts, new shoes and watch too much TV. They complain when it's switched off, bored and irritable until back in touch with their friends. Kiri and Isabel meet daily and keep the reasons for their bursts of laughter to themselves. They ignore James, but he's fine with his measurements and his screens. No one talks about Maya.

Simon dreams of Ruth. Dreams of talking to her. Of holding her. Holding on to her and feeling comforted. He wants to know what she's thinking. He wants to watch her face as she listens to him. His dreams leave him saddened and they take time to dissipate. Once, half awake, he found himself reaching out as she walked towards a welcoming crowd with tears on his face. He felt a strand of her hair slip through his fingers. He rubbed them together, empty, and her accusation started to intrude … 'it might have been something you did … something you did …. something you did.'

It's paralysing and dislocates his thinking.

When Ruth sits nearby to chat he wants to put a hand on her warm arm or thigh, and his heart pounds, his mouth goes dry and inhibition takes a grip he can't dislodge.

There are two problems: wanting what would only hurt and ratcheting up the wanting through proximity. Or maybe it's three problems and the third is wanting her to notice how vulnerable the possibility of rejection makes him feel. How much he needs her understanding.

She seems to be firmly in control. Busy at work and chatty with friends. Focused on practicalities at home. Once again Simon feels he's not worth acknowledging unless he's done something to deserve it. Which doesn't include finding the red trousers. He operates the routines with a protective internal shut-down in place. Fearful of bumping himself where he's still sore.

Their old habits re-emerge. Of intermingling plans, activities, reactions, attitudes. Everything fits together. But when something goes slightly awry, like being late back with the children, the fear of being pushed out comes straight back to life. Full force.

And it's frustrating. Not knowing how to step out of the routine and its particularities into a real conversation. How to reach over the distance that separates them. It was easier to cross bridges with Dani, for some reason. There was less at stake.

'Work's going well,' she says. 'It's fascinating to discover how much rubbish can be turned into something new.' She laughs at the list: plastic bottles into shorts and backpacks, magazines into blocks of insulation, saw-dust back into logs for the wood-burner.

He doesn't tell her about bridges made from recyclables.

She goes on about statistics. Hundreds of containers filled with stuff that's been rescued. As if she was the one cleaning things up and giving them her new start in life. She knows which ideas will sell and which are nearer the fantasy line. She's good at what she does. She's fair and open and others trust her. When the children are in bed she relaxes and chats until it's time for one or the other to go home. To their own beds.

Sometimes it is easy to relax together. Like when she falls into sharing the uncensored flow of her thoughts. She problem-solves out loud as if it was second nature. Which it is. Hers. Not his.

It's a long time before he can raise the subject. There's too much at risk.

He feels better once the autumn winds are blowing the leaves about again. Maybe it's just the passage of time. Internal tensions subside and he feels safer. The shared pleasure of regular live music with Dani helps. Children doing what children do and none of them in danger. No notes of disapproval from Ruth. The evenings together feel comfortable. Maybe that's all she wants. Maybe it's what she trusts she can get.

'Ruth, before you go, can I ask you something?' She's sitting at the kitchen table in his flat checking her phone.

'Of course.' She finishes off a text and it whizzes audibly away.

He turns off the music.

'Is something bothering you?'

He sits down opposite. Takes a deep breath in and swallows.

'What made you think I did something to hurt Maya? What do you think I did to her?'

She looks down at the table with serious consideration. 'I don't think you meant her any harm, but ...' she glances up.

'But what?' Simon has leapt in before she finished. Be careful he tells himself. She hates it when you go too fast.

'Not on purpose. Not intentionally.' Ruth finishes her explanation.

'That's what you said before.'

'I know.'

He's shaking inside. It's hard to know how to go on. 'Hold on,' he says. 'Did you think I touched her? Molested her? Did you believe I'd have done that?'

'No! I didn't. That's not what I thought.'

He takes a deep breath.

'I'm sorry Simon. I should have said so before. I thought you knew.' She puts her hand on his. 'I didn't realise .... Didn't I say I believed you at the time?'

He turns his hand over to meet with hers.

'Maybe. I don't know. It's all a bit of a blur, except that you said, it might have been something you did. We never spoke about what you might or might not have believed.'

His hands go to his face and swipe across his forehead and his eyes. His breathing is shaky.

'Why didn't you ask before?' She takes his hand back in both of hers. It's damp. He shakes his head. 'I'll try to explain,' she says.

She lets go of his hand and looks round the room. 'It's hard to know where to start.' She closes her eyes for a moment.

'It's not that it's difficult to say, it's more that I don't really understand how it works. I think it goes like this. You don't just have to pay attention to others, like you did with James when he was hurt. You need to understand their take on things as well. And how you come over.'

He listens intently.

254

'If you notice what's happening you can think before you act. Reflect before you react. And adjust as you go... ... But it's not easy to learn.'

'How did you learn?'

'I'm not sure. From listening to people? Watching the children. Messages I got as a child. When I'd been horrid to someone at school and Mum told me to put myself in their shoes. Or she would say, don't do that. How do you think they'll feel? And things people did. When I was bullied and my parents knew I was hurt they didn't say much. Dad took me canoeing.'

'I think I understand ...'

He waits until she's ready.

'I think it's about learning how to forget what you want, or need, so you've got the space to tune in to others. Like you did with James when he had nightmares. You thought about what he needed. I think that makes it easier to understand other people's take on things. And how you come over too so you can make allowances for how they are. You change what you do and their reactions to you change too.'

Like my grandfather. Simon thinks he understands.

Ruth touches the back of his hand.

'You need to pay close attention if you're going to understand how people react to you.'

'Me?'

'No. We. Everyone. All of us. It's not just your responsibility.'

It's so complicated, he thinks. Like consideration. Paying proper attention to others. Though too much could be as bad as too little, given what happened with Maya.

'It's true. I didn't understand how Maya felt.'

'No.'

'But no one did.'

'You're right.'

She thinks again.

'Maybe there were signs we missed. Or maybe there's other stuff to know as well ...'

255

'Like?'

'In Maya's case, about the vulnerability of young women. And how what one says and does can be taken in different ways. When one does something like give them lots of time and attention. Being aware of what that might mean to them.'

She looks around before she continues. 'It's not just about paying attention to people. It's about realizing the effect you have on them. Like when you ragged about with the kids at bedtime and I had to settle them down. When your work always came first and mine had to give if there was a crisis. Noticing how people react tells you something about what it means to them. And what you mean to them. Good and bad. It changes how you respond to them. Or shows you how you might change the way you are with them.'

'That fits. And with the way you are with the kids.'

'I don't think your parents had much idea about that sort of thing.'

'I can't spend the rest of my life blaming them.'

'I suppose it's stuff that's harder to learn later on.' She looks directly at him, and smiles. 'Don't know if I could, but you can. I've seen you do it.'

There is so much to consider. When good night comes they give each other a proper hug. He watches as she turns to leave and closes the door behind her.

The aftermath of this conversation sweeps him up in a torrent of images in which two small children rampage around in their pyjamas and refuse to get into bed. He can see himself going downstairs in search of a drink, and Ruth leaving whatever she was doing and going upstairs to calm things down. He can feel the relief he felt then. Now he shudders. He searches for the next stepping stone to take him above the memory-current.

He sits near the window in his sitting room feeling more than usually mixed up. He tries to settle but it's not an order he can obey. He draws the curtains. Talking to Ruth has made him a bit more hopeful perhaps, but more uncertain and impatient as well.

There is a lot to think about.

Things have changed, but he knows that's not the end of it. Change goes in a series of stages. It's as if Stage 1 posed a question (How does this work?), like when Hannah told him he was upsetting people. And Stage 2 was about exploring its meaning (he had no idea how to find out so he just had to keep on striving). Different but related, like two movements of the same piece of music. Stage 3 then got caught up in rough country as it tumbled along. He had to keep his head down. Let it work its way through before Stage 4 arrived and helped him to start identifying the stabilisers. Possibly a slow movement could crystallise ideas. But there's no knowing what's coming next when you first hear the music. No one shows you the way or suggests how things might come together.

Dream on, he says to himself. What about some facts?

Ruth was rejecting, critical and infuriated. Obviously she was fed up with him when she pushed him out. Then everyone stepped up to help James. But how could she dare to believe he'd hurt Maya? How could she even begin to think like that? He was glad to help one of Dani's children. Should he have given Maya less time and attention? And what should he do now?

The mix of hope and fear is increasingly difficult to control.

He'd been pushed out in the cold. Left hoping people would let him back in. Not knowing how to be himself with people. He leans forward, his hands covering his face.

So, what next? Then he remembers how Isabel rode her bike into the hedge. It was useless to tell her how to do it. She had to keep on trying until she'd got her own sense of balance. You can't do that consciously. Or can you?

His thoughts flip back to Ruth. Losing it with her, and the wine glass spilling over when he knocked the table. He moved instantly onto the offensive as she attempted to quieten him so the children weren't disturbed. He was too steamed up to be able to understand her priorities, or where they came from. Now he sees how his reactions made things worse. That he was too wound up to reflect or to understand.

Well, there's been more than enough time to reflect now, he thinks. No doubt about it. At last the jumble of thoughts has settled down and he knows exactly what he wants to do. He sends Ruth a message.

Hi. Can you leave the kids? Meet me at our local Italian?

She can. Ruth said that Friday would be good as both children had sleep overs.

He gets there first and orders a bottle of Barolo. She arrives to join him at the same time as the bottle is being uncorked.

'Hi.' She flings a loose black coat he hasn't seen before over the back of a chair and sits down opposite. She's wearing slim black trousers and a loose-weave top with a Fair Trade label on the outside of the cuff. He smiles at the non-smart smartness of her with her hair loose.

She looks round 'Is this where we came before? When Susie was helping with the kids?'

'It is.'

'Four years ago. More like five probably.'

'Five.'

'Hope it's still good.'

'We'll soon find out. The wine list's been updated.' He's sitting close to the front edge of his chair. He is unsteady and determined to let things take their time.

They choose the risotto, and it's more than fine. The sharpness of rocket combines well with the creamy-cheesiness of the rice. Freshly ground pepper and parmesan on the top. Salad on the side. They eat slowly. She looks relaxed. He wonders when to start and thinks that sooner would probably be better than later.

'Ruth, I'm sorry.' Simon is holding an empty fork, and the finger-tips of the other hand stop playing a silent riff on the polished table as he speaks.

She's surprised. 'What? What for?'

258

'Seriously. I've been thinking. I was totally wrapped up in myself and never thought enough about you. About what you had to do. All the things I was useless at. I'm not surprised you were fed up with me.'

'Oh.' She's looking down at the table. 'Yes. I was. You're right.' She glances up.

'I've been thinking how lucky I am you're still around. Supposing you are that is.'

She laughs. 'I think you mean available!' He doesn't laugh. 'You'd know about it if I wasn't,' she says.

There's more he wants to say. Carefully. 'All that stuff about winning prizes seems so irrelevant. It used to feel as if I had to go on earning a place in everyone else's world, including yours. Now I think it works the other way round.'

'Oh?'

'The more I needed to win the more I upset people. I thought it would prevent you abandoning me when it was really pushing you away. I was so scared of losing you. And the family. And all I could think of doing was pushing on, achieving more and more, without supporting you. So, I'm sorry. I really am.' He looks down.

She looks up. 'Thank you ...'

'Wait ... I know I've got further to go. Lots to learn.'

'I reckon that kind of learning never stops. There's no test to pass along the way. Perhaps the hardest bit is to learn what you really want ...'

'What I want most is you. You and our family. To be back home.' She's looking down. He has to wait.

Then, quietly she says: 'I want the same ... but ...'

'But what?'

'I can't go back to how we were before. This is good, isn't it?' She gives a light laugh. 'Not the risotto. The way we are now.'

'It could be better.'

'What's wrong with it?'

Going to bed by myself. Not waking up with you beside me, Simon thinks, but he just says, 'Nothing. Or rather not being with you enough.'

A hand reaches for the empty plates. 'Everything alright? Shall I bring the dessert menu?' The waiter interrupts.

Simon looks sharply up at the waiter. 'No. Hang on a minute.' He raised his right hand for emphasis. He's so quick off the mark that it makes Ruth's shoulders rise. 'Sorry.' Simon adds as she frowns, and then goes on more slowly. 'Give us a moment. I'll let you know when we're ready.'

'No problem.' The waiter disappears. Unphased.

Ruth is serious. She says, 'That used to bother me so much. Something would go wrong and you'd fire off on both cylinders. Immediately. Before I'd even realised what happened. It was scary. I'd get angry and push you away. Or worried that I'd light the touch paper by mistake.'

'What?' He stops to think. Yes. It was completely automatic. There was no gap left between thinking and doing. 'Nothing I could do about it, then. It was like a reflex,' he says.

'And I felt I'd crossed an invisible boundary and you were away. Furious. Unreasonable. Storming off. Sometimes with no idea what I was on about. Or how I felt.'

'It wasn't your fault, Ruth. Never. Sometimes something happens that makes me feel totally irrelevant. Pushed aside and unaccepted. Superfluous and unacceptable. Not even living my own life.' He scrumples up his napkin and puts it down in front of him. 'Like the first time we talked about what happened with Maya. That's exactly what I did.'

'But not the second time.' She's serious. 'Actually, it doesn't seem to have happened for ages.' Now she's smiling at him.

But something makes her move on. 'I'm still hungry. Aren't you?'

He waves to the waiter. She chooses an apricot tart. He has the cheese. They finish the bottle of wine between them, and suddenly it becomes easy to talk. About how much better James has been.

260

About Isabel and Kiri. More ways of using more of the stuff that used to be called rubbish. Building more bridges.

By the time they walked away, side by side, it sounded as if their lives were filled with perfectly ordinary matters.

They come to her door first.

Our home where she lives, in Simon's view.

He stops and holds her close in a long, warm hug. She looks up. Gives him a real kiss, opens the door and leads him in.

Chapter 32

Simon and Ruth

Simon turns over and nuzzles gently into his sleeping wife's neck. He puts an arm around her from behind and a gentle hand on one breast. She doesn't move a muscle. He closes his eyes. It's not new territory.

She stirs and stretches. The familiar body beside her. She knows exactly where his ankle will be. And there it is. She opens her eyes. His face is so close she has to move back a fraction to bring it into focus.

James barges in. 'Look.' He holds up a picture. Three people eating a smoking eel. Two women, R and I on their foreheads, making horror faces. The boy has a fiendish grin.

'There's no more Coco Pops,' he says.

'Look in the larder cupboard. Should be a new box there.' Ruth makes no attempt to move.

He throws them the fiendish grin and he's gone.

They make love slowly. Take their time. They know the teenage sleep-fest has a firm grip on Isabel.

Simon

'So, I love you because you're wonderful, and clever and funny and relaxed and successful and can see right through me and you help me and I'm here all over again, and it makes me want to laugh aloud.'

Simon is getting dressed. She's still in bed. 'And I forgot to say beautiful. Should have come first.'

'You sound high as a kite.'

'Yup. Aftereffect of apologizing perhaps. Just ask when you need one. Or me.'

'Don't worry about it.' She closes her eyes and turns over.

He does up his cuffs. 'I think I owe Maya an apology. To make things easier for her.' He's serious.

She sits up. 'Doesn't she owe you one?'

'No. Not really. She was only 16.' He turns to go, then turns back to look at her once more. 'Pancakes for breakfast?'

Ruth's stretches. 'Is that an offer?'

'Whatever. You say.'

'Yes please.'

Simon whisks up the pancake mix and sets it aside to rest. He goes to his study, sits and leans back with his eyes closed so as to think without being distracted. When he's ready he opens his computer and starts to compose a letter. It takes more than one attempt to find the right words.

Dear Maya

I am writing to tell you I'm sorry about how things worked out on your placement. It was my responsibility to make sure things went well, so it's my fault not yours that we ended up where we are now.

We both know that nothing happened between us that would worry anybody else, and I've been thinking about how we go on from here. I hope we can as our families have been friends for so long.

You have lots of talent, I hope you get to use it for making houses if in the end that is what you want to do.

It would be good to see you. When you're ready.

Simon

A few days later Simon opens an envelope with a postcard inside. A picture of the Pont d'Avignon. On the reverse:

Thank you. M.

He searches through the desk drawers for an older envelope and another postcard. The bridge in Singapore glowing with purple lights. He places them side by side. Singaporean bling on the left. On the right, an ancient French bridge that ends midstream. A broken bridge. A bridge that ends too soon. Somebody's unfinished business perhaps. Or someone's disaster.

Somewhere people come to dance.

In the Golden Lion Simon and Dani watch the instruments being packed away.

'Same time next week?' Simon says

'Uh-uh,' says Dani without thinking. 'How about we get together here before Christmas?'

'Great idea.'

'I'll see if they've got a table free. Not sure Maya would come but everyone else will.'

'How's she doing?' Simon speaks without thinking. 'If it's OK to ask, that is.'

'It's fine. She's out a lot. Working hard too... doing well. We hardly see her but I suppose that was bound to happen.'

'I'm sorry Dani. Sorry if I accelerated that process. How are you? You and Amit?' Simon was able to ask at last.

'OK.' Dani smiles. 'Actually, more than OK.'

'So glad. He's no longer worrying you?'

'I don't think he's ever going to behave as if he can't have everything. But I have to admit that's one of the things I love about him ... As long as it doesn't go too far. Which I don't think it has. Or did. And he's utterly convincing in his devotion to all of us.' He reaches for his glass but it's empty. 'I think he's relieved that I've moved on too.'

'How do you mean?'

'Songwriting. I love it. It gives me something I had no idea I needed. An ambition that isn't all about caring for others.

You're going to find I'm much less sympathetic from now on.'
He laughs.

'Fine by me ... as long as Jazz nights keep coming.'

'Don't worry. They will.'

Simon opens his front door and hears laughter in the kitchen. He takes something bubble-wrapped out of a bag, undoes it carefully and hangs the Golden Gate Bridge on its hook. Left of the front door. He steps back and tilts the right side up a fraction. One of my wonders of the world. It's got a certainty about it. Both light and heavy at once. Properly grounded. It's an in-between. Doesn't belong wholly to one side or the other.

'I don't know why you like that picture so much,' his grandfather had said. 'But I'm glad you do.' What made him say that? His grandfather must have known that Simon was floating free too much for a child. Not properly tethered until he stepped in. Without him Simon would never have got close to anyone. Without him and Dani he certainly wouldn't have let himself get close to Ruth. That might even explain why he'd never got close to searching for anyone else.

Ruth and Isabel are cooking together. Ruth stirs and Isabel chops.

'Where's the small knife?' Isabel throws hers down.

Ruth looks in the drawer. 'Here. It's just as blunt. The other one's in the dishwasher.'

Isabel fishes it out and rinses it. 'That's better.'

'Hi,' Ruth says, looking up. 'Chili for dinner.' She turns to Isabel. 'Ready with the peppers?'

Isabel scrapes them into Ruth's pot and clatters the board into the sink. Then she walks right past Simon without looking at him and heads for the stairs.

Simon watches her go. 'What's up with her?'

'Teenager'ness. She's 15. What's the problem?'

'She seems to be avoiding me. Or she's angry about something. She leaves the room as soon as I get there. Like now.'

'She's got homework to do. Nothing to worry about.'

'Anything up at school?'

'No. It's fine. She has lots of friends. Happy to have you take them places and pick them up it seems. I don't think there's a problem … though I can't say I like all those piercings …'

'Umm. She disappears instead of hanging about after supper or staying to watch a movie. I miss her.' Another young woman going through the business of growing up? It seems like an uncomfortable road to be on. Hope we get it right for her … uhm … hope she finds her way OK.

The Golden Lion is decorated for Christmas in gold with highlights of red. Strings of lights are hooked up above the bar and round the windows. Music from the improvised stage provides rhythm without interfering with conversation. Red napkins on table mats and lighted candles on the tables. Dani, Amit and Kiri have ordered a pint, a gin and tonic and a tomato juice with extra Worcester Sauce. Ruth, Simon, Isabel and James have just arrived. The young ones aim for the window seat. Isabel has three earrings in one ear and her hair pinned back to display them. Kiri has an enormous striped shirt over skinny black trousers. Simon sees them sit together and hopes Maya will turn up. Someone will be missing if she doesn't and he would feel responsible.

'Hey! Want a taste?' Kiri offers her glass to Isabel.

'What is it?'

'Try.'

'Ooh.' A grin follows the first grimace. 'Love the colour. Can I have one?'

Simon adds another to the order.

'What d'you want James?'

'Coke. Two cokes. Both at once.'

'One's enough to start with.'

They're waiting for the food to arrive when Simon sees a familiar figure unwinding a soft brown scarf as she follows the waiter to a table set for three.

'Look,' he says to Ruth, nodding across the room. He gets up straight away.

'Hannah!' He gives her a kiss on the cheek. 'I didn't know you knew this place.'

'Hi Simon. Well, I don't live far away, you know. And it is Christmas.'

'Come and meet everyone.' He takes her to their table. 'Look who's here!'

'Good to see you Ruth,' Hannah says.

'It's been a long time. How are you?'

'Well. You too?'

'Quiet a moment everyone.' Simon says. 'This is Hannah. She organizes everything at work. Keeps me in line. She's been doing it for years.' The young ones pause a second. He realises as he introduces her to Dani and Amit that Maya has probably told them about her and moves quickly on. James swivels round and holds onto the back of his chair.

'Like to taste my coke? It's got Worcester sauce in it.'

'No thanks,' she says, laughing at him. 'That's definitely yours not mine!' He grins at her and puts his glass back on the table.

'Join us for a moment?' Simon goes on. 'Can I get you a drink?' But then plates of hot food begin to arrive and Hannah moves out of the way.

'Maybe later? Best get to my table or the others will never find me.'

'See you later then,' says Simon. He points to Kiri as the owner of the veggie lasagne. James claims the burger and chips.

When he next looks up, he sees a tall man with a beard lean over Hannah to give her a kiss. He sits down beside her. Their companion is half obscured by the crowd but there's no way that Simon could miss the floppy hair and constantly moving arms. Jason looks utterly at home. What? He's going on about something, with a familiar mix of enthusiastic gestures. There's a burst of laughter and they pick up their menus. Too late. They ask the waitress for extra time. It's odd to see them together. As if they belonged that way.

267

Simon realises Amit is talking to him and he's missed the first sentence. Or even the first paragraph.

'... danger over,' he's saying. It sounds like a conclusion.

Danger? Within milliseconds Simon is flooded with thoughts and images.

1. Dani. Is he telling me their relationship is out of danger? That he's stopped wandering?
2. Maya. Which is most dangerous? that she does turn up? Or that she doesn't? Danger not (quite) over.
3. The Thames Footbridge. The deadline for its completion is now fixed. Danger over. But Amit wouldn't know that.

Luckily, Amit is on a roll. 'The business is exploding. I'm running away with it. I mean it's running away with me. I'm going to be all over the place next year.'

'Oh, that's what you meant.' All over the place? What's new? 'That's a relief. It must be a relief. The business I mean.' Simon is not at all sure what he's said. But Amit is describing the wonderful people of Kuala Lumpur, and the recipes he's collected from them and appears not to notice anything odd about Simon's response. He's wearing pale blue slippers embroidered with gold thread and he taps one foot as he speaks.

Dinners are nearly over. A new band is setting up. People walk about collecting drinks. Simon wants to find out how, and why Hannah and Jason have found their way here together. And who's the stranger with the beard? He sees Hannah at the bar and goes to speak to her.

'Good to see you. And with Jason.'

'Didn't you know? He had nowhere to go for Christmas.'

'Nowhere? I didn't know ...'. Is he that much on his own? I'd never have guessed ...

'He's staying with us.'

'Us?'

'Come and meet Fred,' she says.

'Fred?'

'My husband.'

'Hannah ... I didn't know you were married.'

She laughs. 'I know you didn't. You never noticed the fuss or asked what it was about.'

'When? When did that happen?'

'A couple of years ago.' She looks amused as she turns to thread her way between people and tables to the other side of the room. 'Come and meet him.'

Simon stands still. She's right, he thinks. He'd never noticed anything. Even when she had a long break he never thought to ask. It hadn't occurred to him. That's how far gone he was. Totally wrapped up in his own stuff. Horrifying, given how generous she'd been to him when he upset Jason and the others. When Ruth kicked him out. During the aftermath of James's accident. When the bridge collapsed. And she trusted him over the Maya business. Mollified Marion as well. Dreadful to think he'd taken her so much for granted.

And Jason. He suddenly realized how little he knew about him. There were things he could have followed up but didn't. In the pub after the HSE meeting he'd been too tired. Or he was too distracted, like when Jason brought the tubiframes to James. He would never have thought Hannah and Jason had anything in common.

Standing by Hannah's table he holds out a hand to Fred and can't think what to say.

'I didn't know ... so glad ...' He feels awkward and turns quickly to Jason.

'Hi there. Good to see you.'

'Happy Christmas, Simon.' Jason takes a gulp from his pint and raises the glass. 'Enjoy.'

Simon stands there for a moment, just looking.

Hannah comes to the rescue. 'Sit down Simon. We won't keep you long.'

Fred turns to Simon. 'You're the bridge designer. Right? Things taking off again after the crash?'

'Crash?' Simon tries to delete an image of fallen beams, fingers at his temple. 'It seems the financial world is picking up again. Could be exciting times ahead for us I think.' He pauses. 'Hannah's been wonderful. We seem to be amongst the survivors. So much to thank her for.'

Hannah smiles as she offers him a glass of wine. He looks from her to Fred and back as he accepts the glass and raises it. Then he knows it will be OK. But he wants to apologise to her, later, when he's had time to think about it.

'Here's to you. Good luck!'

That's easier. The embarrassment fades and he finds out that Fred used to play alto-sax. And he's looking forward to hearing the new young singer to be introduced later.

'Do you know who she is?' asks Simon.

'No idea.' Fred replies. 'A mystery.'

Simon returns to the table in the alcove and sits by Dani who's gazing rather vaguely round the room.

'No Maya yet.'

'Yes. Sad,' Dani replies.

He's disappointed Simon assumes. Or maybe he's resigned.

Dani is slow to go on. 'It's making me think of my sister. She was only 12 when she died. You knew about that.'

'Just before we first met.' It's dreadful to have brought this back for him.

'Yes. Her death completely changed me.'

'How? Tell me.'

'That's when I decided that the only thing worth working for was a family. Back then I never thought that would be possible for people like me.' He speaks quietly. 'Amit persuaded me we could

270

do it our way. That it would be OK. And it was. It is. You saw what our family was like.'

That makes sense Simon thinks. No wonder Dani was so distraught … so unable to talk. Or meet. Simon thinks back. When they met up again and they all made friends it was as if they were creating an extended family together. A family that included all eight of them. Then the oldest child left. Ran away. Knowing it was his fault makes Simon clam up. It's a huge effort to find anything acceptable to say next.

'And Maya …' He searches. It takes some time. 'You've got her back now? …'

'Yes. We hadn't lost her. At least I don't think so. But there's something else I've been thinking.'

'Uh-uh?'

'It's crazy to think all you need is a family. That's what writing songs has told me. It's shown me who I am. Like the rest of you. Someone with more than one kind of ambition. Rooted in more than one way. Better balanced. Safer.'

Simon pauses, waiting for him to go on.

'Amit makes me feel like that too.' Dani laughs as he looks up. 'Songs can easily fall apart under construction you know. But they can bring people together as well.'

A shriek turns many heads towards the bar. It's from Kiri and Isabel. They've met a friend who Jason seems to know as well. Perhaps she's the mysterious singer? She has hair a quarter inch long over a perfectly round head and a glossy black strand threaded with gold hangs over one shoulder. She's listening to Jason, who is talking with a high degree of animation. Isabel gives the friend a hug, and all four of them move close to the stage. Simon doesn't recognise her until she turns to find somewhere to sit. Briefly she catches his eye, with the smallest hint of a smile. So, she's alright he thinks. Unless that hairstyle is here to stay. She's certainly got courage. Ruth and Amit are now deep in conversation. Simon turns to Dani.

'Do you see who's arrived?' he points.

'No.' He looks again. 'Oh. I'm so pleased …'. He turns to the other side. 'Amit look. It's Maya …' He puts a hand on Amit's arm. Amit covers that hand with both of his.

Simon blinks. That's who she belongs to. Not to all of us. Extended families are different. They can't be fully inclusive. Maybe they shouldn't be.

'She's got here,' Dani says.

He's about to say more but Joe the band leader calls for silence. 'We have a new star to introduce to you tonight. I think we'll all be hearing more about her before long. Make sure you remember this. It's a one-off special just for y'all at Christmas.'

There's a burst of noise rather than silence as chairs and tables are shuffled around and everyone settles down.

And there on the stage, her big striped shirt abandoned to the sister with almost no hair, is Kiri. Now dressed all in black. Suddenly no longer the child stretching pizza cheese round her fingers but someone on the edge of finding a completely unexpected air of sophistication. She's holding a mic as if it's a natural extension of her body. She puts up a hand to call for silence. She is in charge, and comfortable with it.

'This is something my dad wrote,' she says. The band strikes up, and she starts to sing, in a low and unexpectedly powerful voice.

The urge to fly, to move, to roam
On and on and on
Stretch the mind to break – and make
Solidity … solidity … solidity …
Over and over. Make the leap …
Fly on and on and on …

There's a lot more, and her support team are rapturous and won't let her go. Maya and Isabel synchronise their clapping. Those nearby join in. Simon and Ruth keep time with them from a distance. Joe smiles as he nods to her and Kiri takes another bow. She waits for the crescendo to die away, raises an arm and points.

272

'There he is!' she says. 'There's my dad. Both my dads.'

Everyone turns towards the table in the alcove where Amit forces Dani to his feet.

Soon the tables are pushed back. The musicians get into their stride, and a few people begin to dance. Simon waits for a slow one and holds Ruth close as they move together. He looks down at her.

'Enjoying yourself? Happy?'

'Yes. And yes. Those kids suddenly seem so big. I love to be with them. Aren't we lucky?'

'We are.'

The two families walk down the hill in and out of the light spots made by widely spaced street lamps. At the bottom, when the hugging is over, they separate. James leads the way with Ruth. Simon follows behind with Isabel. He sees James run ahead, then turn back to say something. Then he runs on again, the direction of travel and degree of separation controlled by whatever happens to fall into his head. Her response sets him free, and off he goes again. From this distance they're as insubstantial as animated shadows.

Isabel beside him has gathered herself in. Maybe she's worn out.

'Wasn't that great! I loved Kiri's song. Kiri and Dani's song. Did you know about it?'

'Yes. Kiri told me. She made me promise not to tell.'

'She was so good.'

'Uhmm.'

'Did you enjoy yourself?'

'Ur ....' He waits. She doesn't go on.

'You looked as if you did.'

'Did I?'

Simon stops walking to look at her. She takes another step. Stops.

'What's up, Isabel? What's bothering you?'

'Nothing. Nothing you'd understand.' She's quiet but she sounds angry.

'Try me. I'd like to know …' He sees the others way ahead, still carrying out their coming and going ritual. What's this about?

'Would you? OK. Well, I'm not alright.' She swallows. Takes a deep breath and looks at him straight. 'Having a nice time at a party doesn't make it alright.'

'Make what alright?'

'The way you treat me.'

'The way I treat you? Isabel, I love you. What have I done?'

'Isabel's fine. No need to worry about her. That's what you think.'

'Well, it's true. I'm proud of you. I don't worry about you. You're wonderful …'

'Why d'you have to have problems, or accidents, to get your attention? Like James. It's all about him. Fair enough. I know he was hurt. But I was just supposed to get on with it. No problem here.' One hand flat on her chest. 'No need to look in my direction. Or find out what I'm like. Well … maybe you'll get a surprise one day …'

'But …' What's she talking about? What kind of surprise?

'And it's the same with Kiri. She's the one with talent. So, you're amazed by her, and tell me to practice harder.'

'What? When? Did I? I don't remember doing that.' He's frowning.

'When we were learning one of the songs and recording it. The one with the chorus.' She turns to walk on alone.

'Oh! Don't go Isabel.' He catches up and takes her by the arm. 'I do remember. I see what you mean.' He's sure he told both of them to practice. That message wasn't just for Isabel.

She lets his arm rest where it is for just a moment before she takes hers back.

'I'm so sorry. I didn't realise you felt like that.' It's not comfortable to be on the receiving end of her sceptical look. 'I didn't know that was how I made you feel.'

No answer.

'What would you like me to do?'

'Don't you know?'

274

'No.' I suppose I should, but I don't. 'Why don't you tell me? Tell me what you need.'

'Isn't it too late? That's the way it happened.'

'No, it isn't. It's never too late. I love you, Isabel. You're special and I admire you. Like the way you do your own thing without making a fuss. The way you make friends and laugh with them. The way you always knew what James needed because you're so good at thinking about other people. I've never known you to be selfish. Or resentful. And you're clever. But I've let all that go without saying. I haven't shown you how I feel nearly enough. But I will.'

There's got to be a way.

They walk on together as if there's an imaginary person keeping the distance between them. By the time they get home Ruth has chased James to bed. She turns round as she hears them come in. Isabel first, Simon close behind.

'Hot drink?'

'No thanks. I'm going up.'

'Stay with us, Isabel. Stay and chat. Just a moment.' Simon says. But he's too late. She's gone. He looks at Ruth and shakes his head.

'What was that about?' she asks.

'She's angry with me. She's just told me. Did you know?' He sits down by the table, arms on its surface, fingers outstretched.

'No.' She comes to stand close to him. 'Tonight? Of all nights?' She puts a hand on his shoulder. 'I'm so sorry. What did she say?'

'That I've ignored her. Left her to grow up unassisted. Just assumed she was OK without asking. No need to worry about Isabel, so not noticing any of the good things about her as well as the times when she might have needed help. Or encouragement. Or understanding. That's probably the main bit.'

'She knows we love her ...'

'But that's not enough. At least from me. I'm ashamed of myself. For just accepting her. Without saying so. Without telling her why.'

She puts a hand on his shoulder as she gets up to make two cups of tea: Yorkshire for him. Green tea with mint for her.

'It doesn't change anything. That was a wonderful evening and everyone enjoyed it. Including Isabel. Remember she's 15. Perhaps it's our turn for tumult ahead.'

He takes a sip of tea. So, there's work to do at home. Work that should take priority. This time about winning through rather than coming out top. Perhaps it's not the right moment for the Brazilian competition. There'll be others.

'I need to work out how to put things right. Make her feel better.' He looks up to find Ruth waiting for him. 'What were you thinking?' he asks her.

'That she's strong. This will blow over. We just need to hold steady. Keep in calm waters.' Her words have a confidence and a certainty about them. But that's her. Not Simon.

'Um ... ur ... I don't think that's enough.' He pushes his mug away. 'I've got to try. Think about it. Make sure I don't slip back into bad habits ...'

'We'll manage,' she says.

Simon thinks that if he starts to build from his end he will soon find out if she can approach from hers. That could work.

They sit together. Quietly.

Acknowledgments

My first thanks go to Elizabeth Garner, whose creative writing courses inspired me to attempt something I had always wanted to do, and to the members of our writing group, Siobhan Fraser, Heather House, Ruth Leadbitter and Stephen Lunn.

Jericho Writers has been a source of information about every aspect of writing. I am especially grateful to everyone associated with the Ultimate Novel Writing Course, for the support and encouragement of my tutor Wes Brown, and for the combination of serious ideas, energy and humour in Harry Bingham's Friday emails.

Sam Tindale and Holly Seddon were my earliest readers and helped me on the way without pulling the punches. Mark Wilson explained a number of engineering and bridge-building matters. Any remaining mistakes are mine. Xandra Bingley's kindness, enthusiasm and friendship has helped me to keep going while insisting, correctly, that if I used fewer words I would tell a better story. She was right.

Ann Lamb from Forward Thinking Publishing and Laura Duffy (Laura Duffy Design LLC), have turned my typescript into this book with skill and creativity. To me it looks beautiful.

Many friends have heard about the ups and downs of my journey into the world of fiction. Thank you to all of them, and especially to Cathy O'Neill and Melanie Fennell.

First and last thanks go to my daughters, Sophie and Josie. They have been endlessly supportive and encouraging despite not knowing the story or being allowed to read early drafts. My whole family has been wonderful, and curious. All of you have helped to create enduring images, ideas and memories some of which are reflected in this novel, but none of you has served as a model for anyone who lives merely on the page.

About the Author

Gillian Butler was brought up by a beautiful river in Hampshire and then studied politics, philosophy and economics at Oxford. After working briefly as an economist she came back to Oxford, started a family and re-trained as a psychologist. She has never left.

Over thirty years of clinical experience has left her with a huge respect for the ability of people to change and adapt when confronted with difficulties. She knows that some of the attitudes and assumptions experienced early in life can interfere, and leave a painful and damaging legacy, and that others bring benefits with them. In the face of the many complex threats that now face our world, Gillian continues to believe that problems can be solved if we are able to meet them with knowledge, understanding and appropriate action. Her optimism provides a well of energy that, so far, has not run out. Another of her beliefs is that novels can take over where psychology leaves off. This is her first novel.

gillianbutler.com

Other books by Gillian Butler

Non Fiction

Overcoming Social Anxiety and Shyness

Manage Your Mind, GB with Nick Grey and Tony Hope

Psychology: A Very Short Introduction,
GB with Freda McManus